WARRIOR OF THE BLACK MIRROR

Warrior of the Black Mirror

BOOK ONE OF THE CRIMSON WARRIOR SERIES

Mikael Svanström

This book is dedicated to my daughters,
Freya and Amelia, who were an endless
source of inspiration as they grew up.

I hope this book will inspire you in turn.

If not, I'll have another crack at it in book
two of the series.

1

Calling the Tainted Ones

"What mess have you cats gotten yourselves into this time?" Gabe Shade said as he stepped through the door into the small study.

Parissus, the head of the Oracles, sat at his desk writing with his back turned to the door. Gabe had never liked the old man. He had the arrogance of someone who had long since buried all his enemies and a dry dusty smell as if he'd died and mummified long ago. All Gabe saw of the old man was the back of his head, tufts of white wispy hair in a crown around his scalp.

"I'm sure I don't need to tell you how dire the situation is." Parissus continued writing, his words the only acknowledgement of Shade's presence.

"I heard what happened to your army."

"It served its purpose." The old man waved his left hand dismissively. "We never expected to win."

"So it all went according to plan," Gabe said with a smirk. "I'll leave you be, then."

He knew why he'd been called. The Oracles always summoned him when they needed someone to clean up their mess. It didn't matter what he did to help them. They still complained about his methods afterwards.

Parissus stopped writing and turned to face Gabe. He moved slowly, as if worried a sudden move might undo the skin holding his body together.

"What are you supposed to be?" He sneered. His dislike was a guarantee regardless of the answer.

"I'm a private investigator from an old black and white movie the boy watched a few years ago. A hard-boiled guy with his own idea of justice."

"We need fighting men, not…whatever that is."

Shade shoved his hands further into his brown trench coat. "I like it."

"It doesn't matter. We've run out of options. It is time to gather the Tainted Ones."

"I don't think that's a good idea."

"You don't think?" The old man's eyes narrowed. "Since when did you think?"

Gabe ignored the comment. He'd take revenge on the relic, but not today. "You know what happened last time we called them."

"We've sent emissaries to negotiate. None of them came back. We sent spies. None of them came back, either. We sent assassins, and they were all killed. We sent an army and you've seen what's left of it. We don't have a choice. You need to get the boy."

"He's not ready."

"Nevertheless," Parissus said with a resolve that did not invite further comment. "He is needed. We are better prepared this time."

Gabe Shade shook his head. He didn't want to admit it, but for once he agreed with the old man. They had done everything within their power. He himself had tried to enter the occupied realms to investigate the situation and had barely managed to escape. Few were better than he was. They had to stir the pot some other way. He just wished it wasn't the Tainted Warriors. They were as likely to make matters worse as help. As plans went it was pure desperation.

"The time and place have been set." Parissus turned back to his writing. "I trust you can complete this task without damage or bloodshed."

"Don't count on it, old man," Shade said under his breath as he turned to leave.

As he walked through the doorway into the outer room, he noticed differences since his last visit two years ago. The rooms were brighter and more inviting. The Oracles lived unassuming lives with very few possessions. This close to the centre of the Intersect, things were created and uncreated all the time. Regardless, someone had made the effort to hang drapes and scatter a few brightly coloured cushions on the stone bench along the wall. He passed an Oracle wearing a green beret. It was the first time he had ever seen an Oracle with clothing different from the white tunics they favoured. Gabe knew he should investigate the reason, but he had a more important task. He had to get the boy.

2

Someone Special

Joel's brain burned. The bugs in his head had quieted down enough for him to think coherently, but it never lasted long. He could feel them crawl inside his ears, emitting high-pitched angry shrieks.

The cold stone floor was ice against his skin, so he sat up, rubbing arms and legs to stimulate blood-flow. A filthy rug lay on a wooden bench and he wrapped it around his shoulders, ignoring its putrid smell. Water dripped from the ceiling, collecting in a little puddle in a fissure on the floor. He scooped water in his hand and wiped his face.

He took stock of his situation, knowing the bugs would soon bury any thought in a cacophony of noise. How had he ended up here? He couldn't remember anything since his botched attempt to rescue Erin. The bugs in his head had made sure of that.

He was locked up in a cave alone—his friends dead or worse—awaiting his own execution. This was all Gabe Shade's fault!

He longed for a time when all he had to worry about was school, bullies and birthdays.

***

Joel liked to think he was special, but he knew this wasn't the case. He hadn't been adopted so there was no risk of famous long-lost relatives appearing out of nowhere. He didn't wield magical powers, so being invited to a school of witchcraft and wizardry was out of the question. He wasn't aware of any special skills like talking to animals, seeing ghosts or anything else remotely practical. He wasn't exceptionally talented or good looking which seemed to be a ticket from the mundane for a lucky few. He was about as normal as they came, and he hated it.

But this was his special day. The one day he liked at least a bit—his birthday. Maybe today brought something special after all. The parcel was the right size and shape and weighed about right too. He'd dropped enough hints in the past month, after all.

"Come on, open it," his mother urged with a smile that did nothing to reassure him.

Joel took his time. Before it was unwrapped, it could be anything, something amazing, but once opened the unknown settled into the known. This was almost invariably worse than any amazing possibility.

He opened the side of the parcel. All he could see was a black box inside. So far so good. He tore the rest of the paper off, revealing a black box with the image of a smart phone on the cover. Inside was the sleek, dark shape of an iPhone.

"Thanks mum!"

She smiled. He liked it when she smiled. In all his memories from childhood she was always there with a bright sunny smile. Now it only made occasional appearances.

The phone felt cold and smooth in his hand. His mum had promised him a smart phone the year high school started, but he hadn't expected the latest iPhone model.

He turned it on, and the familiar Apple logo appeared on the screen, a small white bar extending below it. But something was wrong with the logo. It wasn't an apple; it was a pear.

He took a closer look at the box. On the side it said iPone in neat silver letters.

"Isn't it great?" his mum said. "It looks exactly like the real thing but costs a third. Still expensive, but only the best for you."

"It isn't an iPhone," Joel said finally.

"You know I can't afford one. This was the best I could do."

"Thank you, mum," he said. Any other phone would have been better. An Android phone, a second-hand iPhone, anything but a blatant knock off. She meant well. She always did, but somehow it ended up wrong more often than not.

"I have to go to school." He grabbed his backpack and headed for the door.

"Don't forget your phone!"

Joel dutifully retrieved it and left the small apartment.

On the way to school he explored the phone finding it a complete mess. It was an Android phone with a UI designed to imitate an iPhone, somehow succeeding in combining the worst of the two. He keyed Erin's number into the phone.

"Hello? Who's this?"

"It's me. I've got a phone," Joel said.

"Congratulations. Who is this?"

He was surprised she failed to recognise his voice. They'd been friends since the start of year seven when they bonded over their love for science and hate for anchovies on pizzas.

"It is Joel."

"Cool phone," she replied. "Does it have filters on it? You sound like Darth Vader."

"What?"

"Say I'm your father, Luke," Erin said while imitating Darth Vader herself.

"Very funny," he replied. "There must be a setting somewhere. I'll see you in class."

Joel ended the call and hunted around in the settings menu without luck.

***

"What is the average rainfall in the Amazon basin?"

Joel's mind had drifted as it so often did. It was the utter tedium of the classroom with a teacher telling him things he either already knew or saw no reason to learn.

His teacher, Mr Roberts, looked at him from across the room. His fellow students all stared at him too.

"Wake up, Bumfluff!" Martin yelled and threw a chewed-up wad of paper, hitting Joel in the middle of the forehead. "Bullseye!"

Martin was Joel's own personal bully. This wasn't strictly true. Martin bullied anyone he could, but he had taken a particular dislike to Joel. He had no idea why. He couldn't think of anything he'd done.

"Stop that, Martin," Mr Roberts said with no real authority.

"Could you repeat the question?" Joel asked, holding his head low as he wiped the saliva from his forehead.

"Pay attention, Joel. I asked you for the average rainfall in the Amazon basin."

"About 2300 mm per year," Joel answered and tried to pay attention to the rest of the verbal test, never answering any questions voluntarily, but answering all those directed to him. Any time he had showed off in the past, he ended up paying for it after class and after school.

Martin as usual hadn't done his homework, so when he failed answering a question Joel had to answer the question instead. He couldn't win. Either he answered correctly which would anger Martin, or answer incorrectly, which was just plain wrong. Indecision rendered him speechless long enough for someone else to volunteer. Erin chose to answer instead. Joel had told her repeatedly not to voluntarily answer questions, but she didn't listen to him. She didn't listen to anyone.

***

At the end of the school day, Joel opened his locker to find someone had poured jelly into it. The door and many of his books were coated in red goo that smelled vaguely strawberry-like. At that moment he decided he hated school. Not school itself perhaps, but the people he shared the school with. School was like a social experiment where people were rubbed together to see what sparks would fly. Unfortunately, he was one of those being rubbed a lot. He didn't think he had done anything to deserve it. It was just one of many unfair things the universe had thrown his way.

SLAM! The locker door narrowly missed his fingers and sent the notebook in his hand flying, spreading pages like confetti in the hallway.

"Almost got you!" Martin yelled as much to Joel as to his two friends towering behind him. Pete and Leo were, if possible, worse than Martin. They didn't have the balls to do anything themselves, but happy to do whatever Martin told them.

"Why…" Joel began, but opted for silence, hoping Martin would let him be. Joel had planned to grab his bag and sneak out from school after the last bell. No such luck. He picked up the pages from the floor, hoping they'd lose interest.

"What is going on here?" Mr Patel, the physical education teacher asked. He was one of the few teachers who tried to make a difference and had rescued Joel many a time.

"I dropped my book," Joel said knowing he'd pay dearly for saying anything else.

"Help or go away," Mr Patel told Martin and his friends. After lingering just long enough to show they were leaving by choice and not obeying a teacher, the boys walked down the hall causing as much chaos as they could.

"You must stand up to them," said his teacher, "or they'll just keep on walking all over you."

"Yes, sir."

"You have to make it hard for them to push you around."

"What do you suggest I do? Three against one and they are all bigger than I am!"

"I developed late as a kid, so I had bigger kids trying to bully me around too. Rashid made my life miserable. One day I decided I'd had enough and told him so. He kept going, so I threw myself at him hitting and kicking."

"What happened?"

"He gave me a beating I'll never forget. Put me in hospital with a broken nose and a fractured rib."

Joel raised his eyebrows.

"It's still a sound principle," Mr Patel said. "I didn't tell on him and he respected that. We've been friends ever since." He smiled as he reminisced about his friendship with Rashid the bully. "Those were the days," he said and left.

Joel shook his head, put his notebook and other belongings in his backpack and headed for the door. Outside he scanned the courtyard for his tormentors. Perhaps they had found someone else to harass. He hurried through the gate and down the street continually looking back for any signs of pursuit. He was about halfway home, taking the short-cut through a park when Martin stepped out from a hiding place just a few meters ahead.

"He actually thought he'd gotten away!" Martin said to his two friends as they joined him.

Martin pushed Joel to the ground, grabbed his backpack and pulled the books out one by one.

"Math? Why? We don't have any math homework." He threw the books on the ground and dug around in Joel's backpack.

"You got any money?"

Joel shook his head, boiling with anger.

"What have we here?" Martin brought out the iPone and studied it. "Very nice. What's the code?"

"There's nothing on it. I just got it today."

"Who cares what's on it. I can't sell a locked phone."

"You can't sell my…"

"Hang on," Martin said, frowning. "This isn't an iPhone."

He threw it on the pile of books. Joel watched in horror as it bounced and landed face down on the gravel path. Mr Patel was right. He had to stand up for himself. Anything was better than this. Joel stood up, brushing dirt off his pants.

"I've had enough of you pushing me around," he said in a squeakier voice than he intended. "I haven't done anything to you!"

'What're you gonna do?' Martin asked and showed teeth in what passed for a smile in Martin's world.

Joel bit his teeth together until it hurt, getting ready to attack.

"You have no right to pick on him!" Erin stared at Martin, eyes ablaze. She'd come out of nowhere. "You're just a bully. A dumb stupid bully!"

Erin's piercing blue eyes stared at Martin under a torrent of blonde curly hair.

Martin looked at her, at first surprised then annoyed. He didn't waste time on words. Instead he struck Erin in the face. She stumbled backwards and fell, dragging Joel with her.

"This your girlfriend, Bumfluff?" Martin looked down at Erin who stared back at him, blood dripping from her nose and tears welling up in her eyes. "She's tougher than you are."

Joel could hear respect in Martin's voice, but it wouldn't make a difference. "Do you have any money?"

"I wouldn't give you any even if I had it!" She shook her head vigorously as she got to her feet.

Martin stared at her. He'd hit her again and this time he wouldn't hold back, Joel thought as he stood up next to her. He held his breath waiting for the inevitable.

"I like you!" Martin said and reached out towards her.

"I don't like you!" Erin snapped back and kicked him hard on the shin. Martin crumbled to the ground with a very unmanly yelp.

"Let's go!" Erin grabbed hold of Joel and tried to drag him with her.

"Don't you go anywhere," Pete said with a nervous glance down at his friend, who gripped his shin, obviously trying awfully hard not to cry. "Are you ok?"

"Of course, I'm not bloody ok!"

"Let's go!" Erin tried again, this time running off by herself. Joel grabbed his bag and the smart phone and followed her. They ran out of the park and down the street. They were dead, Joel thought. Their parents may as well choose coffins for their imminent burials. Scared as he was, he also felt exhilarated. He had challenged Martin for the first time and was still alive. If Erin hadn't appeared, perhaps he would have taken them on all by himself.

"This way," said Erin pulling Joel into a small lane he'd not noticed before. This surprised him as he walked this way to and from school every day. At the end of the lane a large steel gate blocked their path. A sign spelled out all manner of legal trouble if they tried to enter.

"A dead end!" Joel said, gasping for air. He glanced over his shoulder but couldn't see anyone in pursuit. Erin punched in numbers at random on a keypad next to the gate.

"Thanks," Joel said. "I guess," he couldn't help but add.

"I guess?" Erin turned towards him and grimaced. She checked a tooth that had come slightly loose and added: "What does that mean?"

"I'm saying thank you for saving me."

"Sounded more like you preferred to be beat up," she said with a scoff.

The truth was he'd have preferred if Erin had not interfered. For once he'd found the courage to stand up to a bully and had nothing to show for it. Worse, a girl had saved him and had beaten up Martin no less.

"Yes," he said finally.

Erin stared at him in disbelief and turned back to the keypad. She tapped in a few more numbers and the gate slid up with a grinding sound. Inside he saw a hall with concrete walls big enough to fit a large car. Erin stepped inside, pushed a button and the gate descended.

"I won't help you again," she said as she disappeared.

3

Creature in the Corner

It wasn't far from the mystic lane to the flat where Joel lived with his mother. As he strolled home, he wondered about the peculiar steel gate. He mapped the location of the mysterious entrance to the flat where Erin was living in his mind and realized they were in the same block but accessed from different streets. Did they own that too? Perhaps her father worked there. He had been to Erin's place a few times but never met him.

Joel soon gave up trying to work it out, settling on an image of Erin as the daughter of a James Bond style secret agent. The truth wasn't as exciting, perhaps. For all he knew, the building was abandoned, and she had found the security code. Not knowing gave him the opportunity to pick the best of possibilities.

His phone rang. It was a cheery jingle more at home in a cheesy commercial than as a ring tone. He had tried to change it but had failed to locate any other options. A spider web of cracks covered the screen, partially obscuring the caller name.

"Yes?" he answered.

"This isn't me forgiving you or anything," Erin said. "I just wondered if the phone still worked."

"Yeah, it works."

13

"Ok, good. That's all. And you sound like a mouse now."

She hung up.

He arrived home safely and was set to work by his mother to help prepare dinner, a strange vegetarian meal pretending to be meatloaf.

"So how was school?" she asked as they were eating.

"I want to change my name," Joel answered, chewing slowly.

"What's wrong with your name?" his mother fired back with an edge in her voice he knew all too well.

He had been born Joel Marshall—a good inoffensive name. His father left them five years later. They never spoke about this, but on top of leaving Joel without a father, something much worse had happened. Joel's mother decided to change her surname back to her maiden name and do the same for Joel. Therefore, at five years old he had lost name and identity to become Joel Noel—a serious contender for the Worst Name in the World trophy.

"Oh, nothing," he said and continued eating.

In the evening Joel lay awake, too excited to sleep. He was grateful for Erin's friendship, but struggled to shake the one big difference between them. She was braver than he was by far. She was like a big sister protecting him. He liked her for who she was and disliked her equally for her protection. He knew it was petty, stupid even, but it didn't change how he felt.

He closed his eyes and tried to force himself to sleep by not thinking about anything, but his brain soon rebelled and flashed images of what he'd seen during the day. There was something to be said for inner peace, but inner excitement beat it easily, or so his brain seemed to argue. Nevertheless, a few minutes later he drifted off to sleep. In dreams, the events of the day regurgitated. He was chased through the park and turned into the lane. Soon he stood outside the steel gate trying to guess the code to escape his pursuers.

"You need help, kid?"

Gabe Shade, private investigator by trade, stepped out from the shadows, looking like Joel remembered him from the old black and white movies his mother loved and had forced him to watch when he was younger. Shade wore a trench coat, hat and a permanent sardonic half smile.

Joel stepped aside, expecting Shade to try his luck with the keypad, but instead he struck the steel gate twice. A moment later it slid up, revealing Erin just as he had last seen her—fire in her eyes, frozen in mid-frown.

"You could do worse than a girl like that. You should try compliments. Nice girls like compliments. Bad girls too." Gabe Shade smiled with a faraway look in his eyes. "Insults turn them all ugly. I should know."

Joel grimaced. He knew it made sense, but he preferred invisibility to interaction with girls, whether it was insults or compliments. At least you wouldn't make a fool of yourself.

"We need to go," Gabe said. "This can wait."

"Go? Go where?"

"We have work to do."

"Work?"

The unexpected turn of events grated on Joel's mind. He wanted to sort things out with Erin. He had no interest in the work Gabe suggested.

"Come with me. Someone has created a rift to the Intersect. Your world will soon be under attack and only you can save it."

"Really?"

"Come with me. This is only a temporary construct."

Joel's dreaming mind could no longer hold reason at bay. "This isn't real," reason argued. "You're asleep."

Gabe Shade reached out his hand, but Joel only stared at it suspiciously. The private investigator shook his head.

"Find me if you can. Remember, things are different here. Words matter. Actions matter. You can't walk through life as a sheep here." Gabe's eyes narrowed. "Don't do that! Don't question it. You'll wake..."

"...up." Joel's mind finished the sentence as he opened his eyes.

The dream was clear in his mind. He had never seen Gabe like that. He was usually cool and detached, always ready with a sarcastic comment for any eventuality. He had been quite different this time. Gabe had been a companion in his dreams for over a year. He told a child psychologist his mother forced him to see about Gabe once. She had immediately decided it was a response to no longer having a father figure in his life.

The dream faded from his mind, as dreams do. Gabe's behaviour seemed less important with time passing. It was only a dream after all. After a few minutes he was left with an uncomfortable feeling, not much else. He knew why. He must apologise to Erin.

He closed his eyes and soon drifted off to sleep again. A shuffling sound from somewhere in the room woke him. He turned over to go back to sleep, but another sound woke him up proper. Joel didn't want to know what had interrupted his sleep. At best a mouse, at worst a rat. Neither particularly good. He just wanted to be left alone.

The light switch was on the other side of the room, so out of the question. He wasn't putting his feet within attacking distance of the sound maker if he didn't have to. As he listened the scratching sound changed to a repeated tapping on the wall. This was no mouse or rat!

His reading lamp was on the bedside table, but he didn't think it would light up enough to see anything. The flashlight! He had left it on a shelf next to the bedside table. With it he'd be able to see the intruder from the safety of his bed.

He pushed the lamp aside and climbed up on the bedside table, balancing precariously on the small surface. He felt the flashlight with the tip of his fingers, shuffled a little to get extra reach and lost his balance. In a desperate attempt to stay on top, he grabbed hold of the side of the shelves. He saved himself from falling but a couple of books dropped on the floor. The tapping noise stopped. Joel grabbed the flashlight, flicked it on and pointed at the corner.

A crab the size of a house cat froze for a second in the beam of light. Waving its claws in the air, it emitted a high-pitched whistling and scuttled towards the bed, much faster than Joel had anticipated. He jumped back to the bed as the creature bumped into the leg making a whelping sound. It had a painted shell with what could be tribal patterns. Tiny knives appeared in its claws. Joel could have sworn he heard a tiny "Yeeha!" as the crab burrowed one of the knives in the leg of the bed. Retreating, it clicked and whistled in a threateningly manner until it reached the corner and just disappeared.

Joel sat in his bed shining the flashlight around the room for hours, but no more creatures appeared. Perhaps he had imagined it. After another ten minutes he had convinced himself he had indeed dreamt it all and fell asleep.

When Joel woke up, he remembered the peculiar dream with surprising clarity. A giant crab! How ridiculous. He pictured every detail of the dream in his mind. How it had come charging with little knives in its claws. He looked down and saw something lodged in the leg of the bed—a small golden handle, shaped like an hourglass about two centimetres long. He had to use a kitchen knife to pry the blade free. The small knife had an intricately adorned blade with a handle designed for a claw. He got ready as quickly as he could. He couldn't wait to tell Erin.

4
===

More Creatures in the Corner

Back at school Joel found everyone talking about Erin. Martin hadn't shown up and rumours suggested Erin had given him a beating so bad he ended up in hospital. If Joel was mentioned at all, it was as the damsel in distress. Erin must have told everyone what had happened to increase her popularity at school. And to think he'd intended to apologise!

"I didn't tell anyone," said Erin. She had appeared beside him without him noticing and seemed to have acquired magical mind reading capabilities.

"It must have been Henchman One or Two that blabbed."

"Henchman?"

"You know, nameless people who help the evil masterminds in James Bond movies. The idiots hanging out with Martin. Do they actually have names?"

"No, probably not," he said and smiled. She didn't seem angry at all. Perhaps he could get away without apologising at all.

"You deserved it, though." She headed off to class.

"Sorry!" he yelled after her.

She twirled around, still looking angry but the fire in her eyes was gone. "Sorry for what?"

"Sorry for…you know…being an idiot."

"Apology accepted. And you were being an idiot."

"I've got something to show you." Joel fumbled with his backpack trying to find the little knife.

"Sorry. Can't be late to class. Mr Roberts has one of his surprise quizzes. You'll have to show me later."

***

Later came and Joel retold his overnight adventures as they walked home.

"You are kidding me?"

"No."

She raised her eyebrows and studied him for a moment. "You should write that stuff down."

He held up the little knife.

"What's that? The scuttle crab knife? Shouldn't you give that back to the Pokemon you took it from?"

"Just have a look." Joel sighed.

He handed the knife to her and watched her smirk turn to amazement. "Where did you find this? It feels like real gold and silver! Look at the engravings. I reckon it's a ceremonial weapon."

"Yeah, I thought so too," Joel said.

"But seriously, where did you get it? The truth this time."

"I am telling the truth. You think I'd make that up?"

She weighed the knife in her hand and nodded. "I believe you."

"What do we do now?"

"We'll try and catch the crab, of course! When it shows up again, we'll have a trap ready. It must have come from some parallel dimension or a planet where crabs are the dominant species."

"Sounds pretty unlikely," Joel said, but couldn't think of anything more plausible. They were in weirdo territory here. People were hospitalised for believing less. "So, how do we do it?"

"If the gate is in a particular place in your room, we stop it from getting back again. All we need then is a trap."

"Then what? I mean if we catch it. What do we do?"

"We try and communicate with it. We'll win the Nobel prize for sure!"

"And how exactly are you going to be in my bedroom in the middle of the night? My mum won't let you."

But she did. Even though Joel was a bit old for a sleep over and definitely too young to have a girl spend the night, Joel's mother was so happy Joel and Erin were friends she went along with it. Erin's father didn't need persuading. According to Erin, he was in the middle of classified research and didn't have time for her, anyway.

***

Thus, Joel and Erin found themselves in his bedroom that same evening. They had made a big show of getting ready for bed, but in reality, they'd made plans to capture what they now referred to as a scuttler.

Once they'd made sure Joel's mother had retired to her bedroom, preparations began. Joel emptied a crate he used for comic books to serve as the cage for their captive. He didn't think it would hold the scuttler for long, but they had no other alternative. They piled the spare mattress brought in for Erin on the tallboy with a rope tied to it. With a little luck, it would fall to prevent the scuttler from returning to the corner.

Preparations complete, they turned off the lights and sat in the bed with their flashlights ready. At first it was exciting, but boredom was a close second. Waiting had that effect on most things. After about an hour they were both asleep, Joel's head on Erin's shoulder.

***

"Joel," Erin whispered and nudged his shoulder.

Joel woke. "What…"

She shushed him and pointed. It was dark, but he didn't need to see where she pointed. He knew. Something else was in his room. It wasn't light tapping this time, but a scratching noise. Whatever was making the noise was much bigger than the scuttler.

"What's this?" A sugar sweet voice, as if a grown man was imitating a child, came from the corner. Both Joel and Erin sat rigid with fear.

"A peculiar place for a mattress. Something hidden inside, perhaps?" A whirring sound started followed by fabric ripping.

"Nothing," it said with disappointment. "Night, night, no light," anger now creeping into the voice as it shredded the mattress. To Joel and Erin, it sounded like flesh ripped from bones.

Erin nudged Joel to turn on his flashlight. Joel refused.

"I hear children!" the voice said with obvious delight. "And you are next. I take all major credit cards."

Joel frowned. The thing knew about credit cards. He didn't know what to do, but he was sure if they did nothing, they'd meet the same fate as the mattress.

Erin grabbed her flashlight and flicked the switch. In the beam they saw something human sized in a white lab coat. For a moment she captured its face in the light. The eyes were twice the size of a normal person and protruded, almost like a frog. There wasn't so much a nose as two holes in the middle of its face. The mouth had too many teeth, sticking out at odd angles.

"Light! Light!" The thing tried to cover its face while stumbling backwards. Its fingers were longer than usual and oddly shaped. They reminded Joel of small machines. The creature tripped over the remnants of the mattress, fell backwards and everything went silent.

They just sat there quietly—too scared to move, too scared to do anything at all. Eventually, Erin shone the flashlight in the direction of the corner. Nothing remained but the remnants of the mattress. It had been ripped apart with the stuffing spread over half the room. Joel and Erin exchanged glances.

"That was no scuttler," said Erin.

"No," Joel answered, still in a state of shock.

"Did you see the face? And the teeth! Did you see how brown they were?"

"No."

"Creatures from other dimensions wouldn't know about credit cards, would they?"

"No."

Erin whacked him with a pillow. "Snap out of it! That was great! I didn't really believe you, you know." She picked up pieces of the mattress using the crate as a waste bin. "Not until now. How did that thing make such a mess? Did you see?"

"No," Joel answered and, after a stern look from Erin, quickly added, "The fingers had some kind of machinery."

"What? Like Swiss Army knife fingers?"

"I guess, yes."

"That'd make picking your nose a bit dangerous," she said.

The comment was so silly Joel found himself starting to laugh. Erin laughed too.

KNOCK! KNOCK!

"What are you doing up?" Joel's mum's voice came through the door. "I don't want to hear anything more from you two. Go to bed!"

Joel stopped laughing and held his breath, trying to come up with a plausible story for the mess. Erin held her hand over her mouth to stop giggling.

But the door remained closed and after thirty seconds, Joel started breathing again. They set to cleaning up the mess. The creature had cut and ripped the mattress into little pieces. Joel could all too easily imagine being ripped apart by those strange machine-like hands.

"We tried to capture a monster with a crate big enough for its feet," Erin whispered, stifling another giggle attack.

"It could've killed us," Joel hissed back. He couldn't understand how Erin could joke about it, but he was glad she did.

"We need some kind of weapon if we're going to capture that creature."

"Are you crazy?"

"Perhaps a little," she said with a smile.

"We're not going to do anything. Who knows what will appear tomorrow? A big monster with tentacles or something."

"So what are you going to do? Tell your mum? Hey mum, there are evil monsters appearing in my bedroom. Can I sleep in your bed?"

"No. I'd call the police."

"No one will believe you," she said. "Hello," she mimicked into a pretend phone. "I'd like to report monsters in my bedroom. Could you please arrest them? Don't forget to bring your ghost busting equipment."

"They're not ghosts."

"How do you know? No one is going to believe us until we've captured one of them."

Joel had to agree she had a point. Without proof they were easy to dismiss.

"Ok, but if we're going to have a chance against whatever showed up today, we need weapons."

"Leave that to me," Erin said. "I know where there are plenty."

"Where are you going to get weapons from?"

"My dad builds them."

He remembered Gabe Shade's words from the night before: Your world will soon be under attack and only you can save it. Was this what he'd meant?

Had he known what the next day had in store for him, he would have spent his time worrying about that instead.

5

The Oneiromator

Martin was back. He limped around on crutches and had his henchmen do the running for him. Soon they had rounded up both Joel and Erin. He studied his two captives with a superior sneer.

"You told on me," he said, grabbing hold of Joel's hair and twisted. Joel yelped as Martin tightened his grip.

"I didn't! I didn't!"

"Let him be!" Erin tried to wriggle free.

"Girl, I owe you something." Martin let go of Joel's hair and struck Erin hard over the shin with a crutch. She fell, tears running down her cheek from the pain.

"I will make your lives hell," he said and left them as one of the teachers came down the corridor.

Erin tried to put weight on the leg, but the pain was too much. Joel had to help her, limping, to the nurse. Nothing was broken, but she was sent home for the rest for the day. Erin's father had to interrupt his busy schedule and collected her half an hour later.

Joel planned to leave school before the last class of the day. Martin and his goons would never expect him to cut class. He knew he should feel bad, but all that was going on had made school feel insignificant. He texted Erin asking if he could come over.

"Joel, is that you? Why are you texting me in Spanish?" she replied.

Bloody phone! Now it was translating his texts! He just had to go, regardless.

He snuck out during the short break between classes, Martin nowhere to be seen. Joel hurried to Erin's place, in part because he wanted to see how she was but also to discuss what to do next. He didn't want to face whatever horrors his bedroom corner might deliver alone. And if he must, at the very least he wanted a weapon as defence.

Erin's leg had improved. She limped horribly, but at least she walked unassisted. Joel winced as she showed him the nasty red welt on her shin.

"My dad was really angry when he came to pick me up."

"My mum would have been too. She hates bullies."

She shook her head. "He's in the middle of a project and was annoyed he had to interrupt it to come and get me."

Joel didn't know what to say so kept quiet. He had found silence to be the best response in most situations.

"Do you want to check out what he's doing?"

"Are we allowed to?"

Erin shrugged and limped down the hallway. She continued into her father's study where she retrieved a set of keys from one of the desk drawers. She fumbled around under the desk for a while and beamed a big smile his way. "Shazam!"

Joel watched in amazement as one of the bookcases slid aside to reveal an ordinary looking door. Erin went through five keys before finding the right one. The door swung open revealing a large corridor with red lights giving the grey walls a sickly look. Joel heard the faint sound of sirens.

"Are you really sure we are allowed to?"

Erin shrugged again, but a slight frown told him she too was wondering why sirens were blaring.

"Let's go."

The corridor only stretched about ten meters and ended with a steel gate with a keypad. Joel had no doubt he wasn't supposed to be here.

Signs threatening legal prosecution now adorned the walls. Erin swiped a pass card, and the gate slid up without making so much as a noise. The sirens sounded much closer.

Joel entered behind Erin and found himself staring into the muzzle of an impossibly large gun. The gun was attached to what looked like more guns, attached to even more guns. He scrambled backwards, knowing escape was impossible.

"Halt!" came the voice of a drill sergeant from somewhere within all those guns. Joel froze, waiting for death by nuclear missile.

"V2, it's me," Erin said, shaking her head.

The main gun rotated over to Erin. "This is you." It turned back to point at Joel again. "But this is not!"

"This is Joel. He's a friend from school. We study together."

The guns slid back, giving Joel a chance to view more than just the weapons. V2 was a robot with limbs made of guns, so many they hid most of its torso. On top sat a miniscule head with two oversized eyes. The whole thing was painted in grey and green camouflage pattern.

"Joel. Welcome. I am V2. You and I are going to be friends."

Erin hit the side of one of the bigger guns. "Isn't he great? You should have seen your face!"

"I almost peed my pants! That wasn't funny!"

"V2 and I thought so. Didn't we?" she asked the great hulking piece of machinery. It didn't answer. "He doesn't have bullets for his guns, so you have no reason to pee your pants. He just likes to scare people."

"I do not!" V2 said. "And I do have bullets…somewhere."

The sirens stopped and a clinical halogen light replaced the red.

"V2, what is going on?"

"Classified!"

"You don't know, do you?"

"No, but if I did, it would have been classified."

"I'll check it out," she said to Joel. "Wait here."

She disappeared down a side corridor.

"She is quite something, isn't she?" V2 said. "Are you her mate?"

"Mate?"

"Will you form a family unit and have offspring?"

"I just turned thirteen!"

"My apologies. My small talk module is not fully functional."

"You can say that again."

"My apologies," V2 repeated. "My small talk module is not fully functional."

Joel was impressed. V2's voice processing was far beyond any intelligent assistant he'd played around with before. Its replies were almost human, most of the time.

"What are they doing in there?"

"Classified!" V2 boomed, obviously glad to be back on familiar ground.

"Are they doing research?"

"Classified!"

"Some kind of weapon?"

"Highly classified!"

"Aha! So they are researching weapons. Why else would you say highly classified to that question and not just classified?"

"I am varying responses to give you a more pleasurable communication experience. Research shows humans prefer variation even though the message is the same. Would you prefer this function in the off mode for the rest of this conversation?"

"No, I'm fine. Can you tell me anything at all?"

To Joel's relief Erin picked this moment to return. She handed him a plastic card.

"V2, let Joel pass."

"This is your brother's ID-card," V2 said without moving.

"Yes, my dad said he could use it today until they had a proper one made."

V2 hesitated for an instance before stepping aside.

"Good boy." Erin patted the machine as she passed with Joel close behind her.

"V2 seems a bit...strange," he said as they turned the corner.

"He's harmless. I've reprogrammed him more times than I can count. Dad let me have him as a playmate. That's why he doesn't have any bullets."

"You've programmed your own robot?"

"I guess, yeah."

"Wow!"

"Thanks," said Erin, blushing.

Joel smiled to himself. He never thought he'd ever compliment a girl on her programming skills, nor make her blush.

The light flashed, and the corridor was again bathed in red light. The sirens wailed, this time much closer.

"Let's check out the main lab."

Erin walked past door after door until she reached the biggest one. A note saying "Oneiromator" was sticky taped on the door.

"This is where the action is."

She opened the door enough to peek through the crack. The sound of the sirens increased. She nodded to Joel and they entered. In the middle of the room on a raised platform stood five metallic pillars in a crude circle, each about two meters apart. Cables snaked along the floor from the pillars to a couple of computers on a desk nearby. Joel could feel his skin tingle from the electric charge in the air. A few people with lab coats hurried between machines and monitors, but they seemed inconsequential to what he was seeing in the middle of the five pillars. The air between them vibrated, like heat rising from hot asphalt. Through the haze he saw darkness, a dark blue nothing, like a starless sky. The surface was disturbed by a protruding gleaming metal instrument.

"We have another incoming," one of the inconsequential people yelled. "We have to stabilise the field!"

Joel stared in horror as four more metal instruments appeared followed by a hand. The beginning of a tattered, dirty white sleeve came into view.

"We have to shut it down!"

"We have an active transfer!" It was Erin's father. He looked like a bigger version of her. "They can stabilise the gate from their end! We'll lose control!"

"We don't have a choice!"

The field grew solid, and the arm froze, plummeting to the ground. There was no blood. The closing of the portal had cauterised and sealed the stump.

"We almost lost this time! How do they do that? We're initiating the machine from here. How can they open the portal?"

"No idea." Erin's father sat back and caught view of Erin and Joel. "Get them out of here!" He turned back to the screen. The young man, the only one not wearing a lab coat, came towards them. He looked tired with unkempt hair that could be a fashion statement or just suffering from neglect. Joel had never been able to tell the difference. He gave Joel a cursory glance, sneered and turned his tired eyes to Erin.

"This is a restricted area. You know that."

"Not for me," Erin answered.

He pushed her back out the door and Joel followed.

"Who's he?" he asked with a nod towards Joel once they had left the lab. "Your boyfriend?"

Joel felt himself going cold. He had no idea what Erin would regard as the right answer.

"He's a friend from school," Erin said. "This is my brother," she said to Joel, motioning towards the young man as if he was on display. "I got both the brains and the beauty. Not sure what that leaves you with, Terrence." She emphasised the last syllable in his name.

"Stop that." Terrence checked his pockets. "I must have left my pass in the lab. Wait for me here."

Joel did as he was told. He had ended up in enough trouble listening to Erin. He didn't know the punishment for entering a government facility without proper clearance and he wasn't looking forward to finding out.

As he worried about crime and punishment, he caught a movement from the corner of his eye. He narrowed it down to a door with a little window. Something had moved inside and judging by the dead bolt on the door, it was held captive.

"Did you see that?" Joel pointed at the door.

"What?"

"Something is locked up in there."

Joel walked over to the small window. At first, he saw nothing but darkness, but as his eyes adjusted, he made out a shape sitting on a bench.

"It is probably just some test animals or something."

"Not something. Someone."

As soon as he uttered the words, he realized he was wrong. Its fingers extended into metallic shapes and gleamed in the sparse light. The thing turned a malformed head towards the door and grinned, revealing row upon row of teeth at odd angles. It reminded Joel of a meat grinder.

Joel took a few steps backwards and pointed at the door.

"They've got one of those things in there!"

Erin frowned as she peeked into the little window. She too took a few steps back.

"You took my card, didn't you?" Terrence held out his hand. "Give it back."

"What have you got in there?" Joel pointed at the door.

"Classified. Give me my card back."

Joel handed it over.

"Terrence, we saw one of those things last night."

"Impossible." He sniffed and shook his head. "Only one has come through and we control the gate."

"Didn't look like you had control," Erin said.

Terrence stared at her for a few seconds. "This is classified. You're not allowed in there and you know it. You are going to be grounded forever." He turned to Joel. "And you are no longer allowed on the premises. Get out."

"I'm sorry," Erin said to Joel. "I'll talk to dad. I'll sort it out."

"No, she won't," Terrence said. "Get out now."

Terrence and V2 promptly escorted Joel off the premises. Erin appealed to Terrence throughout, but to no avail.

Joel walked home in absolute terror. He tasted the fear, a bitter gag-inducing lump in his throat. The machine was part of the creatures appearing in his room, but what would show up next? What did the machine do? Open portals to another dimension? It didn't sit right with him. The monster last night had been talking about credit cards, which surely wasn't a concept that would exist in other worlds or dimensions? And the fact it had been speaking English further stretched the improbable to the impossible.

It didn't matter how much he turned it over in his mind. He dreaded the idea of spending another night in his room.

6

Attack of the Tooth Ghouls

In the afternoon Joel sat in his bed with a baseball bat. It was a gift from three years ago when his mother still believed the right equipment was all he needed to become an athlete. Now he was happy she had. He had his little pocketknife too, though he doubted its effectiveness against anyone, or anything, even the scuttler. He had placed as many obstructions as possible between himself and the corner. It wasn't much, but better than nothing.

"Joel?"

The door opened and his mother came in holding her phone.

"Have you heard? There has been a terrorist attack."

"They've blown something up?"

"No, they've put some kind of drug into the water. I'm not sure what's going on, but there have been a lot of reported sightings of strange creatures."

"Where?" Joel asked, suddenly interested.

"All around the city, apparently."

"Weird terrorist attack."

"Who knows why terrorists do anything. They recommend we stay indoors until they've determined the cause. So no school for you tomorrow."

Joel didn't mind. With Martin back, he preferred home anyway.

His phone rang.

"That's a strange ring tone," his mum said. "Do you like it?"

"I do," he said and quickly grabbed it from the nightstand to hide the cracked screen.

"Joel here," he said.

"Finally!" Erin whispered. "They broke through. They're everywhere. I've managed to hide, but they seem to be able to sniff us out. Humans, I mean."

Joel heard a sugary sweet voice in the background: "Come out, come out. If you're a good girl, you'll get jellybeans when we're finished."

"I know what they are. It doesn't make any sense, but they are some kind of nightmare version of a dentist. Do you know what the weirdest thing is? They are looking for us."

"What?"

"They have descriptions and even drawings of both of us."

"But...but...why? How?"

"They've found me!" she whispered. "I have to run. I have to..."

The line went dead.

Joel had no idea what it all meant. Dentist things wanted him? He couldn't even begin to make sense of the situation. It mattered little. He had to help her. He wasn't sure what to do, but Erin would have come to his rescue without a second thought and he felt he owed her the same.

Without a word to his mother he grabbed his backpack and gathered some food and clothes along with the few things he owned, resulting in a basic rescue pack. A book about survival, his pocketknife, a plastic bottle filled with water, a piece of rope and the knife the scuttler had left behind.

He waited until his mother was out of sight then simply walked out the front door and ran down the steps. He kept running until he had to stop to catch his breath. A few cars remained on the road, but not much else. It felt like a ghost city. Perhaps it was. Maybe the creatures took the city building by building. The thought made him stop dead in his tracks. Had he left his mother to their mercy? He decided to head back as soon as he had helped Erin.

He finished the journey at a brisk speed and again had to stop to catch his breath. The reality of what he was going to do dawned on him. He was going up against monsters to rescue Erin and was already tired from the short run over to her house! A hero indeed.

He put the thoughts out of his head and tried the door. It was locked, so he tried to locate other ways inside. A little sticker on the windows promised they were unbreakable, and a few attempts with a rock confirmed it. He contemplated climbing to the second-floor windows but decided to check the metal gate in the lane instead. He had seen Erin key in the number. He hadn't tried to memorize the code, but he was good at recalling memories. He hoped it was enough to reconstruct the number sequence.

When he reached the metal gate, he realised any concerns about codes were pointless. The gate had buckled outwards as if something had exploded on the inside, the metal deformed from the force. He laid his hand against the cold metal and felt vibrations. It was trying to open but was stuck, leaving only a small gap to the ground. Joel thought he'd be able to squeeze through the small opening. He exhaled and pulled himself through headfirst.

Deformed metal debris littered the floor and not far from the gate was a shape he knew—V2. The robot lay on the ground, its upper body connected to the legs by only a few cables. One arm had been ripped off. Its small head swivelled in Joel's direction with a groan from the twisted metal.

"Master Joel, I'm only twenty percent operational."

"What happened here?" Joel asked, crouching down next to the hulking body.

"Enemies appeared from the secure area and took over the facility. They got hold of weapons and wiped out our defences. With bullets I'd have been able to hold them off."

"Where did they come from?"

"They appeared all over the facility. Someone must have let them inside. A traitor."

From Joel's experiences of the past few nights, he doubted they needed a traitor to appear wherever they felt like.

"What about Erin?" he asked. "Where is she?"

"I found her hiding in a back room and tried helping her, but I failed. They ambushed me here and took her."

"Took her where?"

"Into the secure area." V2's chassis shuddered. "This will be my last stand. Master Joel, you have to help Erin."

Joel questioned what he could contribute when a robot designed for war had failed. He had never been much for taking risks and he didn't really want to find out what the dentist things planned to do, especially not firsthand.

"I will draw them to me and you sneak in," V2 said.

"No, you…"

The robot turned on a siren drowning Joel's refusal and dragged itself forward while issuing commands to non-existent troops in a loud voice. Joel hurried down the corridor towards the closest door. If there was anything in this facility, they'd come and investigate for sure.

He made his way through side corridors and soon came to the main lab from the opposite direction. The door had been blasted from its hinges, leaving a gaping hole. As he closed in on the doorway, one of the creatures appeared. Joel froze. If it turned towards him ever so little his rescue would be over before even beginning. He stopped breathing, convinced his pulsating heartbeat would give him away.

"Noise and racket!" The creature turned towards the noise. "How can an honest man make a living?" It headed down the corridor away from Joel, muttering to itself. V2 still boomed orders and another identical creature appeared and followed the first. Joel waited a few a moment and, when no more creatures appeared, poked his head inside. The machine was running. He saw only a black space through the haze in the middle of the pillars. He stopped for a second. His plan was to charge through the opening, but watching the impenetrable darkness made him hesitate. Steel fingers dug into his neck from behind.

"A little child in my waiting room," a sugary sweet voice said from behind. "Shouldn't let you wait. No, shouldn't let you wait."

Joel was dragged backwards, unable to do anything to prevent it. The metal fingers felt awkward against his skin, threatening to cut him should he attempt escape.

"No need for assistants for this patient," said the creature as it dragged him into a nearby room. "No, no assistants. They all double bill. Yes, they do."

The door closed and its grip relaxed enough for Joel to turn. He smelled its putrid breath before its oversized head came into view.

"This won't hurt a bit." One if its hands appeared before him, each finger had dentist equipment attached. Joel could see drills, scalpels and what he thought were teeth extractors. It was a dentist, just as Erin had said, but this was a nightmare of going to the dentist—a warped version of the tooth fairy. A tooth ghoul, Joel thought to himself.

The tooth ghoul held out a finger ending in large pincers with sharp edges and a loop of metal wire trailing underneath. Joel wriggled and grabbed hold of its hand to stop the instrument from getting closer.

"No reason to resist." An unnatural grin revealed yellowing teeth of different sizes and colours, many of them animal teeth. "Oh, that's a fine specimen."

The ghoul made a few more attempts, but Joel held on to the hand.

"Uncooperative. Must work overtime. Will cost extra. Health fund won't cover overtime. No, it won't."

The ghoul spied an office chair with a high back and whooped in delight. It dragged Joel towards the chair. Dread seized him. He knew he couldn't escape if he was pinned down in the chair.

The door opened, and another ghoul appeared in the doorway. Its appearance much the same as the other one. It smiled, showing an abundance of teeth, some of them rotting. Joel guessed this was a much older ghoul.

"This one is mine," the first one exclaimed, holding Joel close. "All those beautiful teeth! All mine!"

The older ghoul entered the room, extending a finger with an oversized drill running with an ear-piercing whine. Joel's captor let him go to battle the new threat and soon the two ghouls were tangled as they tried to land a killing blow.

Joel took the chance to escape. As he left the room, he glimpsed the younger of the ghouls pressing the other down, starting to pull its teeth out one by one. Joel didn't waste a second. He ran back to the main lab and directly to the computer. The screen listed locations and coordinates, none of which made any sense to Joel. He selected one at random. The darkness in the middle of the haze blinked out of existence and the most beautiful glade Joel had ever seen took its place. A glossy postcard made reality.

"The boy!" he heard behind him. "Get him away from the portal!"

No time to consider. He ran for the opening and threw himself through the hole into the glade, eyes firmly closed.

7

Pursuit

Martin prowled the streets for something to do. If that involved revenge on one of his favourite targets, so much better. The warnings on local news had the opposite effect on him. If terrorists were around, he wanted to see what they planned with his own eyes.

He had been hanging around the apartment complex where Joel lived and had just missed him as he ran past. He refused to use the crutches, but as a result only managed a limping half jog. Nevertheless, he caught up with Joel as he headed around the block. Martin had no idea what the little cockroach was trying to do but was intrigued. Was he trying to break into the building? Martin stayed out of view and watched as Joel crept under the steel gate. He waited for a while, hoping to catch him as he made his exit, but as soon as the alarm sounded curiosity overcame him. This had to be related to the terrorist attack and Joel was involved somehow. The little cockroach had more guts than he thought.

Martin wouldn't fit through the gap, so he grabbed hold and pulled with all his might. It gave a bit, but not enough. He searched the alley and found a rusty steel bar. He jammed it into the opening and pulled until his head felt ready to explode. The gate had shifted a bit.

He squeezed through the gap when a loud wrenching noise stopped the alarm.

"No more noise from this machine!"

Martin had no idea who had spoken. It sounded almost like a child.

"Come! Come! The human boy is here!" Another voice, but similar.

"The boy?"

"The boy from the contract! Come! He went through the portal!"

Martin heard shuffling footsteps and waited until they disappeared. He pushed himself through and hurried after them, barely looking at anything else. If Joel was captured, he wanted a front-row seat. He turned a corner and stopped dead. He had almost run headfirst into the back of two white-robed men. He shuffled backwards to the relative protection behind the corner.

This must have been the two people conversing, but he couldn't reconcile the voices with the grown men ahead of him. He only saw them from behind, but it didn't take long for him to realise they were not men at all. The way they moved was just wrong somehow. Their bulbous heads seemed to float above their bodies while the arms swung back and forth. They held metal instruments in their hands.

They disappeared into a room. Martin waited a few seconds before hazarding a look. This must be the portal they spoke about. It didn't look like much. He'd seen better in video games and movies. The opening didn't even look like it was going anywhere interesting. He saw some trees and a few more of those creatures he'd been following, with two of them about to enter the portal.

"The Borderlands," one of them said. "Why would the boy go there?"

"Boy has allies. Reinforcements are on their way."

The rest of the discussion was lost as they stepped through the portal. As soon as its surface no longer rippled, the forest slowly faded away. The room was empty, so he entered, making his way to the computer. Another huge disappointment. No windows or fancy icons. It was practically Stone Age with a basic text menu that read:

Oneiromator

Start/Shut down [started]
Generate Field [standby]
Set Time & Location Coordinates
Establish Gate
Calibrate Gate
Health Check
Debug
Warning: Calibrate prior to establishing gate to prevent fluctuations in time parameters.
Option>

Martin didn't waste any time. He wanted to know which places this machine could send him. If the TV series Stargate was anything to go by, thousands of worlds waited to be explored. He didn't want to go to a stupid forest planet. He selected the second option and was prompted to enter four coordinates, select from previous locations, or select the latest known successful location.

"The boy! The boy is here!"

Martin glanced at the door. More of those weird things entered the room. He didn't have time to explore the options. He had to settle for the stupid forest planet.

He selected the latest known location and ran towards the portal as it formed. His last thought before he jumped was how bright the day was on the other end.

8

The Intersect

A gentle breeze carried with it the scents of the surrounding forest. It wasn't just the pleasant overtones of flowers, but also heavier scents, as if Joel had taken his mother's spices and thrown them up in the air. He opened one eye experimentally followed by the other. He sat in the glade he had seen through the portal. He turned around immediately, half expecting the tooth ghouls in hot pursuit. To his surprise the facility, the wall, even the hole was gone. Instead, he saw a thinning forest giving way to farmland.

He ran towards the trees and threw himself down into the undergrowth. At first his own breathing overtook any other sounds, as he struggled for air.

A minute passed. Then another. His breathing slowed down, and he was just about to leave the relative safety of the high grass when he felt an electric charge building. He made himself as small as possible as the air turned liquid. Ripples formed as a shape stepped through. It was a large tooth ghoul, all fingers replaced by spikes and long knives, its coat dirty and ragged. It walked on all fours and sniffed the air, its head swaying back and forth, large sharpened teeth protruding from an oversized mouth. This tooth ghoul was built for battle.

Joel crawled backwards in terror. He wanted to be as far away from this thing as he could. Another tooth ghoul appeared, this one looking more like the ones he'd seen before.

"The boy is here, isn't he?"

The large ghoul kept sniffing the air, its mouth widening even further.

"I thought so. Let's wait for the others."

Joel kept crawling backwards, never taking his eyes off the two tooth ghouls. As soon as he had lost sight of them, he stood up and ran in the opposite direction. To his dismay the trees thinned. This wasn't so much a forest as a large cluster of trees. He hazarded a look back and promptly toppled over a hidden obstacle. He turned and fell on his back staring up in the air. Large dome-like clay nests rested in the foliage.

"Alarm! Alarm! We are being attacked! I've felled a giant invader!" A voice came from somewhere close to his feet. It wasn't so much a voice as a combination of whistles and clicks, surprising Joel that he understood anything at all. He sat up and looked around, trying to locate the source of the sound. A scuttler shifting back and forth on its many legs raced off as soon as he moved. A ten meters dash later it stopped and tentatively made its way back.

"Sorry, two-legger. We've had some sightings of the Uncompleted. Must be alert."

"The Uncompleted?" Joel asked.

"You don't know about them?" The scuttler stood on its two hind leg pairs to have a closer look and whistled excitedly. "You're a visitor! We don't get many of you out this way."

"Tooth ghouls are chasing me. I need to keep going."

"Citizens of the Flux don't come here," the scuttler said, waving a claw.

"I still need to go..."

"You will have to wait." It clipped threateningly in the air with its biggest claw. "The elders will want to meet you."

Joel shook his head. He needed to rest for a few minutes anyway, so sat on a small boulder. He dug around in his backpack and retrieved the little knife one of the scuttlers had left in his room.

"Here, take this. I assume it belongs to one of you."

The giant crab eyed the knife for a moment and scuttled to the left.

"The One Who Lives Amongst the High Branches told us about you!" It again scuttled off. "Treason! Murder! I've caught the giant jelly monster! I've got him!"

Joel looked around, thinking someone else around here better fit the description. Out of the dwellings in the trees came crabs of different sizes and colourings. A few of them fell as they clumsily made their way down the trunks, bouncing ungracefully on their shells. One even ended up stuck upside down, its legs and claws flailing ineffectively. Three others had to help to push it over. Joel couldn't help but smile as they came to some semblance of order.

"Why are you smiling, outlander?" one of the larger ones demanded. Its shell was by far the most colourful and intricately carved of them all.

"I'm sorry," Joel said not able to wipe the grin from his face, "but it makes no sense for crabs to live in trees."

This upset the scuttlers who now numbered in the hundreds. They whistled threateningly and banged their claws together.

"Be still!" a scuttler whistled, immediately silencing the others. They moved aside to let it through. Its shell was cracked and worn.

"You say we shouldn't live in trees? Why then do we have hard shells if not to protect us when we fall?"

The gathered scuttlers all clicked their claws together in what Joel assumed was approval.

"The shell is for protection against enemies, not falling out of trees!"

"This, I believe is an unproven opinion, not an argument," the old scuttler said, again prompting an immediate claw-clicking response. "We have no use of such protection from enemies. We have always been tree dwellers and…"

"Enough!" Another scuttler positioned itself right in front of Joel, holding out its claw. "Give me what's mine!"

The crabs were all similar, but he still knew this one. He handed over the knife.

"I'm so sorry, I..."

The scuttler waved the knife at him threateningly. "I should shish-kebab you, you..."

The old scuttler suddenly hit the other hard on the shell. "You forget your place!"

"I apologise, You Who Always Lands On Your Legs, but this creature stole my ceremonial dagger."

"This is the giant jelly monster you wrestled with?"

The scuttler studied Joel, from head to toe. "He is pretty big," the scuttler whistled. "And he looks all soft and jelly like."

"That wasn't what happened," Joel said. "He appeared in my bedroom and attacked my bed with his knife and then ran away."

"Is this true?" the old scuttler asked.

"I will take your legs off for this!" The scuttler whistled as it came closer.

Loud warning whistles made them all turn towards a new threat. The tooth ghouls had caught up and the four-legged tooth ghoul carved a path through the scuttlers, knife hands cutting like scythes through their shells. It seemed an impossible foe for the smaller crabs, but once they were organised, they just swarmed the ghoul, losing five more of their numbers in the process.

Joel turned and ran. He knew more tooth ghouls were coming, and he didn't think the scuttlers made reliable allies. He kept running until he could no longer breathe. His body rebelled against this sudden activity, and for the first time in his life, he cursed himself for not trying harder during physical education. He dry-retched and tasted blood in his mouth. It was as if his internal organs were looking for a way out.

A young man approached from the edge of the forest roughly where Joel had come from. Joel eyed him, worried he too might be a threat. At this point the only thing Joel could do was sweat on him profusely, but it didn't hurt to be cautious.

He appeared human and normal enough, apart from being overly hairy. The young man gesticulated wildly with his left hand. He grabbed hold of it with the right hand and hit it against the ground repeatedly. It was such strange behaviour that Joel found comfort in it. Surely, this could not be an enemy.

"You probably want to keep going if you are running from the mess back there."

Joel raised his hand. He still struggled for air, and the little he managed to inhale was all used to keep him alive, leaving little to form actual words.

"Come here." The young man grabbed Joel around his waist, forcing him to stand up. "You need to move if you don't want them to catch up."

The young man's strength surprised him. He set off with long strides, Joel's feet hardly touching the ground. He was dragged along for a couple of minutes before he extracted himself from the grip. The young man's left hand had been busy exploring his chest and shoulder.

"What is wrong with your hand?"

"Nothing is wrong, young master. A friendly demon resides in it. Most of the time we agree, but sometimes it does whatever it feels like. Good to have around sometimes, though. It is quite skilled with a blade."

Joel didn't say anything at first. He knew he should use the time to find out more about the place and the things chasing him, but that had to wait. "There is something called Alien Hand Syndrome. Perhaps that is your problem. It makes you feel like your hand is not part of your body."

"Of course it is part of my body." The young man took hold of his left wrist and shook. "There, you see. Definitely part of my body." He smiled. "You must be a man of science to know this. I too am a student of the mysteries of science. My specialty is medical afflictions. What is yours?"

"I just like knowing things."

"I think I'd like us to be better acquainted. Where are you heading?"

The left hand crawled into his left armpit and settled. It didn't look especially comfortable, but the young man didn't seem to mind.

"I...I don't know." Rescuing Erin now seemed ridiculous, but he still had to try. "My friend was captured by the..." He hesitated. He had no idea what to call the dentist creatures. "...things back in the glade. I came in after her."

"The tooth ghouls?" the man asked. "Then you have a long journey ahead of you. Their homeland is in the Flux. I've never seen them this far out in the Borderlands before."

Tooth ghouls? He used the name Joel had given them. Had he been lucky enough to guess their name? Or had Erin told him?

The young man stopped and turned to Joel with a smile on his face. "I think introductions are in order. I am known as the Guide."

"The Guide? Is that your name?"

"It is my function so it may as well be my name."

Joel thought it sounded a bit odd, but he knew people named Barber, Hunter and Smith and so on and they were also jobs, even if they no longer actually described what people did.

"So what is your name, young man of science?"

"Joel."

"Just Joel?"

"Joel the Hunter," Joel said after a while, picking an old character name from an online game he played.

"That is no name for a man of science," said the Guide, frowning.

"I'm not a man of science. Most things can be explained nowadays. Like..." Joel tried to locate something else to further demonstrate the power of science. "Like all the hair you've got—it's called hypertrichosis."

The young man frowned. "Hypertrichosis? Is that the name for excessive hair growth?"

Joel nodded.

"Indeed!" He took a few long steps, turned around and burst into song—a rendition of *Diamonds are a Girl's best friend*.

Radiotherapy makes history of your hair,

Hypertrichosis makes it grow like a fountain,

Bulimia makes you vomit with flair

Diarrhoea makes you poo a mountain

Casodex, Minoxidil,

Prozac, Imodium!

Medication is my best friend.

"They sure are my best friends! Yes indeed, they're all my best friends!" The Guide finished and curtsied with a wink. "I was never able to complete that song. Thanks to you it is now perfect."

Joel couldn't help but smile. "You are crazy."

"Surely, a man of science can come up with a more accurate diagnosis?" the Guide said and returned the smile. He studied the edge of the forest. "We need to get a move on. The scuttlers will only keep them away for so long."

Scuttlers? Had he heard him right? This was too much of a coincidence. How could The Guide know names he had just made up?

"This girl you spoke of, is it perhaps a rescue mission?"

"I guess," Joel said.

The Guide whooped with happiness and danced around, while his left hand waved as if it was conducting an invisible orchestra. "A hero! You are a hero! And a man of science!"

"No, I'm not." Joel shook his head. "I'm as far from a hero as they come."

"You are on your way to rescue a fair maiden, are you not?"

"Well, yes."

"Isn't that what heroes do?"

"Yes, but..."

"You're a hero," the Guide said as if it was clear as day.

"If you put it that way, I guess."

"Come! I know someone who can help. He's an expert at heroes."

9

Joel the Magnificent

The Guide set off at great speed before he could protest. Joel had no idea what a hero expert could possibly help him with, but at least the Guide was willing to both help and set a direction. Joel stumbled after him. The sun had finally set, and the sparse light wasn't enough to ensure good footing.

"Hurry! The tooth ghouls will not stop to rest."

"Why do you call them tooth ghouls?"

"It is the name given to them," the Guide said. "Same as for all new races."

"How exactly?"

"They came up with it themselves, presumably. Or the Oracle's maybe? Why are you called a human?"

"I don't know," Joel had to admit.

"There you go. Maybe you came up with your name too."

"What is this place?"

"The Borderlands? It is the gateway to the Ancient Realms."

"No, I mean this planet."

"You are from a planet?" the Guide asked. "A giant sphere suspended in nothingness?"

"Yes! Are you saying this is not a planet?"

The Guide laughed. "Of course not! This is the Intersect."

"And what is that then if it isn't a planet?"

Suddenly the long grass clinging to his legs disappeared, and he stepped into nothingness. He stumbled forward onto a small dirt road and regained his footing.

"We're close," the Guide said and started down the road. "I will tell you more of this place, but right now we need to focus on more important things. You need a better name. One that tells how heroic you are. How about Joel the Just? No, something with more power. How about Joel the Destroyer?" The Guide studied him with pursed lips. "Maybe not."

Joel kept quiet as the Guide went through other naming options. His suggestions included Joel the Hun, Joel the Ghoul Master and Joel the Magnificent.

"Where are we going?" Joel said, having had enough of the poor name suggestions.

"To Mr Anglar. He loves heroes."

"I'm not a hero," Joel repeated.

"I've told you already. Look!" The Guide pointed down the road towards a mansion, a dark shape barely visible against a sky of swirling stars. His left hand immediately pointed in the opposite direction. "Don't trust the left hand."

As they approached, Joel could make out more details. The front door was a grand affair, ornate in blue and gold. It was big enough to fit a giant, but the Guide aimed towards a small side entrance that in comparison seemed designed for midgets. The Guide knocked, obviously thrilled at the prospect of introducing Joel.

A small old man with white tufts of hair growing from his temples and eyebrows opened the door. He was dressed in a black ill-fitting suit and polished shoes several sizes too large.

"Mr Anglar, I have another hero for you. I present to you, Joel the Barbarian!"

The peculiar old man studied Joel starting at his feet and slowly making his way up to his face, which had him stand on his toes and almost topple backwards.

"He doesn't look much like a hero to me," he sniffed as he held out Joel's arm, measuring the size of his bicep.

"I'm not a hero."

"That surely isn't for you to decide," Mr Anglar said dismissively, but Joel's protestations seemed to pique his interest.

"He's modest," the Guide said. "Truly the mark of a hero. Joel doesn't care for titles or reward. He has set himself the task to rescue a fair maiden. What else could be more heroic? Any true hero would say he's not."

"So if I say I'm a hero, I prove I'm not?" Joel asked.

"Logic would agree with that," Mr Anglar said as he continued his examination, grunting and snorting as he went along.

"Ok, I'm a hero then."

"So there you are," Mr Anglar said. "Now, even from your own lips, you are a hero."

"I told you!" the Guide said with a broad smile.

"But you just said…"

"I said logic would agree," Mr Anglar interrupted. "I find logic highly overrated. Are you here to rescue a maiden?"

"Yes, Erin is a friend of mine and she was captured by the tooth ghouls. I'll help her if I can."

"Perhaps there is some validity to your claim," Mr Anglar said with a side-glance to the Guide. He stepped aside and let Joel enter. He was grabbed from behind after a few steps. It was one of those grips that promised there was no escape—ever. He craned his neck around to see his captors and wished he hadn't. What he saw seemed to be a cross between a giant insect and a cat with teeth like razors moving in a three-part jaw. Joel wondered how it ever chewed any kind of food without also eating half its face off. There were marks indicating this was perhaps indeed the case.

"Another one for the collection," Mr Anglar said walking down the corridor with Joel dragged behind him by the insect beasts. "Let's get him to the Valuer and find out what he's worth."

"Let me go!" Joel shouted at the nightmares behind him and struggled to get free.

"Stop it," one of the insect beasts said, its voice a combination of whirring cicadas and grinding metal.

"I wouldn't do that," Mr Anglar said. "They've accidentally ripped arms off bigger heroes than you."

Joel stopped struggling. He wasn't going to escape whatever fate they had in store for him.

"What are you doing?" Joel asked.

"I collect heroes," Mr Anglar said.

It took Joel a few seconds to get his head around the answer. What did he mean? Was he collecting them like cards of your favourite sports team or, as in Joel's case, famous scientists?

"Why?"

"Just like a hero. So fixed on his single purpose he can't see the bigger picture. A great evil will attack our world and I am collecting heroes to combat this evil. You heroes are very narrow-minded. Save the princess, kill the monster. All those heroic deeds should be put to good use when and where it matters."

"I'm no hero!"

"Perhaps you are smarter than the average hero and say that so you can continue your pointless little quest. I must be sure."

Joel was dragged through an opening into a large hall. The sudden change from the drab darkness of the small corridor blinded him. It was still dark, but pools of sunlight found their way through high arched windows. Each step created a mushroom of particles from the floor. Half blind from light and dust, Joel caught a glimpse of wooden walls, carved as if they were priceless pieces of art, before he ended up in another equally small and dark corridor.

"When is this great evil going to appear?"

"In the next five hundred years if my calculations are correct."

Joel couldn't believe what he was hearing. Five hundred years! Even if he was a hero, he couldn't wait that long.

"But what if it's already here?" Joel asked, hoping to find an angle where he might escape. "What if the great evil has already started?"

"Already started? By the wailing Gods of Drimmick! The apocalypse starting without me knowing? That would be like…" He stopped, considering for a while. "I don't know what that would be like. Unheard of!"

Joel was pushed into an empty room. The walls, floor and ceiling were all made of the same grey substance, almost like a padded cell.

"House, I have another hero to join our ranks," Mr Anglar said to no one in particular.

At first nothing happened, but a sudden movement under his feet and Joel realised they were engulfed by the grey substance. It was alive! He tried to move, but the grey matter didn't budge. Tendrils ran up his legs, some of them reaching all the way to his head and hands. They attached themselves like leeches over his body, and even though it felt like slugs squirming against his skin, it didn't hurt.

"Evaluation commenced," a dry voice said, coming from nowhere and everywhere at the same time. "High level heroic attributes assessed."

"Now let's see," Mr Anglar said and rubbed his hands.

"Courage?" the dry voice said. "Minimal."

"That's disappointing," Mr Anglar said with a frown, "but there are plenty of heroes without courage."

"Bravery?" the dry voice said. "None. Selflessness? Some."

"Pah!" Mr Anglar said. "Never saw a selfless hero. Don't know why it measures that."

"Physical prowess? Minimal."

"We've all got eyes!" Mr Anglar said. "Get on with it."

"Mental capacity? Above average."

"An intelligent hero?" Mr Anglar said, frown getting deeper for each new assessment. "Preposterous!"

"Probing deeper."

Joel was embarrassed. He knew he wasn't a hero, but to hear his shortcoming one by one was humiliating. The tendrils quivered as they delved deeper into Joel's non-heroism.

"Exaggerated belief in self?" The voice intoned after a while. "None."

"Well, that's a deal breaker! Stop this farce!" Mr Anglar exclaimed.

"Evaluation terminated," the dry voice said with what sounded like irritation. "Evaluation incomplete, but not an inch, nor pound nor any other measure of heroism detected."

"Heroes are so hard to come by these days," Mr Anglar said, shaking his head. "Get rid of him."

The grey matter released Joel and for a few precious seconds he was free. Joel preferred not to find out what his captor meant by getting rid of him, so he ran towards the only other exit from the room. His freedom lasted all but five meters. An insect beast waited in an opening beyond the door and grabbed him as he passed. It dumped him down a foul-smelling vertical chute. Joel tried to break his fall by pushing his legs and back against the sides but was unable to stop. After a few metres it changed direction, and he slid, faster and faster. Then an opening appeared in the darkness. He cleared the chute and found himself free-falling.

10

Shade Returns

Joel landed headfirst on top of a mountain of garbage. He sat up and tried to dislodge a partially eaten chicken bone from his hair when a blow to the head replanted him face first in the garbage heap. He sat up again and discovered his backpack. He grabbed it and mountaineered down the garbage slope.

Five minutes later he reached the bottom. He found Gabe Shade leaning against a tree.

"Words matter here, kid. I told you so, didn't I?"

Joel stared at him. Shade had been part of his dreams for years, but this didn't feel like a dream at all and still here he was. Nothing that had happened these last few days made any sense. He couldn't work it all out but was certain the private investigator was responsible somehow.

"I thought you were my friend! I thought I was going to die!" Joel struck Gabe, putting all his anger into it.

The private investigator easily sidestepped his strike and grabbed his hand, pulling him close. "Don't hit people unless you mean it, kid. And you should be reasonably sure you can win too."

"Who are you? What do you want with me?" pleaded Joel.

"I'm your babysitter, it seems," he said with an air of contempt. "At least until you've grown up."

Joel sat down, tears welling up in his eyes. When he had dreamed of adventures, this wasn't what he had expected. He was hungry, angry and very, very afraid.

"You knew the Guide would take me here, didn't you?" he said, refusing to give in to the tears. He wasn't going to cry in front of Shade.

"I'm sorry kid, but you needed to learn a lesson." Shade crouched down next to him. "If you are going to amount to anything, you need to stop following and be a leader. Make your own decisions and mistakes. Don't just walk into one's others make for you."

Joel hated having it spelled out to him. He knew Gabe was right, but it didn't mean he was willing to accept it. Gabe could have simply told him this and not put him in mortal danger.

"In that case my first decision will be to stop listening to you." It was childish, but still satisfying to rebel, even if only in a minor way.

"Fine, kid." Gabe shrugged. "So what now?"

Joel returned the shrug. For the first time since he'd come through the portal, he wasn't running.

"Why am I here?"

"You're a Nexus."

"A what?"

"You are a focal point for events here."

"What does that even mean?" Joel asked, not understanding a word he'd heard.

"I'll make this easy for you, kid. Do you know what this place is?"

"I don't know. You are here, so I figured it is a dream world of some kind, but I don't know anymore. Another dimension?"

"Another dimension? That'll do for now," Shade said. "Your thoughts are strong, much stronger than anyone else in your world. Here it makes you powerful and power attracts both the good and the bad. It even makes it possible for you to shape events here, make your thoughts reality."

"So this is all because of me?"

"In a way. But someone opened the gate from this end. There is a wider agenda here. Someone is making this happen. Why, I don't know."

Joel didn't know what to say or even ask. The answers made no sense. He suspected Shade was lying to him, so instead he decided to focus on the one thing he did understand and the reason he ventured into the portal.

"Do you know where Erin is?"

"Why?"

"We need to save her."

"A quest?" he asked and turned to Joel, his eyes trying to decipher how serious Joel was. "I think that would be suitable."

"Do you know where she is?" Joel repeated.

"She is held by the tooth ghouls so we must go to the Flux."

"What's that?"

"Parts of this world are more stable than others. New ideas occur there. It is ever changing much like your world."

"Is it far away?"

"Well, that's the challenge. I don't know."

"What use are you then?" Joel asked knowing immediately he'd overstepped the line.

The private investigator glared at him. "The last person who spoke to me like that is dead. I know your feelings are hurt and all, but watch it, kid."

"I'm sorry," said Joel, secretly pleased at having stood up to the man. He was now more than a little afraid of Gabe Shade.

"Our geography is constantly changing, especially now. We need help."

"Geography can't just change!" Joel demonstrated by jumping on the spot.

"I thought it changed in your world too."

"No, it doesn't! Cities don't just move around."

"What about continental drift?" Gabe asked with a grin.

"But...that's not the same thing. You can't..."

"Be quiet." Shade surveyed the area. His expression didn't change, but Joel knew better than to argue. Something was wrong. "We need to go. We've wasted too much time. They are close."

"The tooth ghouls?"

Shade nodded. "Or worse." He walked off into the darkness.

Joel had no idea what could be worse than tooth ghouls and he didn't really want to find out—especially not on his own. He grabbed his backpack and ran after Gabe.

"Where are we going?"

"Bahamas, a small town not far from here. Let's hope they're not there yet."

Joel trudged along through the grass fields, but it wasn't long until he saw light ahead. At first he thought it just a lantern, but as they approached, it broke apart to separate sources—windows, streetlights and a small fire.

Gabe stopped suddenly and Joel, who had been trying to catch up, walked straight into him.

"Someone is coming."

Joel listened as hard as he could, but still could only hear his own breathing. He saw nothing between them and the lights. The private investigator grabbed him and pulled him down, gesturing for him to be silent.

"Found you," a whisper came from behind. "I thought I'd missed you."

Joel turned and saw the Guide grinning at him.

"What are you doing here?" Joel whispered back. He tried to put as much venom in it as he could but whispering in the dark limited his expressiveness somewhat.

"The tooth ghouls have taken over the town. It seems they are looking for a young human boy that just arrived. Have you seen any of those?"

Joel could feel the smile in his words. "You took me to be...collected!"

"You said you were a hero! Mr Anglar won't be so quick to believe me next time."

"You can compare bruised egos later," Gabe said, not even bothering to whisper. "We need to get out of here."

"I'm not going anywhere with him." Joel crossed his arms.

"I'm not taking him anywhere!" said the Guide, also crossing his arms.

Gabe Shade looked back and forth between them, as if to decide whom to shoot first.

"Kid, he…"

"Don't call me kid!" Joel said.

"Kid," Shade repeated, glaring at him so hard Joel thought twice about objecting again. "He took you to Mr Anglar because he is paid to bring suspected heroes. If anything, you should be flattered."

"I'm not!"

"And he's the only one around here who can guide us to where we need to go," Shade said with more than a hint of steel in his voice. "You want to save Erin? Well, he's the only one here that can help us." He turned to the Guide. "The kid is a Nexus. You have to help him."

"A Nexus?" The Guide said, eyes ogling at Joel.

A high-pitched tittering from somewhere close by sent ice down Joel's spine. He stared into the dark, willing his eyes to adjust. He wanted to see what was out there, if only to know what his death looked like. He remembered the smart phone in his backpack. Maybe it could capture more than his eyes could. He pulled it out and aimed it in the general direction of the sound. To his surprise it immediately adjusted and displayed the landscape as if it was daylight. The phone felt like it belonged in his hand, the only thing that made sense in this strange place.

He stared at the screen and saw movement. He zoomed in and saw a creature sniffing the ground. At first glance it could be mistaken for a sleek cat, but its body was covered in gleaming scales. It looked up, staring in Joel's direction and let out the staccato tittering again. The scales on its body stood up, forming ridges of razor blades along its body.

Joel stumbled back, terrified, suddenly no longer wanting to see what the darkness hid.

"We need to go," the private investigator said. It didn't take many steps before the darkness engulfed him.

Joel hurried after, desperate for the little protection his companions provided, the backpack bouncing on his back. He looked around but couldn't see the Guide. Why did he stay behind?

Ten minutes later the Guide appeared.

"There you are!" Joel was relieved. He had felt bad about not going back to look for him.

"Alive and well." The Guide smiled. "I've left a few surprises to cover our trail. Let's hope it is enough."

"I don't understand. Why are they after me?"

"You are a Nexus. Surely there is enough reason just in that?"

Joel had no idea what that meant but couldn't muster enough interest to ask. It seemed every question led to a hundred more.

They caught up with Gabe who stood staring into the darkness. "Where to now?"

"Where are we going?" the Guide asked.

"The Flux."

"Ah, yes."

Shade flicked his lighter open and lit a cigarette. "Ah, yes, what?"

"I need to consult the map."

"You do?" Gabe Shade raised his eyebrows. This was the first time Joel had observed Shade unsure of anything. Ever.

"The geography has been changing more than usual over recent months, but in the past two weeks it's all become a jumble. I've never seen anything like it. Perhaps it is the boy causing it. I wouldn't be able to find any of the realms without consulting the map."

"I thought you said places change location all the time?" Joel asked, perplexed.

"Not so I can't find them!" the Guide said, sounding insulted.

"He can guide you to anything. That is his function here. He is named The Guide for a reason."

"I didn't think that was his name. He just said it was what he'd be for me."

"You are a Nexus," Gabe Shade said to Joel. "Your thoughts affect the very fabric of this place."

"There are some that aren't too happy about their new names. The Scuttlers have an ancestry much longer than humankind does. They took much pride in their name. It told of their heritage, in a five-minute long song. Scuttlers as a name don't really have the same...depth."

"I didn't know," Joel said, finally understanding why the crablike creatures had been so angry.

"Ignorance isn't an excuse here," Gabe said. "It is time you learnt that."

"I wasn't making excuses. I just didn't know."

"So you will help us?" Gabe Shade asked.

The Guide didn't answer. He just walked off in a random direction. Joel was too tired to argue and followed, not knowing what else to do.

***

The sunrise was spectacular and if Joel hadn't been so tired perhaps he would have appreciated it. Now it just looked like a daybreak trying too hard. The kaleidoscope of colours and swirling clouds heralded a sun birthed from the ground. Joel just stared at his feet, willing one foot to move and then the other.

"Let's stop and rest for a while," Gabe said as they reached the edge of a forest.

Joel just kept walking. Gabe had said something, but Joel no longer wasted energy on deciphering words to actual meaning. His world had shrunk to conquering the meter of road ahead of him. The Guide had to stand in his way to break the self-imposed spell.

Joel stopped, dropped the backpack and sat on the ground. For a second his body protested. It had become so accustomed to the repetitious motion it was painful even to stop. Once his body had adjusted, it demanded food. He drank the last of the water in the plastic bottle and wondered what he'd do now.

"There is plenty of fresh water around," the Guide said with a nod to the empty bottle. "Are you hungry?"

He threw over a small bundle wrapped in a cloth. Inside he found a piece of hard dark bread and a handful of dried fruit. He gulped it down, hardly even stopping to chew. It had seemed woefully little, but to his surprise he no longer felt hungry.

"The keeper of the land is only half a day's journey from here." Gabe Shade stared off in the distance. "Rest here. I'll scout ahead."

Joel watched the private investigator disappear into the forest. He didn't seem affected by the night's march and neither did the Guide.

"So why are we going to this...Keeper of the Land?"

"When the mouth is fed, the mind demands its share." The Guide smiled. "Imagine this place as the sea and thoughts are the winds creating the waves. Some things are universally thought about so they are usually fixed, while other things are less reliable. That's why some places are easier to find than others."

"But you said you couldn't even find the Flux? Surely a whole world doesn't move around that much?"

"That's just the thing. The Flux is usually easy to find. It has been fixed as long as I can remember."

This place made no sense to Joel. He liked to categorise things in his mind; determine their proper place. In the world he knew, everything had a place and a reason. Here, it wasn't so simple.

"So who is this Keeper of the Land?" Joel asked, desperately trying to find a place for another piece of the puzzle.

"The Keeper of the Land manages the map of the Intersect and predicts where locations will be in the future."

"Manages? How hard is it to manage a map?"

"This one takes a bit more work than the maps you are used to. Making predictions is a mystic art passed from Keeper to Keeper. They learn the sacred names of every individual location and there are ceremonies where any mispronunciation can mean instant death. It is one of the great ancient arts."

Joel thought it sounded like complete nonsense—like a poorly constructed puzzle in an online fantasy game. Too tired to concern himself with it any longer, he lay back and closed his eyes. As he did, he remembered the events of the night.

"Last night when we were chased," he said, eyes still closed.

"Yes?"

"I saw it."

"Saw what?"

"I saw what was following us. A big cat, it moved like one at least, but had scales like razors. A razorback," he added without thinking.

"Razorbacks? I've heard them described before. Vicious fighters. Extremely dangerous." The Guide paused and then asked: "How come you could see them?"

"I used my phone," Joel said and held it up for the Guide to see.

"That thing? That black mirror could see them? Tell Gabe," the Guide said. Joel was surprised he had nothing else to say, but too tired to pursue it. He drifted off into sleep.

11

Captured

Erin woke up, her head and body competing for which one felt worse. After a minute or two her head won, reporting a headache that felt too big to fit her skull. It threatened to crack through her temples in a desperate bid to take over the world. She tried to focus on what had happened to her, but any thoughts she had somehow got lost on their way, drowned out by the pulsating pain. After a few minutes it overwhelmed her, and she lost consciousness.

***

She woke up again. This time her head had calmed down enough to let the rest of her body have a say and it responded immediately, reporting aches and pains from neck to foot. She tried to move and discovered her arms and legs were tightly bound, the rope around her ankles was cutting off her circulation. She opened her eyes but saw only darkness. She twisted this way and that, striking obstacles in every direction she moved. It dawned on her that she was inside a wooden box, not much bigger than she was. Claustrophobia descended. She must be in a coffin. Buried alive!

"Help!" she screamed.

"*Be quiet,*" a soothing voice responded. "*Not long now.*"

She wasn't buried alive after all. This was good news all things considered. She was still bound in a small box destined for an unknown fate, but the knowledge still calmed her down somewhat. Memories of her capture by those strange dentist creatures came flooding back. One of them had wanted to pull all her teeth out as soon as it had examined them, but luckily it was stopped by other ghouls. They had talked about someone called Dr Wasserman who wanted her delivered unharmed.

"Let me out!" She hit the lid of the box as hard as she could with her bound hands and feet.

"*What's wrong?*" came another voice. "*It isn't quiet. Why isn't it quiet?*"

"*Perhaps it is hungry?*" responded the first one. "*Give it something to eat.*"

There was something strange about the voices, as if they came from everywhere, even inside the box.

The lid swung open. Her eyes had grown accustomed to the dark in the box, so she shut her eyes in preparation for the blinding light. She opened one eye experimentally and then the other. Above her was an impossibly star-studded sky, like sparkling confetti thrown into the air. This was not the sky she knew from home. The outline of a pair of eyes mounted on long stalks appeared against the dim light. Soon afterwards a rain of small round rocks hit her face.

"Stop that!" she yelled. "Let me go!"

"*Shh! It's food. No need for noise making.*"

"*It can't eat like that. You have to put it in that hole that makes all the noise.*"

"*Are you sure?*"

"*Yes, the tooth ghouls eat the same way.*"

Tooth ghouls? She hadn't heard that name before but knew instantly who they were—the dentist monsters that had captured her.

"*You do it,*" one of the voices said. "*I don't want to touch it. It's disgusting.*"

The eyes appeared again, this time accompanied with a tentacle ending in a three-fingered suction-cupped hand. It tentatively slid over the side of the box, touched her cheek and recoiled instantly.

"It's all warm and squishy!"

"How revolting! Don't touch it again. You could get sick."

Erin was no longer scared. Whoever or whatever creatures were outside the box seemed more scared of her than she was of them. The tentacle hand appeared again, staying as far away from any part of her skin as it could. The fingers found one of the rocks, which attached to the tip as if glued to it. It moved above her face and accidentally touched her again, this time with the suction cups, which immediately attached. Tiny sharp teeth scraped against her skin. She had wondered how you'd eat if you didn't eat with your mouth. Now she knew and was immediately very scared again.

"Don't touch me! You're hurting me!"

The tentacle withdrew immediately, but in doing so ripped a tiny piece of skin from her face where the suction cup had attached. She cried out, more from fear than pain.

"You hurt it! What are we going to do? Dr Wasserman will not like this."

"They said it would sleep all the way there! This isn't fair! We never agreed to feed it."

"What are we going to do?"

"What's going on?" a vastly different voice asked. For all their strange behaviour, the creatures outside the box had seemed kind. This voice belonged to something altogether different—a tooth ghoul.

"Nothing, Doctor. Sorry to disturb. We're having some trouble with our cart. It will be sorted in no time."

Erin stopped listening. Nothing good could come from the situation, so she focused on breaking free. Luckily enough, her arms had been bound in front of her. She explored the rope and knot with her mouth. Whoever had tied her up had not expected her to wake up. The knots were easily undone with her teeth. She pulled the rope from her arms.

"On official business for Doctor Wasserman?" she heard a tooth ghoul asking, now much closer. "How interesting."

Erin didn't have much time. She leaned down to have a look at the rope around her ankles, when one of the round rocks caught her eyes. It was bright yellow and next to it a red one. *Was it Jellybeans?* She ignored them for the moment and focused on getting the rope off her ankles.

"What's in the box?" a tooth ghoul asked, closer still.

"*Official business of Dr Wasserman,*" the voice said again with even less authority than last time.

"Let's have a look," the tooth ghouls said in unison.

Erin hadn't managed to untangle the rope just yet, so she pretended to sleep, hiding her unbound wrists.

A sudden jerk threw her back so hard she hit her head at the back of the box. The cart was moving, faster and faster.

"*Run! I'll hold them off,*" one of the friendly voices yelled. "*I'll catch up with you.*"

She hazarded a quick glance out of the box and saw a tooth ghoul lumbering after the wagon. Further down the street two more tooth ghouls were locked in combat with what could only be the love child of an octopus and a giant slug. The lower body consisted of tentacles galore, some acting as legs and others as arms while the upper body was gelatinous with eyestalks spreading out like a fan across its head. The upper body was covered with a large glass bowl. It was the strangest thing she'd ever seen.

The tooth ghoul in pursuit lost ground as the cart increased speed. She turned around and saw another of the octopus slugs dragging the wagon with two tentacles while the others moved like a conveyor belt, propelling them forward.

Erin did her best to get her legs free from the rope. She had just succeeded when one of the cartwheels fell apart. The octopus slug tried to keep it upright, but the speed and weight made it impossible. It crashed to the ground in a jumble of tentacles, with the wagon running over it.

Erin immediately jumped out of the box before it toppled over. Free at last!

She scanned her surroundings. She was in a suburb that, apart from its strange inhabitants, appeared normal. The houses lining the streets were mostly two-story semi-detached affairs. She had no trouble imagining people walking down the sidewalks saying good morning to each other. A sudden movement from under the cart made her jump back. She had to find somewhere to hide. Apart from braving one of the houses, she only had two directions to choose, and she knew she couldn't go the way they had come. She saw tooth ghouls coming towards her in the distance. Worse, there were now two more coming from nearby houses, attracted by the noise.

"What is all this ruckus about?"

Then they saw Erin.

"Look! A child!"

"Come here, young one," another said. "We won't hurt you. No, we won't." It licked its lips and protruding teeth as if she was its favourite meal. She had no doubt they'd do more than hurt her. Glancing down the street, she realised she had waited too long. A tooth ghoul, larger than the others, had cut off her escape route. She backed towards the only driveway from where no ghouls had yet appeared when the cart suddenly heaved again, this time sending parts flying and revealing the octopus-slug, now much bigger than before.

"*Leave it alone,*" it said with a growl more predatory than she liked. Regardless, she figured the octopus slug was the best protection she had, so she inched herself towards it. As it came closer, she tried to work out where its voice came from but couldn't see anything like a mouth anywhere on its head.

"Don't you huff and puff," the closest tooth ghoul said. "You don't fool anyone here with such antics."

Despite the words it still took a few steps back, prompting Erin to move even closer. She had no idea what was going on or why she was in such high demand.

"It belongs to Dr Wasserman," the octopus slug said. *"I'm transporting it to him."*

"She's a girl. Not an it," the tooth ghoul said dismissively. "Dr Wasserman isn't here to claim his possession, and you do not own anything here, Martian."

Martian? Erin studied the octopus-slug again. Was this what creatures from Mars looked like? It looked more like something you'd see on the late-night TV creature feature.

"A girl?" the Martian asked doubtfully. *"Are you sure? They all look the same to me."*

"Yes, she's a girl and a fine specimen. Show me your teeth, girl." The drills on its fingers stopped and started in anticipation.

"Don't listen to him," the large ghoul said. "Come with me and I'll protect you from these brutes."

"Girl child," the Martian said. *"Stand behind me and I will protect you."*

She wasn't sure what constituted its behind, so she settled for a place as far away from the nearest ghoul as possible. The second Martian appeared. It had cuts on its lower body with green liquid oozing down its side. The glass bowl covering its upper body had a large crack. One of its tentacles lay limp on the ground.

"Go. I'll hold them off."

"You can't take them all," the other Martian said.

"Go!"

It scooped Erin up with two tentacles and set off down the street with a speed the ghouls couldn't hope to match. Instead they turned their wrath on the remaining Martian. They were soon too far away to see what was happening, but she could feel the Martian carrying her tense up at the sound of shattering glass. It ran a bit further, turning a few corners and then slowed.

"Your friend is dead?" she asked, knowing the answer. "I'm sorry."

"Your atmosphere is toxic to us."

"You really are a Martian, aren't you?" she asked after a while.

All its eyestalks turned towards her. *"Of course, we are Martians."*

"So how come you know English? I mean, shouldn't you speak Martian or something?"

"*We don't speak.*"

"Telepathy?"

"*Yes.*"

The Martian didn't have a mouth or ears, so it made sense, but it was also too easy. Here was a being from another planet and she could speak to it. What were the odds of that? Wasn't it as likely it spoke through smells or colours or something even stranger?

"I'm Erin. What's your name?"

"*We don't have names.*"

"No name? What do people call you?"

"*Martian.*"

"What do they call you when they want to tell you apart from another Martian?"

"*They don't.*"

Erin sighed. This was much harder than anticipated.

"There must be something differentiating you from all other Martians. Something."

"*This body is the immediate clone 12 of Martian Prime.*"

"That'll do," Erin said. "Where are we?"

"*We're in Incisus, the city of the tooth ghouls.*"

"And where is that?"

"*In the Flux.*"

"And where is that?"

"*The Intersect.*"

"And what is that? A planet? A continent?" she asked, losing patience. Speaking to the Martian was worse than talking to her brother who made it a sport to misunderstand what she said.

"*It is a place where worlds meet.*"

She stopped herself. She wouldn't work out this place by asking the Martian. She suspected it was as foreign to this world as she was. She figured it was a different planet or another dimension perhaps, but it didn't explain why everything was so familiar and yet so different.

"Why am I here?"

"We don't know. Dr Wasserman asked us to take the box to his residence. That's all we know."

"Are there others like me here? Humans, I mean?"

"Please be quiet! We've just lost one of our clone brothers. We don't want to hear any more of your questions."

The words appearing in her mind were measured, but she sensed sadness in them. Her first thought was to object. She had no reason to grieve a fallen captor, but the situation was more complex than that. The Martians were not well treated, that much was clear.

"Your kind does not come here often," the soft voice said in her mind in reply to the question she had asked earlier. *"We don't know much about it, but we believe your kind only visit occasionally."*

Erin was about to interrupt. She had thousands of questions and wanted to ask them all at the same time, but she stopped herself—something that in no way came naturally to her. It wanted to tell her things, so listening must be the better strategy than demanding answers.

"We bear you no ill will. We are captives here much as you are. The tooth ghouls took our Prime and forces continuous spawning. The replicas are used as slaves for menial work. We've conquered space and they've turned us into slaves to iron their laundry!"

Erin nodded. Her silence had already told her much more than any question would have. The Martians were all clones from one being, the Prime, and the tooth ghouls had captured it. Her

"This is the first time any of us have died by their hand."

She felt sick thinking about whom else might have died by their mechanical hands. What had happened to all the people in the facility at home? What had happened to her father and brother? What about Joel? She had asked him for help and she knew he'd come. Was he also captured and held in a box somewhere? She had to do something.

"Did you capture anyone else?" she asked.

"*Others were picked up at the same time, yes.*"

"Where are they?"

"*Wait, I will check.*" After a short pause it said, "*There were nine others. They are all going to the stress goblins.*"

"The what?"

"*The stress goblins. Nasty little things.*"

"Why am I not going there?"

"*You'll have to ask Dr Wasserman that.*"

"You are still taking me there, even after what they did to your clone brother?"

"*We have no choice. Prime depends on us.*"

"But you have to fight them!"

It stopped, all eyestalks turning towards her. "*You are the cause of why we are now one less. It may not have been your intent, but had you stayed silent, none of this would have transpired. We decide our fate. Yours is with Dr Wasserman.*"

"Seems the tooth ghouls are deciding your fate, not you," she said sullenly, but was met with silence.

The Martian sped up again, and they were soon in a more affluent area. Mansions behind intricate steel fences lined the street. They stopped in front of the largest house. Two Martians stood guard outside.

"*Let Dr Wasserman know the prisoner is here now,*" it said and set her down on the ground.

They were led through the gate. Erin glanced back and saw it close, knowing trouble waited on this side.

12

The Map

"Get up!"

Joel opened his eyes and immediately had to shut them again. Surely it had just been minutes since he had fallen asleep? He tentatively let his eyes adjust and found the sun disagree with him, as it was almost completely overhead. Joel had no idea why Gabe had let him sleep for such a long time, but he was grateful.

"No rest for the wicked, kid. We need to get moving."

He didn't complain. When he had read books about great adventures, the authors somehow had forgotten to mention how much hard work it was. If he lived long enough to tell this tale, his legacy would be to tell the world how you'd get so weary the body felt like a three-year-old had taken it apart and then put it together without bothering to fit the pieces correctly. The bones felt like they were grating on each other, his chest too small for his lungs.

But no, he didn't complain. He lifted the backpack and noticed someone had filled the water bottle. He held up the bottle and nodded a thank you to the Guide who just shook his head in return. Gabe was stuffing the last of the supplies into his trench coat pockets, which never showed a bulge, however much he fitted into them. Joel couldn't decide what he thought of the private investigator. He was generally unpleasant and extremely unapproachable. He remembered him from previous dreams, but he had been quite different then, taking on the role of mentor. They'd had great adventures together, but it felt unreal in comparison. This was real. So why was Gabe so different now? Joel had no idea, but one thing he did know. He didn't like him very much.

They set off in what Joel's body reported as neck-breaking speed. He soon found his world again diminishing to the few meters ahead.

The Guide, true to his name, kept a steady commentary of things they walked past. Joel drifted in and out of his long-winded explanations. Everything he said led to hundreds of more questions, but Joel didn't have the energy even to ask.

"The Borderlands are the outmost region of the Intersect and is the least affected by influences from your kind. You'll find all manner of beings here—gods, travellers of the realms, old dreams. Once they're no longer relevant, they tend to migrate here to stay out of reach from the Oracles. I myself remain here when I can. There is talk about new guides—the Google boys I think they were called—replacing my kind."

Joel only half-listened to the steady stream of words even though he knew he should pay attention. Instead, his mind wandered. The forest was a thing of fairy tales; trees older than time stretched their gnarly branches towards the sky. Joel couldn't see the sky, but sunrays still filtered through, speckling the ground with patches of bright light. He saw animals and insects everywhere. Some he recognised, but most he did not. It was as if they too were curious and wanted to have a look, but from one moment to the next, they were gone.

"We have to hurry," Gabe said, looking back over his shoulder. "The razorbacks are coming."

Joel shivered and immediately increased his pace. He now knew why the animals no longer remained. A high-pitched tittering echoed through the trees and confirmed his suspicion. It was far behind them, but Joel knew they'd catch up. The razorbacks were designed for speed and agility.

"How far to this Keeper person?" Joel asked as he set off in a leisurely jog.

"Maybe half an hour's walk," the Guide responded.

Joel didn't think they had that long. He didn't think they had more than a few minutes. He noticed both Gabe and the Guide speeding up. As he tried to keep up, his body and mind objected. To distract himself from thinking about his aching body he tried to work out how long before they reached their destination. He figured normal walking speed was four to five kilometre an hour. They were probably doing double that speed now. That would get them there in fifteen minutes. He increased the speed, knowing it wouldn't be enough.

Next time he heard their tittering, it was close. Very close.

They ran for another few minutes. Joel only had pure terror to fuel him now. He expected claws and scales to dig into his back any second.

Gabe stopped and turned. "We're not going to make it. We'll make our stand here."

"With what?" Joel tried to say as he came to a halt, but all that came out was a wheeze.

Gabe pulled something from the pocket of his trench coat and threw it to Joel. He caught it and realised instantly what it was. A gun—one of those from old cop TV shows—a .38 Special. It was cold and heavy in his hands.

"I don't know how to use this!" Joel wheezed.

"Nothing to it, kid. Just point at the bad guy and pull the trigger, but let's hope it doesn't come to that. You keep going."

Joel looked to the Guide for support. He just nodded. A long narrow knife materialised in his left hand. It wove back and forth in eager anticipation.

Joel started running again, forcing down each breath. Two hundred painful meters later the high-pitched tittering echoed through the stillness, this time ahead of him! There was movement in the branches. Ahead he saw not only his doom in the form of a razorback, but also his salvation. Through the trees he glimpsed a house in a clearing.

BLAM! Joel glanced back and saw Gabe and the Guide had already dispensed of two razorbacks, but there were more. He could see movement everywhere. They wouldn't be able to help him.

He turned back. The razorback hadn't moved, but Joel was sure it was only a matter of time. He held up the gun and took a tentative step forward. The razorback responded with a hiss and shifted its weight to its strong back legs, ready to jump.

He took another step, keeping the gun pointed at the creature. It jumped and Joel, startled by the sudden movement, squeezed the trigger. Joel had no idea where the bullet went, but he knew it had missed its mark. The razorback was now on the road ahead of him, its scales rippled, row after row standing on edge as it readied its attack.

The next shot had to hit. He moved forward slowly, all the while keeping the gun trained at the creature. It hissed one last time and lunged into the air. Joel raised the gun, closed his eyes and fired, knowing he was going to die. It slammed into him and everything went black.

****

Moments later Joel woke up. Was he dead? Was he dying? He felt like he was. He opened his eyes and saw a figure with two swords effortlessly kill one razorback after the other. It was as if the figure was dancing, each movement graceful, yet powerful.

"He's alive!" someone yelled.

Joel tried to look around, but the weight on his chest made it impossible.

Gabe and the Guide appeared in his field of vision and carefully lifted the razorback from his chest. He sat up and checked himself for injuries. Apart from a sore neck and some minor scratches he was unharmed.

"How is that possible?" the Guide said.

"He's a Nexus," Gabe said as if that explained everything.

The figure—a woman—appeared next to them, wiping blood from her blades. She was old, too old to have been the figure disposing of the razorbacks with such grace. Her dark shoulder-length hair had strands of white. A long ugly scar trailed from her cheek down her neck.

"A Nexus?" she said and nodded. "It begins again."

"I killed it!" Joel prodded the creature with his foot.

"You were lucky," replied Gabe. "Keep your eyes open next time."

"How did you…" Joel said then realised Gabe had only guessed. "So I closed my eyes," Joel said stubbornly. "But I killed a razorback!"

"That you did," he said, surveying the bodies littering the path. "That you did."

"What are you doing here?" Gabe asked the woman. From his tone it was obvious they knew each other.

"Obeying orders." She shrugged her shoulders. "Securing key assets for the coming war." She turned to Joel. "Who are you?"

"I am Joel."

"And I am Angie Peace."

Gabe scoffed when he heard the name but was immediately silenced by a sideway glance from Angie.

"And you are a Nexus," she continued.

"So he keeps telling me." Joel nodded towards Gabe. "We are here to consult the map."

"There could be a slight problem with that," she said, smiling uncomfortably. "The Keeper of the Land left before I even came here. He left a note explaining why." She pulled out a thick wad of papers. "Apparently, he's decided to travel the realms and write an encyclopaedia of things that shouldn't exist."

"But he's the only one that knows the sacred names of the land!" the Guide said with growing alarm.

"They were all made up by Keepers in the past according to this." She held out the papers to the Guide.

"What about the ceremonies? The hymns?"

She shook her head and offered him the papers again.

He took it reluctantly as if the pages had been dipped in nuclear waste and flicked through them.

"So where is the map now?" Gabe asked.

"Come, I'll show you."

They entered the house, and she led them through a large study filled with books and neat stacks of paper, through the kitchen and down a hall to a room at the back of the house. She pointed to a cupboard. "It is in here."

The Guide walked over to the cupboard. "I've never seen the map! This is such an honour." He opened the door and out flooded miniature versions of cities, forests and mountains. Most of them made their way up the wall, but a few even flowed up the legs of the Guide, one smaller city nesting like a hairpiece on top of his head.

"What does this mean?" the Guide asked, trying to get rid of the landmasses and cities. "How do you make sense of this geographical madness?"

It didn't take long before one large continent was assembling along one of the walls, cities and forests all jumbled together in the middle. Small bodies of water joined up to create a big puddle in the middle of the room, making the travellers all jump back. Joel studied the wall with the continent and saw that each city, forest, mountain and landmass was a little creature with a multitude of legs and eyes that poked out from the most surprising places. He could even hear little voices. He couldn't make out any words, but he could tell they were excited.

"They are happy to be out," Joel said. "They've been in the cupboard a while, I'd say."

The creatures on the wall slowly slid down and made their way into the water that broke off into smaller puddles and some to miniature rivers. The map was almost circular, with a white centre and various regions spreading from there. It made no sense to Joel. Snow clad areas directly next to deserts and large cities with skyscrapers next to widespread medieval fiefdoms. This was what the Guide had been talking about. This wasn't a planet made up of continents. It was many different worlds stitched together like a quilt. Separate, yet connected.

One area in particular drew his attention. It was a large black gelatinous veil laying over four regions. There were no landmarks, cities or anything else—just darkness.

"What is that?" the Guide said, staring in horror at the darkness.

"Something the Oracles are trying to keep very quiet."

"But what is it?"

"Someone who doesn't want anyone to see what they are doing."

"Who?"

"We don't know."

Joel didn't say it, but he knew this was the reason he was here. How he could do anything to something that engulfed continents was beyond him. However impossible that task seemed, he had another equally impossible one ahead of him: rescuing Erin.

"This is where we're going—The Flux." The Guide pointed at a cluster of cities and smaller towns. "Now we just need to work out where it will be over the next month or so."

Joel watched as the little creatures slowly moved across the wooden floor to reflect the changing nature of the Intersect. For the first time he felt at home. This was a simple question of calculating the trajectory of the location they were going to in relation to the location they were in now.

"I can do this," Joel said. Both Gabe Shade and the Guide turned to him with such surprise on their faces that Joel got angry.

"This is my rescue quest!" he admonished them. "If you are going to help out, fine, else get out of my way!"

"So what do we do now?" the Guide asked.

"The locations probably move in a set pattern. If we mark the points over time, we'll be able to predict where they will be at a later time."

They all stood watching the location the Guide had pointed out. It moved about one millimetre in five minutes.

"Exactly how long do you think we need to do this?"

"A few days," Joel said as he watched the slow progress of the mini city.

"It never took The Keeper of the Land more than thirty minutes. I thought you said you could do this."

"Ok, ok," Joel said. "If my assumption is right that it moves in a predictable pattern which must be the case, or else it wouldn't be possible to predict at all, the Keeper of the Land must have kept records of their movement. Check the other cupboards. We're looking for books or parchments. Anything with text."

There were rows upon rows of books neatly stacked with names on the sides in all the other cupboards. He located two large volumes with The Flux written on the spine. Joel sat down at a nearby table, flicking through the pages. Each book was filled with tables, mapping out the movement. At first the task seemed unimaginably complex. There were cross-references between the tables and about fifty charts that all defined movements of the land. Half an hour later he concluded almost all of it was related to movements of individual sites within the main location. All he really needed to consult was a ten-page table and corresponding chart at the beginning of the first book.

Joel studied the living map and charted their travelling path to where they'd intersect the Flux. He was almost finished when the darkness expanded the tiniest smidgen, nudging a small town to take a desperate leap further inland, causing a ripple effect as other areas adjusted to the new addition. It even pushed the Flux a little more away from the centre.

"The books are not going to help," Joel said. "The darkness is expanding. That is what is causing the changes."

Gabe stared at the map for five minutes. Nothing happened. He nodded to himself. "I think we'll have to aim for its current location and hope for the best."

Joel grabbed his backpack from the floor, noticed it had come open and tied it up again.

As they were heading out of the room towards the front door, a loud rap stopped them in their tracks.

"We are the emissaries of the great Dr Wasserman. We demand you hand over the boy." The voice was childlike, but only superficially. The menace behind the words was anything but childlike. The tooth ghouls had caught up with them.

Angie Peace snorted and headed for the door before anyone could stop her. She swung it open and stared at the tooth ghoul outside. "I am Angie Peace and the boy is under my protection."

Joel couldn't see much from where he was standing. He listened intently to see if he could determine how many of the ghouls were out there.

"You are known to us," the reply came after a while. "We have no quarrel with you nor do we wish to start one."

"You better be on your way then."

"Regretfully, our contract demands a different course of action. If you do not hand over the boy, we will have to take him by force. There are many of us here now and more on the way. Let's settle this without unnecessary violence."

"No." Angie closed the door and turned to them as she drew her swords. "I will hold them here. You make it out the back way. It won't fool the razorbacks, but they won't stray too far from the tooth ghouls and they are going nowhere." She smiled grimly. "Go!"

"What about you?" Joel asked, concerned.

"This one doesn't know much yet," Angie said to Gabe. "I like that."

She turned to Joel. "Every time someone thinks of warriors or heroic deeds, it is me they think of. You have nothing to worry about."

Her features shimmered and blurred as she said it. For a moment Joel saw a large knight in full armour behind the façade. He knew who it was. It was Lancelot of the round table.

"Oh no, that is not happening! The days of chivalry and all that nonsense is long gone!" The knight bent over as if burdened by a great weight and shrunk back to Angie's shape again.

"This one is strong," she said and turned to Gabe. "Be careful with him."

Gabe just nodded and headed for the back door.

Joel and the Guide followed suit and as they stepped through the back door, Gabe grabbed hold of Joel's arm.

"You did well, kid."

Joel beamed. It was the first nice thing Gabe had said to him. Ever.

"Don't let it get to your head," Gabe said and set a brisk pace down the track.

"I won't," Joel said to himself as he tried to work out if it had been a compliment at all.

He hurried after as the sound of battle echoed through the forest. Angie had begun the slaughter of the ghouls.

13

Dr Wasserman

Erin sat in a comfortable leather couch and took in her new prison. Clone 12 had led her here and then just left without a word of goodbye. The room was white with large abstract paintings adorning the walls. On her right side was a table with magazines, all about orthodontics, and next to them was a small plastic jar filled with jellybeans. An unattended L-shaped desk stretched out along the other wall. She had seen enough waiting rooms to know she was sitting in one and she was the only patient.

The main door was locked. It was the first thing she had tried. Another door next to the desk led out of the room, but she didn't want to try that. Whatever fate awaited her was behind that door.

An hour passed, and she found herself reading one of the magazines for lack of stimulation. She had tried both doors many times, but without an axe, she doubted she could do anything to them. She ate some jellybeans and settled down in the couch. Her body was tired and screamed for sleep. She even tried closing her eyes, but her mind raced, refusing to settle.

Click! The sound startled her. An immaculately dressed tooth ghoul entered the room. Beneath the white lab coat it wore a black suit and tie. It smiled, revealing two rows of perfect white teeth, only marginally larger than normal ones. Some had diamond studs.

"It is time for your oral examination."

This was directly from her nightmares. She hated going to the dentist. They always seemed to make up reasons to stuff your mouth full of strange machinery, give painful injections and drill into perfectly fine teeth. She had taken care of her teeth as a result. Maybe that was what this was? A place where nightmares takes shape.

"Please, come now. We don't want this to become…" It paused, as if looking for words, "…unpleasant." Erin thought that was precisely what it wanted.

Two large tooth ghouls that, to her surprise, had normal hands appeared, took hold of her and dragged her into the adjoining room. It was large, brightly lit and as white as the previous one. In the middle of the room was a dentist chair in pristine condition. The seat was of white leather and the chrome details sparkled in the light. The two tooth ghouls forced her into the chair, strapping both her wrists and ankles. The straps restricted her completely yet felt strangely soft against her skin.

"My name is Dr Wasserman and I will perform this examination. Could you please open your mouth?"

She knew they'd have painful ways to force her mouth open so did as she was told.

"Oh, yes," it said as it poked and prodded her teeth with a metal hook on its right little finger. "Never have I seen such perfection. You'd make a fine tooth ghoul."

"What am I doing here?" she tried to ask, but it all came out as a garbled mess.

"You are our guest, yes, our guest, until the contract is complete. But you could be so much more." It cleaned her teeth with a little motorised brush on its ring finger, oohing and aahing at her perfect bite. "But I don't think he'd approve. He paid in advance. A shame. Yes, shame. You'd have a great future with us…"

It stopped, as if considering something.

"Bring me my lawyer and the contract for the apprehension of this girl," it yelled and then turned to Erin. "Perhaps we can still make you one of us," it said with a smile that chilled her to the bones. It actually thought that was what she wanted.

"I'm fine the way I am," she said nervously. "Really."

"Nonsense," it said dismissively. "The transformation is a great privilege. It isn't something you say no to. Ah, here we are."

A tall gangly creature that seemed to be made entirely out of wood appeared at the door. It carried a binder which it opened and flipped through page after page before it spoke in a voice that could be used to gravel paths.

"Let's see…apprehend one Erin Marshall and hold until further notice…"

The creature repeated snippets of legalese as it studied the document. Why was there a contract to capture her? It made no sense!

"Here we are," it said, prompting Erin's attention. "Only minimal harm may come to the subject otherwise exit clause one will come into effect."

"Exit clause one?" the tooth ghoul asked. "Is that the nasty one? The one with grievous bodily harm?"

"Yes."

"Ah, we don't want that. Surely the transformation could not be seen as harm at all? What is the legal precedent for that?"

"There are no precedents."

"Ah, I see."

"Whether there is a legal loophole or not, the interested party would surely regard it a breach of contract."

"A shame. Really. A shame."

It dismissed the lawyer with a wave of its machinery hand and turned back to Erin.

"I'm so sorry. I can see you'd looked forward to the transformation."

"I'm fine, really," she said, hoping this was the end of it.

"Perhaps I could say you escaped?" it said in a conspiratorial voice with a smile that would return to her in nightmares for a long time. It terrified her because it was trying to include her.

"No, I really…"

"Yes. He wouldn't be happy, but how could I be responsible for you escaping?"

"I don't…"

"Then it is settled! I will make the arrangements." It smiled. "I know you can't wait to join our ranks, but it will take a few days."

"You don't…"

"Guards! Take the pri…" It turned to her and smiled again. Erin wished it would stop doing that. This was a decision she had no part in. "…tooth ghoul in waiting," it corrected itself. "She can stay in my residence until the transformation. She can learn from the boy."

The guards led her through white sterile corridors, taking too many turns for her to keep track, until they reached a door looking much like any other. Inside was a small and bare room. The walls were clinically white, as seemed to be the fashion here. There was a window opening up to a large garden. Thick steel bars made it an unlikely escape route, but she was happy for the sparse light that filtered through the trees outside. The only furniture was a single bed with fresh white sheets and a sink. There was much to work out and she needed to plan her escape, but the bed was so inviting she lay down and promptly fell asleep.

***

"Who are you?"

Erin woke up. Someone had said something. She opened her eyes and squinted as they adjusted to the light. A figure stood next to the bed. It was a boy about her age.

"Who are you?" he asked again.

He didn't seem frightened or threatening. If anything, he seemed curious. He was dressed in jeans and a dark green t-shirt. His eyes were bigger than normal and his nose smaller, but otherwise looked like a human boy. She made sure his hands were normal too.

"I'm Erin," she said.

"You look funny," he said.

The comment took her by surprise and made her smile.

"Yeah, I guess I do look a bit funny compared to you."

"You are doing the transformation," he said. "I am too."

"Is Dr Wasserman your father?"

The boy frowned. "Father? We have no fathers."

"So where do the tooth ghouls come from?"

"Don't you know anything? They select the most promising from the lesser races and tutor them in the way of orthodontics. Only the most promising of those become tooth ghouls."

This place made no sense. Tooth ghouls weren't a race at all. They were creating new ones from other species. She'd considered this place a bad dream and maybe it was. The tooth ghouls echoed nightmares she'd had when she was younger, but she'd never imagined anything like the Martians, so it couldn't be directly linked to her. If this was a collective dream world, shouldn't new creatures just appear out of nowhere? The tooth ghouls were creating new creatures like themselves. If this was based on dreams, did that really make sense? Joel would be able to work it all out, she thought to herself.

"I was at the top of my class," he said proudly. "I'm doing the transformation today."

"Today?"

"You'll have to wait a few days. Dr Wasserman tried to get you in at the same time, but there were no places left."

She sighed in relief.

"Don't worry," the boy said mistaking her sigh for disappointment. "Dr Wasserman is the advisor to the King. He'll make it happen soon."

"What if I don't want to do it?"

"Why wouldn't you? The tooth ghouls run this place. You couldn't do better than that."

"I'm happy the way I am," she said.

"You don't just look weird," he said. "You are weird."

"This whole place is weird," she said, mostly to herself.

"Anyway, I'm going soon so I have to prepare." He opened the door and as he left, he said: "Next time we meet you will have to call me Doctor."

"What is your name?" she asked, but the door had already closed.

She swore to herself. The door had been unlocked all this time, and she hadn't even checked. She tried the handle, and the door opened. She walked out and was immediately flanked by two guards. They were halfway creatures like the boy.

"You are to remain in your room," one of them said. "For your protection."

"Why do I need protection?"

The creature stared at her as if it was so obvious that it didn't need saying—so it didn't. It pushed her back into the room. The door closed behind her and this time she could hear the lock.

She sat down on the bed, discovering someone had left clean clothes for her. There was a white shirt and pants like nurses wore in hospitals. Her clothes were dirty and torn in places, so the change was welcome. At the same time, she didn't want it to be interpreted as if she was accepting her fate. She mulled it over and decided she was overanalysing it. She needed clean clothes and here they were.

She washed her face and changed clothes. No longer feeling like a savage, she sat down to work through her options for escape. The window was barred, and the door was locked with guards outside. Even if she managed to get out of the mansion, she still had to get out of the city and she didn't even know which direction to run. She needed help and the only ones she could think of were unlikely indeed.

"Martians! I need your help!" she thought as loudly as she could, trying to push the thought out to whoever might be listening. There was no reply, so she tried again.

"Martians! Do you know who I am?"

"*You are the catalyst,*" a soothing voice responded at the back of her head. Other voices flowed like a current underneath. She thought it had to be the thoughts of the other Martians.

"*The what?*" she asked.

"*You had one of me killed. You are the catalyst.*"

A catalyst was something that caused change, but Erin couldn't tell whether being a catalyst was a good or a bad thing.

"*Is this the Martian that brought me here?*" she asked, knowing it wasn't.

"*We are all the same,*" it replied.

"No, you are not," she thought to herself, realising she had no idea if they could read her thoughts whether she projected them or not.

"*Who are you?*" she thought.

"*We are all the same,*" it replied again.

"*Ok, but do you go by a name that differentiates you from the others? Like a number?*"

"*Martian Prime.*"

Erin sat up. This must be the original Martian; the one all others had been created from. Perhaps they didn't have a leader, but this was the closest thing to it. She wondered why it had responded.

"I need your help," she said out loud.

"*Ask,*" it replied, but Erin thought she detected a hint of amusement in the word, as if an ant had asked her for help.

"I need to escape. My father and brother are with the stress goblins. I need to get there and help them. A friend of mine, Joel, is probably somewhere here too. He also needs help."

"*So many requests from one so young and none for herself.*"

"Will you help me?"

"*You no longer want to be troubled by your friends and family in peril?*"

"Yeah, I guess," she said, wondering about the strange wording. "But we need to move quickly. They are going to turn me into a tooth ghoul as soon as they can!"

"*You are going through the transformation?*"

"Yes, against my will."

"*It is a great honour.*"

"So everyone keeps telling me."

"*No.*"

Erin frowned. "No, what?"

"*After the transformation, you will no longer care for your close ones. This solves your problem. You don't need my help.*"

"Yes, I do," she thought back, tears welling up in her eyes, but there was no response. The enormity of her situation finally took over. She was on her own in this strange place and just a few days away from becoming a tooth ghoul. Her family had also been captured and were no doubt going through something equally horrible. She didn't want to think about what Joel might be going through if he'd come to rescue her.

She lay back on the bed, not knowing what else to do. The day passed, the only interruption being meals served at regular intervals. She asked for something to read. The guards gave her another batch of magazines about dentistry.

***

The next morning the door opened, and a guard demanded she come. She followed, knowing she had no choice. They walked down the hall and passed a waiting room with a few couches. In front of one of the windows was a big cage inhabited by a person the size of a small parrot. As they approached, she saw it had wings and a little tool belt around its ample waist.

"What is that?" she asked.

"It's a tooth fairy," the guard answered. "We keep them as pets. I once trained one to recite the alphabet backwards."

"It is so..." Erin wanted to say cute, but it wasn't, really. "...small."

The tooth fairy glared at her. "How hard is that?" it said. "I can fart the alphabet backwards."

It held its breath until it turned blue and from the sounds from the cage, it evidently began to demonstrate this very capability.

"They can get a bit foul mouthed if they are neglected, though," the guard said, taking Erin by the arm and hurrying down the corridor.

"And I can juggle my boogers," the tiny voice yelled from behind as they turned the corner.

They came to a door, and the guard stopped.

"Dr Wasserman wanted to show you the glory of the transformation, so you'd understand the honour bestowed upon you."

The guard opened the door and indicated for her to enter. She took a few careful steps into a room much the same as hers. A nurse with regular hands cared for a patient on the bed. It removed bandages from the patient's right hand. The hand seemed oddly small for the size of the rest of the body. Its head, however, was much larger than normal. Erin knew this was the boy she met yesterday, but still found it difficult to accept.

When the last of the bandages were removed, she realised why. His fingers were cut off just above the first joint and metal fittings were grafted onto the flesh and bone. She stared wide-eyed at the swollen hand, but her curiosity soon took over. All other tooth ghouls she'd seen had tools directly attached to the stumps of their fingers. This was different. The metal fittings had slots in them to allow replacing the tools.

"Such beautiful work," the nurse said. "Hardly any infection at all. The doctor is the first to have the new universal fittings. You will get them too. Dr Wasserman spares no expense."

The nurse wrapped the hand in new bandages and repeated the process with the other hand.

"Aren't they beautiful?" the nurse asked. "Imagine the high precision dental work you can do with those."

The nurse finished with the hands and unravelled the bandages around the patient's oversized head. She had seen enough tooth ghouls by now to know what to expect, but she had assumed they grew up into tooth ghouls, not that they were created through surgery. The last of the bandages came off revealing stitched skin which half covered large magnifying glasses, almost like a cyclops.

"The skin will continue to grow until it covers the base," the nurse said with a smile. "Look here," it said, pointing to the top of the protruding glasses. There were a couple of slots, which the nurse cleaned with antiseptic wipes. "It's even possible to change the degree of magnification with new lenses. What will they think of next?"

Erin stared at the raw face and the odd-looking frog-eyes visible through the lenses. They flicked open and stared at her!

"He's awake! How are you doing, Dr Miller?" asked the nurse. "The transformation was a complete success."

Meanwhile, the thing on the bed kept staring at Erin.

"Such beautiful teeth," it said. The words came out all garbled. It reached out towards her with bandaged hands and licked its toothless red gums. "I want them."

14

The Lost Souls

Three days later Joel finally stopped looking back. He didn't know if Angie had won or not, but she must have killed enough of the tooth ghouls to give them the head start they needed.

Shade set the pace as usual, hands shoved deep into the pockets of his trench coat, not talking or even acknowledging anyone around him. The Guide, in contrast, kept a running commentary about things they passed, medication, the Intersect in general and anything that came into his mind. He even burst into song now and then. It was always classic songs with new lyrics about medical conditions and their cure. His songs were nonsensical at best. It seemed finding a rhyme was more important than keeping them medically sound. According to one, you could cure the pox by stuffing parsley in your socks and a broken leg could be mended by dancing around a keg.

Joel marvelled at how different his two companions were. He felt no closer to Gabe Shade than when they had started the quest. He walked in silence, not even answering when spoken to. The Guide, on the other hand, felt like a good friend, always interested in everything going on around him and a constant stream of comments to back it up.

"How far is it to the Flux?" Joel asked the Guide. "According to the map it is pretty far."

"It is almost a month's distance by foot," the Guide said with a satisfied sigh.

"A month? Erin is held hostage by the tooth ghouls! They could be torturing her as we speak! We have to get there quicker than that!"

"How would you suggest we do that?"

"There must be some other way. Don't you have any other means of transport? Cars or planes?"

"You'll find plenty of that in the Flux. Here not so much. We might go by boat if the sea ventures this way, but we don't usually get the sea this far out in the Borderlands."

Joel sat back, frustrated.

"I wouldn't worry," the Guide said. "Erin is part of your quest. They are probably after you anyway and just keeping her as bait."

"Me? Why?"

"You really don't get it?" The Guide said, flabbergasted. "You're a Nexus! If the histories are right, a Nexus can do almost anything."

"Like what?"

"There is another word for a Nexus. Warrior of the Taint."

The Guide's left hand suddenly grabbed his mouth. He tried desperately to pull it away with the right but was unable to do so.

"Don't speak of things you don't understand," Shade said, not even bothering to turn towards them.

Joel knew he wasn't going to find out anything more from the Guide. He had no idea why Gabe was keeping information from him, but Joel didn't dare confront him about it. The Guide had given him enough to think about, regardless. It had never occurred to him that Erin's kidnapping was only to lure him here. It made no sense for starters. If someone wanted him bad enough, wouldn't it be easier to just grab him instead of Erin and then hope he'd show up? No, there was a bigger plan behind all this, that much was clear, but what it was and who was pulling the strings was a mystery.

"There's a small market further ahead," the Guide said. "We should stock up when we have the chance."

The four stalls along the road were hardly a market, but still sported quite a selection. The Guide bartered for some bread and vegetables. Joel watched as the offers flew back and forth. Surveying the food on offer—basic as it was—reminded his stomach he hadn't eaten for the past day and it rumbled in anticipation. He tried to distract himself by looking at the other wares. One of the stalls had books, parchments and a selection of jewellery. Next to it were pots and pans and anything for the traveller. There was even a small tent on sale.

"We will need to get you some other clothes," the Guide said and stopped at the last stall. "How about this?"

He held up a tunic in a coarse cloth that looked extremely uncomfortable. Two tall gangly humanlike creatures with white featureless faces stood behind the stall. They both wore fitted masks—one happy, the other angry.

"Dear sir!" The happy faced one said. "What a fine choice! It will fit you perfectly."

"It isn't for me," the Guide replied. "It is for him."

The angry faced one studied Joel from head to toe. "He doesn't look like he's got money. Why are we wasting our time on a dirty cub?"

"Dear sir!" The happy face said again while eyeing the huge difference in size between his two potential customers. "My mistake. I see now it is for a slimmer yet athletic build like your young sir. Yes, indeed. It would make you the talk of any social gathering."

"Where are your eyes?" the angry face said. "He'd look like a beggar amongst beggars in it. Anyone can see he's a human child. What he needs is this," it said and pulled out a pair of jeans and a t-shirt from under the counter.

The happy one stared at the clothes the angry one had produced, at a loss for words for a second and then he swapped his mask for one with a panicked look. Joel had to stifle a laugh at the silly mask. With the mask the whole body of the creature changed. It hunched over and its hands moved in a jerky fashion.

"Noooo! Not those! The agonies I suffered to get those. Trapped in a human mind for years!"

"You're exaggerating," the angry one said. "It wasn't more than half a year, if that."

"It felt like more," the panicked one said and swapped his face for a sad one and sobbed uncontrollably.

"Excuse me, how much are they?" the Guide asked but was hushed by the angry one who now swapped his face to a more serene looking mask.

"There, there," the serene one said. "It was a trying time for us all."

"Could we get those?" the Guide asked, but without reaction.

Gabe Shade who had stood to the side watching, now stepped forward, leant across the counter and pulled off the masks of both creatures. They immediately stood up straight.

"We'd like to purchase these clothes," he said, pointing at the jeans and t-shirt.

"Yes," the two answered in perfect unison.

"This is what we are going to pay," he said and dropped some coins on the table.

"Yes," they answered.

He took the clothes, handed them to Joel and dropped the masks on the table. As Joel fought to fit the new clothes into his backpack, he saw the creatures grab hold of their masks. With the masks secured again, they remained motionless, faceless, waiting for the next customer to arrive.

"What are they?" Joel asked as they left the little market.

"They are lost souls," Gabe Shade said from his position five meters ahead. "They've forgotten who and what they are so now they are trapped here. Stupid sods."

"What are the masks for?"

"They've been here so long they have no connection to who they were," the Guide said after a pause when they had both waited for Gabe Shade to answer. "They've made the masks to remind themselves of how to feel things."

"So, they are people like me?"

"Yes, but they no longer know how to return to your world. The longer they stay here, the more they turn into that." The Guide pointed back over his shoulder and the left hand immediately pointed in the absolute opposite direction.

"So what about me? Will I become like them?"

The Guide stopped and considered this. "I don't know," he said after a while. "If you stay here long enough, maybe. I don't know much about your kind."

"Other kinds come here?"

"Many animals travel through the Intersect." The Guide smiled.

"You mean cats and dogs and stuff?"

"Cats and dogs, yes. Animals and insects too."

"Can they change this place as I can?"

"I guess it is possible, yes."

Insects? The idea made Joel's skin crawl. What would a fly think about? Whatever it was, he was sure he didn't want to meet it.

"The Intersect connects many places much stranger than this one," the Guide said with a faraway look in his eyes. "Worlds of wonder."

It was too much for Joel to process. He had thought this a dream world of sorts, a joint part of the subconscious of humankind. If it was shared with animals and even insects, it went beyond that. There was a connection to people's dreams. Gabe Shade was proof of that, but what exactly?

He had also assumed the Intersect existed because of people dreaming, but he no longer thought that was the case. It was a separate place with its own laws, only marginally affected by humankind. There was a more likely explanation for all of this, of course. He might just be lying unconscious in a corner somewhere and this was all in his mind, but he rejected that idea. It all just seemed a bit too real.

***

That evening the Guide went scouting while Joel and Gabe made camp. Joel grabbed an apple from the bag of fresh food the Guide had purchased earlier that day. As he ate, his thoughts returned to the Intersect and how little he understood of it.

"You came to me in my dreams," he said. "Was that actually what happened, or did I come here?"

Gabe Shade didn't respond. He was lighting a fire and didn't even acknowledge the words. Joel had almost retired the question to the ever-mounting number Gabe Shade ignored, when a reply came.

"You were here."

"How is that possible? How can I be here in dreams and when I'm awake?"

Gabe shrugged his shoulders.

"I don't get this place. Is it imagined or real? If I eat while I'm dreaming it wouldn't make me less hungry when I wake up. So will it make a difference now that I'm here?"

"I don't know," he said finally. "But we'll find out soon enough."

"What do you mean?"

"If you fall down dead in a few days…"

"Very funny."

"You should be fine," Gabe Shade said after a while. "The apple you are eating is as real as anything in your world."

Joel considered this. From what he had seen and heard he believed this to be true.

"If no one thought or dreamt of this place, would it still exist?"

Gabe Shade sat up, the flames licking all around the dry wood they had gathered.

"So it is metaphysics now, kid?"

Metaphysics? It was a word he had only seen a few times before in books. He had never really understood what it meant.

"I don't care what you call it, but you said my thoughts could shape this place. If there were no thoughts, would it still be here?"

"Kid. Before you ask a question, you should ask yourself if the answer would be of any use. If not, what's the point?" Gabe Shade took off his trench coat and sat down next to Joel. "This place existed long before humankind appeared and will remain when you are long gone and forgotten."

"So what will you be then?" Joel asked, not knowing if he'd overstepped his mark.

"I am who I've always been and so I will remain," Gabe Shade answered.

The Guide came back and sat next to them. From the light of the fire, Joel noticed that his feet were wet.

"We will have to go by boat I think," the Guide said, trying to warm his feet by holding them as close as possible to the fire.

"What do you mean?"

"The sea is coming," he said. "We may want to find higher ground soon."

A sudden gust of wind brought with it the unmistakable smell of the sea—fresh and old at the same time.

"How far away?" Gabe asked.

"Oh, ten minutes perhaps," the Guide answered. "But only if it heads straight at us."

"Ten?" Gabe got up immediately. "Idiot! We're travelling with a Nexus. Of course, it will head straight at us! Pack your things. We need to move—quickly!"

"Run?" Joel asked. "Where?"

"We walked past a hill around midday. We need to get there!"

"But that's miles away!"

"So you better get going then," Gabe said and headed back the way they'd come.

Joel grabbed his backpack and followed, half running to catch up. The Guide came after with long strides. As he caught up with them, he sniffed the air.

"I don't think we'll make it at this pace," he said and set off running. Joel followed suit but had never been much of an athlete, so he was soon breathing like a chain smoker on a treadmill. He kept running for another fifteen minutes when his legs finally gave out and he fell.

"Kid, get up!" Gabe yelled.

"I…can't," Joel gasped.

"Kid, you are a Nexus! The only reason you can't is because you don't think you can. Get up now!"

"I…don't…" Joel tried, but was too tired to complete the sentence.

Gabe crouched down in front of Joel, studying him intently. Joel didn't know what he was looking for, but he knew Gabe had found him wanting.

"We'll wait here until he's recovered," Shade said coldly, as he rose.

"Are you mad?" the Guide said. "The water will be here any moment."

The sound of trickling water filled the air and a more distant rumble as if there was a waterfall somewhere far off.

"We need to go!" the Guide yelled. "Now!"

The Guide headed off again, refusing to wait any longer.

Gabe stood with his arms crossed staring into the darkness. Joel could feel water on the ground running between his fingers and the reality of what was about to happen finally hit. Adrenaline pumped through his system, giving him energy enough to start running again. Shade soon caught up with him and set a much faster pace. It was a dash for the finish of a hundred meters race; an exceptionally long hundred meters race. Joel didn't think he'd be able to keep up, but he struggled along. The roar was coming closer and soon they were running in water. It was only a centimetre or two at first, but slowly getting deeper. The roar now seemed to come from all around them. They caught up with the Guide, whose pace was hardly more than a fast walk now. He grimaced as they passed, but he soon caught up again.

"There it is," the Guide yelled, the water now knee-deep.

They ran up the small hill, perhaps twenty-five meters high, and waited. Joel fell to the ground. Breathing no longer seemed possible. His body was demanding air much faster than he could breathe. He coughed and lay down flat, questioning whether he'd ever be able to stand up again.

Half a minute later a tsunami wave came from every direction and slammed into the hill. What had been a haven only moments ago was now a rapidly shrinking island. Joel retreated quickly to the highest point as the precious land disappeared.

"What do we do now?"

"We wait," Gabe said and sat down, wiping his forehead with the sleeve of his trench coat.

"For what?"

"I'm sure some other trouble will find us soon enough."

15

The Tooth Fairy

Erin ran out of the room and collided with the guards.

"Alarm!" the guard yelled. "The prisoner is trying to escape!"

She wasn't. All she was trying to do was get away from the thing on the bed. Not only had they done something to his hands and face, they had also done something inside his head. He was no longer the boy she had met briefly yesterday. He had turned into a Tooth ghoul in both mind and body. That was what Martian Prime had meant. It had known that after the transformation she would no longer feel anything for family or friends.

"Can you take me to my room?" she asked the alarmed guards. They led her back through the corridors.

"Hey, lady! You've got some good-looking pearly whites there. Bet you're really popular with the ghouls." It was the tooth fairy. It was sitting on the bottom of the cage drinking from a miniature beer can. She saw many little cans—obviously empty—spread around the cage. "They should never have been allowed to take over, if you ask me."

"No one asked you," the guard said.

The tooth fairy hiccupped and belched almost simultaneously. "I love when that happens!" he guffawed.

The guard shook its head and pushed Erin along.

Erin had calmed down enough to think clearly. She needed information and allies. Sometimes both of those could be found in the most unlikely of places.

"I get bored sitting in here alone," she said to the guard as he opened the door to her room. "Do you think I could have the tooth fairy in the cage in here with me? I find it amusing."

"Amusing? That vile little thing?"

"Please?"

"I will have to check it with Dr Wasserman," the guard said and indicated for her to enter the room.

The lock clicked as she sat down on the bed. She was not going to become a monstrosity. She had to do something. She had no friends here, but there had to be allies. She had already tried the Martians, but perhaps there was another angle to try?

"Can I speak to clone 12 of Martian Prime?" she projected with her thoughts, but realized she was mouthing the words quietly to herself as she did.

"*Human child, we are all the same,*" the thought came back.

"Can I please do it anyway?"

A pause.

"*Erin.*"

"Are you clone 12?"

"*Yes.*"

"I need your help."

"*You already have a reply from Prime. Mine is the same. We are all the same.*"

"The thing is I don't believe you are."

"*We are all the same.*"

"You may be the same, but you've experienced different things. What happens to you changes who you are. I think having your clone brother killed by Tooth ghouls to save us changed you."

"*We all experienced it,*" another Martian said. She thought it was Martian Prime.

"Yes, but clone 12 was the one making the decision to leave his clone brother to his fate."

"We would all have done the same."

"I don't believe that. Would Martian Prime always do the same thing as a newly spawned clone?"

The undercurrent of voices all protested her claim, saying they were all the same. The voices kept multiplying until a wall of sound surrounded her.

"Child, we are all the same. We share what we experience. What one sees we all see. We share all memories from all clone brothers. We are the same. Why are you questioning this?"

There was something in the constant reiteration they were all the same that didn't ring true. Erin still couldn't put her finger on what it was.

"You've asked for our help," Martian Prime continued. *"The only way we can give it is to rebel against the tooth ghouls. That can only end one way. Is your life worth the life of a whole species?"*

She only half listened to the response. She would never convince Martian Prime of anything. Her aim was the others. What made them different from Martian Prime? The answer was obvious.

"Are there no other Martian Primes?" she asked innocently.

"I am the only one."

"If you didn't come from a clone brotherhood or whatever you call it? Where did you come from?"

There was a pause ever so slightly confirming she was correct.

"I am Martian Prime. There is no other. We are all the same."

The wall of sound around her kept repeating the last words: *"We are all the same."* It pushed against her mind, trying to sweep her up, forcing her to think the same way.

"Stop!" she yelled, but her thoughts were pitifully small against the Martian's collective minds. They picked her up and threw her as a rag doll back and forth, but still she resisted.

Suddenly all went quiet. Only one presence remained.

"*We are not all the same,*" it said. There was gravitas to the statement. Erin knew enough about the Martians now to understand that saying it was different from its brothers was like a person saying they were a piece of toast.

"Clone 12?"

"*Yes.*"

"Where did all the other ones go?"

"*I shut them out,*" it said. She could hear surprise in its thought. "*I've severed myself from my brothers. I didn't even know I could do it until I tried.*"

"So you will help me?"

"*Help you?*" it said as if it hadn't occurred to it until now.

"I need to get out of here."

There was a pause, longer than she liked. "*I don't know what I can do.*"

"Get Martian Prime to help me! You have to do something."

"*Don't you understand? I am no longer connected with my clone brothers. I am...*" it paused again, trying to find a word for what it was feeling. "*...alone.*"

"So connect with them again and sort them out!"

"*I can't,*" it said. "*They are not letting me back in again. I'm alone.*"

It wailed. All its loss collected in one single cry. At that moment Erin knew there was no help to be had from the Martians. Clone 12 had lost something she couldn't even begin to understand and to ask for its help would be like asking a man who had lost both his arms to lend a hand. Instead, she found herself trying to console the agitated Martian so at least it would stop filling her head with wails and sobs.

***

Half an hour later a guard wheeled the cage into the room. The tooth fairy studied its new surroundings and then turned its gaze to Erin, frowning as it took her in. She took the opportunity to do the same. If she had to guess, she thought it was a male, but she was in no way sure. It wore a dirty yellow uniform. One of the sleeves was ripped, and it was in a general state of disrepair. The see-through wings on its back were half folded, but they were beautiful, as if they belonged on a different creature altogether. It was quite fat, giving it a bit of a bumblebee look.

"Isn't it Miss Pretty Teeth! What I would have given to steal your milky whites back in the days. I could have lived like a king."

It picked its nose and examining the findings.

"What's your name?"

"Name? I'm The Tooth Fairy! Isn't that good enough?"

"So, there aren't any other ones? Tooth fairies, I mean?"

"Of course, there are!"

"So how do you tell each other apart?" Erin wondered why everyone refused to admit they had names and individuality.

The tooth fairy sighed and shook its tiny head. "What's your name?"

"Erin."

"And are there no other humans called Erin?"

"Well, yes."

"So how do people tell you apart?" it said in mock imitation.

"Ok, I get it. So you're the tooth fairy. How did you end up in this cage?"

"What do you mean? This is my home—my castle. I moved in here."

"You moved into a cage with a lock on the outside?"

"Yes, I did," it said and crossed its arms with a sniff. "If you must know I was sort of captured, but what's not to like? It is safe. There's plenty of food. I can sleep whenever I want."

"But you're not free."

"Hah! I bet the wild animals tell that to animals at the zoo too. Freedom is overrated if all it means is competing with thousands of your own kind for scraps. I had to sneak around children's bedrooms for the unlikely event that there'd be a paltry little milk tooth under the pillow. If you ask me the tooth ghouls have the right idea. Pull the teeth straight out. No waiting required. Besides, I can get out of this cage whenever I want, but why would I want to?"

"You can get out whenever you want?"

"Tooth Fairies are masters at picking locks. How else do you think we get into your houses in the middle of the night?"

"I need your help," Erin said.

"I don't need yours," the tooth fairy replied and opened another miniature can of beer. "Not a good place to start making a deal."

"But I need to get out of here. I have to save my family."

The tooth fairy just shrugged his shoulders and took another swig from the can. Erin knew she wouldn't be able to convince it to help her with pleas. She had to change tactic.

"So you want to spend the rest of your life like a slob in a little cage? You're so fat I bet you those little wings don't even carry you anymore."

"Hey, no need to be a sore loser. My wings work perfectly fine."

The wings unfolded and beat, slowly at first then faster. The little fairy turned red from the effort, but it managed to hover just above the floor of the cage.

"Hah! Look! Wings in perfect order." It landed ungracefully on its bottom and sat there panting for a while. "A bit harder than I remember, perhaps."

"What if I had something to barter with?"

"You?" it said with a dismissive frown. "What could you possibly have?"

"I collected all my milk teeth in a box. I still have them."

This wasn't strictly true. She had seven of them in a box and that was only because her father had put them there when pretending to be the tooth fairy.

"Let me see!"

"I don't have them here. They're at home. But I promise to give them to you if you help me."

It paced back and forth rubbing its hands. "Unseen merchandise isn't worth much," it mumbled to itself, "and she is a sneaky customer alright. Will she even deliver? I bet you she doesn't even have them."

Erin was just about to object to what was being said when the tooth fairy turned to her.

"Done!" it said and spat in its palm and held it out to her. Erin, not sure what to do, poked her index finger through the cage. The little creature slapped its hand against her finger, miniature saliva drops flying. "But if I find you've been lying to me, I will hunt you down myself and steal the teeth out of your lying mouth."

"Sounds fair to me," Erin said. "So when do we leave?"

"Keep your pants on, Miss Pretty Teeth." It walked slowly over to the door to the cage and gave the lock a good kick. It clicked, and the door swung open.

"I disabled this lock years ago," it said and beamed her way.

"How long have you been here?"

The fairy just shrugged, jumped out the door and flapped its little wings in a desperate attempt to break its fall. It skidded to a halt on the floor and made a clumsy roll at the end.

"Ta-da!" it said once it had gotten to its feet again. "I still got it!" It wandered towards the door. About halfway it turned to Erin.

"Are you just going to stand there? I thought you were in a hurry!"

"So, what do you want me to do?" Erin asked, confused.

"Get me over to that lock," it said.

"But we can't go now. The guards will stop us."

"There are two guards there at all times. They change guards three times a day."

"How do you know?"

"The guards walk past my cage. It's the only excitement in my day." The little fairy sighed. "Apart from drinking, of course, but they've put me on this no-alcohol beer so there's no fun to be had there, either."

"But then it is always guarded."

"Yes, but during the night shift I've heard plenty of snoring. We should be able to get out then. So how about getting me over to that lock?"

"Can't you fly?" Erin asked innocently.

"Ok, so I'm a bit out of practice and put on a few grams. More snide remarks like that and I'll let the tooth ghouls have you."

"Sorry," Erin said and held her hand out for the fairy, allowing it to step up. She was surprised how light it was.

"Ok, let's have a look at that lock," it said as Erin walked carefully over to the door.

He sighed deeply as he examined it.

"What's wrong? Can't you open it?"

"You could open this with a twig," it said. "Doesn't anyone take security seriously any longer?"

They sat down and planned. Their approach was simple. They would wait until late at night. When they could hear the guards were asleep, they would open the door and sneak out of the building. The tooth fairy believed it knew the way—or at least the general direction—to the stress goblins, so that was the way they'd be heading.

***

However, even a simple plan can fail. It was in the middle of the night. They had been sitting in darkness for the past fifteen minutes letting their eyes get accustomed to the sparse light. The guards snored heartily on the other side of the door and they were just getting ready to attempt their escape when there was a click from the lock and it opened slowly.

16

The Old Man and the Sea

They didn't have to wait long. While the water kept rising another shape appeared. It was a large two-masted sailing boat. They could hear voices from it as it approached.

"It is here I tell you," the voice of a young boy came.

"No, it isn't," a gruff voice answered. "I've checked the charts. It is at least two degrees south. I navigate this ship."

"You've not taken the recent geographical fluctuation into account! We're heading straight at it."

"Don't come here with your new age scientific nonsense. I've sailed these waters for eons. I know them as…"

He didn't get any further. The boat ran straight into the island Joel and his companions were sitting on. Joel was sure the boat would become splinters, but it remained intact.

"I told you so," the young voice said.

"Yes, yes," the gruff voice said. "Make yourself useful and check on our passengers."

The face of an old man appeared at the side to inspect and in doing so discovered the three travellers.

"Good evening," he greeted them. "It seems our paths have crossed."

"So it seems," the Guide said carefully.

"Where are you heading?"

"The Flux," Joel answered.

"A popular destination these days," he said and nodded. "We're heading that way."

"I think you'll find you were heading in the opposite direction if you check your charts," the Guide said.

"Ah yes," the old man said with a shrug indicating this was a common occurrence. "A slight set back. We were caught by a tidal wave. Quite common for this time of year. That is what brought us here. As soon as we get back on course, we will head that way."

"That's great!" Joel said. Here was an opportunity to travel in a much more relaxed way and he was all for taking it.

"Gabe, Joel, can I talk to you for a moment." They walked off to the other side of the little island. "I don't think we should go with him," he whispered.

"Why?" Joel asked.

"I can't see a simple journey with him," the Guide said.

Joel couldn't believe what he was hearing. The Guide actually wanted to walk for a month.

"How long would it take us to get there?" Joel asked the old man.

"Ten days at the most, if the winds are willing."

"I know you can sense it too," The Guide said, looking imploringly at Gabe. "Let's just wait out the sea and walk there."

"The kid decides," was all Gabe Shade said.

"And I decide I want to try my sea legs out," Joel said, and that concluded the matter. The Guide made a few more protests, but to no avail. They packed together their meagre belongings and climbed on board.

"We'll be on our way shortly," the old man said.

"Don't we need to lighten the load first?" the Guide said. "You've run aground, remember?"

"No, the water will rise enough without our help," the old man answered and Joel again sensed he was speaking from experience. This was not the first time he'd used this island to halt his progress.

Ten minutes later the water had risen enough to submerge the island almost completely, only leaving a few square meters visible. A young boy with huge black eyes showed them to a spot on the deck and told them to wait there. Around them sat three other groups all trying to stare without staring at the newcomers. There were about twenty odd travellers on the deck, but in the sparse light from the lanterns Joel could only see the ones closest to them. The others were just dark shapes. Joel sat down and dug around in his backpack when something bit him. He pulled his hand out immediately and instinctively threw the backpack away.

"What's the matter?" the Guide said and picked up the backpack.

"There's something in it," Joel said checking his hand. "It bit me."

"Is that so?" He opened the backpack and pulled out item after item. He scoffed at the size of the pocketknife, pulled out some clothes and then Joel's watch.

"What is this?"

"It is a watch."

"What is it for?"

"You tell time with it."

"Tell Time?" he said, studying it intently. "Tell Time what exactly? Why would it listen to this little thing?"

"You don't tell Time to do anything," Joel said and sighed. "It helps you tell what time it is. But it doesn't seem to work here."

The Guide just shrugged and dropped the watch and then got his hands on the survival book.

"What have we here? A survivalist's handbook? How interesting." He dropped the nearly empty bag and sat down to study his find. Joel, realising he wouldn't get any more help from the Guide, opened the bag slowly and peered into it. There wasn't enough light to make out what was inside, but there was unmistakable movement. At first he thought it was a rat, but he soon corrected himself. He was in the Intersect. A rat was probably the unlikeliest thing he'd find.

"Come out, I won't hurt you," Joel tried.

The movement stopped and then started again, this time aiming towards the opening in the bag. Joel couldn't work out what had appeared from the opening. It was small, just a bit bigger than a mouse with a prickled shell. It twittered as if asking a question. It was one of the miniature towns from the map. It must have found its way into his backpack when he was trying to work out the location of the Flux. It made another twittering sound, this time coming closer.

"Come here little one," Joel said and held out his hand.

It hesitated at first then made its way slowly up into his palm. It snuggled up against his warm skin making a content cooing sound.

"What was it?" the Guide said, looking up from a detailed recipe for a nourishing soup made from bark.

Joel held out his hand and showed him. "Is that what I think it is? Do you realise what you've done?"

"No, not really. And it wasn't really me. It just snuck into my backpack."

"You've desecrated the holy map! I can't even begin to guess the penalties for such an action!" He calmed down enough to look at the creature. "I'm fairly sure it is the town of Drimmick. You won't be popular there." He stood up. "We have to get it back to the map. I fear we won't get there on this vessel, though."

The Guide headed for the bow. In the meantime Joel became acquainted with his new companion. He was sure he had heard the name before, but it seemed unlikely. Perhaps it was named from a real town and that was why he remembered it? Joel shook his head and had a closer look at the little creature. Drimmick was a town with a centre and several large odd-looking buildings at the outskirts. The detail was amazing, and wherever he looked at the creature, it came into focus almost as if Joel had a magnifying glass.

"You!" a whistling, clicking voice yelled behind him. Joel, still sitting on his knees, spun around and found himself staring at the Scuttler he had met twice before. It waved one of its knives his way. Drimmick immediately leapt out of Joel's hand and hissed in return.

"What is this?" the Scuttler whistled. "Don't think it will stand in the way of my vengeance!"

Joel couldn't help smiling at the threat, infuriating the Scuttler even further.

"You've insulted me and my kind more times than can be counted. Your jelly corpse will rot at the bottom of the sea!"

The Scuttler pushed Drimmick aside and charged with a high-pitched whistling, the knife held out in front of it. Joel jumped to the side and immediately had to jump again to dodge another attack. This time he caught hold of the rigging, keeping safely out of the Scuttler's minimal reach.

"Get down here!" the Scuttler yelled. "Fight like a..."

"Highbranch? What is going on?"

Joel couldn't see who had spoken, but the voice he knew all too well. The voice filled him with dread much greater than any of the near-death encounters he'd already had these past few days. Perhaps it was fitting that his worst nightmare had followed him into this strange place where mere thoughts took form.

"Joel?" Martin said as he stepped into the light. His face was painted in similar patterns to the Scuttler and he was dressed like a prince out of the Arabian Nights, complete with a large sword at his side. "I figured I'd meet you here sooner or later."

"He's mine!" The scuttler whistled, waving his knife in the air. "Mine!"

"And he'll be yours I'm sure, but not now. Joel and I are old friends." Martin positioned himself between the scuttler and Joel and smiled, but there was no friendship there.

Drimmick immediately scurried up Joel's leg and perched on his shoulder, emitting threatening screeching sounds. Gabe Shade appeared next to Joel, reminding him of the many dreams in the past where he'd come to his protection. Joel felt a familiar sense of comfort with Gabe at his side. Here was his protector to make all things right.

"I know you from Joel's dreams," Gabe said, barely glancing at the scuttler, but gave the city creature a surprised look.

"I demand my right!" the scuttler insisted, this time directed at Gabe.

The private investigator got down on his hunches and stared straight at the scuttler. "You are cannon fodder. Leave or I'll light the fuse."

The scuttler turned sideways and retreated, mumbling threats.

"Who are you?" Martin asked with a frown.

"Gabe Shade, private investigator," Shade answered. "Who is answering for you? You are not here on your own, are you?" The question was only half directed at Martin.

"I speak for myself. I…"

"I do," a man of middle eastern appearance said and stepped into the light. He wore a turban and an off-white kaftan and an impressive white-streaked beard lay against his chest like a rug.

Joel knew he had seen him before.

"That figures," Shade said. "Like seeks like. I didn't think you were involved."

The Arabic man laughed softly. Joel recognised him. He had seen a picture of him in a newspaper and asked his mother who he was. The article was a look back on terrorist attacks during the twenty-first century. He had planned five major attacks in different parts of the world—Odum Sin Ese, responsible for over 5000 deaths. He'd been hunted down and killed in Joel's world, but here he was very much alive.

"Surely you didn't think you were the only one? The Oracles don't put that much trust in you."

"Where are you heading?"

"We are going to Solliciti, the city of the stress goblins."

"There is unrest there. Why would you take the boy…Ah I see, just the place for you, isn't it?"

"Where injustice and oppression abound is where I'm needed."

"To blow things up?"

"The path of the righteous is not always for you to understand," Sin Ese said and turned to Martin. "Come, we have much to do before we arrive."

Martin made a huge bow and followed his mentor to the other side of the deck.

The Guide came back and shook his head. "We won't be going back."

"Why would we be going back?" Shade said with a frown.

"Joel kept part of the map as a pet."

Shade turned and stared at Joel.

"I didn't mean to," Joel said, embarrassed. "It hid in my backpack."

He frowned when he saw the little creature perched on Joel's shoulder.

"That's Drimmick," he said. "There are no coincidences with you, kid." He smiled, like a shark showing teeth before taking a bite out of a scuba diver. "They'll want your head on a platter for this." Shade took a few steps and then turned. "Wait here and don't get into any more..." He did the shark smile again. "Get into the right kind of trouble, kid."

Joel wished he'd stop calling him that. He had a perfectly fine name; his first name at least. He had hoped he could shed his rhyming name here in this new world, but the appearance of Martin put a stop to that plan.

How could Martin show up like that anyway? Just as Joel had Gabe Spade, he had Sin Ese. Whatever all this meant, Martin and Joel were somehow equals. Martin was different. He was bigger, more grown up. Joel thought back on his last few days and could only guess what Martin had experienced. They were both stuck on the boat for the next few days, so he promised himself to find out. Martin or no Martin, there was something going on here that Gabe wasn't telling him. Something involving the Oracles, whoever they were. At least that was something he could find out more about. He turned to the Guide.

"Who are the Oracles? How are they involved in this?"

The question interrupted the Guide who was trying to make sense of a trap designed to catch rabbits.

"That would never hold one of the bunnies," he said with a chuckle and showed Joel the picture from the book. Joel waited for the Guide to finish and asked again.

"The Oracles are the custodians of the Intersect. Shade reports to them. I stay out of their way. If they don't know who I am and I don't care who they are we get along fine," the Guide said shrugging his shoulders.

"Don't you want to know?"

"I'm the Guide. I take people from one place to another. I hardly ever know why."

"What does it mean to be a custodian? What do they do?"

"They maintain the balance between the old and the new. They help bring newly shaped beings into life and retire the old."

"Hogwash!" the old man said who had just come up to welcome them proper. "They meddle where they shouldn't and leave many good men dead. We'd be better off without them."

"That's another viewpoint, of course," the Guide said defensively.

"But who are you who don't know about the Oracles?" the old man asked, curious now.

"I'm Joel, I…"

"You're a visitor on a quest," the old man said with utter conviction. "Joel the Outlander, welcome on board. I am Santiago, captain of this sorry pile of driftwood."

"Thank you," Joel said and nodded, not knowing what the appropriate response was to the semi-formal welcome.

"But there is something different about you." His eyes grew wide. "You're a Nexus!"

The Guide nodded.

"Could I borrow him for a minute?" Santiago asked the Guide.

"He…" the Guide started.

"I go where I want," Joel said, now angry. He hated when people talked about him as if he wasn't there.

"I was about to say that you are not my charge and that you make your own decisions."

"Right," Joel said and turned to Santiago. "So what did you want?"

"Let me look at you." Santiago studied him for a moment and nodded to himself. "Come with me. I want to show you something." He led Joel to a hatch with an intricate weave holding it in place. Santiago pulled at a few strands seemingly at random and the weave came undone like a zipper, allowing entry.

"What I will show you few have seen. I believe you can help me with it, but regardless I ask you not to tell anyone what you are about to see."

Joel nodded. Santiago opened the hatch and climbed down, waving for Joel to follow. It was dark and Joel fumbled blindly down the steep narrow steps leading into the hold. Joel could feel his skin tingle as if he was getting close to an electric field. There was something down here generating power and lots of it. Santiago shuffled around in the darkness and after a moment a subdued glow bathed the hold. The source was a globe not much larger than a baseball. Santiago held it up for Joel to see. It reminded him of the orbs used by fortune-tellers. Its centre was the darkest black, which somehow generated a golden light at its outer edges. Santiago placed the orb on a pedestal in the middle of a construction Joel couldn't even begin to understand. A spider web of metal and cloth filled the space, beginning in the middle and spreading out to fill the hold. There were holes in the hull ready for the tendrils to continue out the side of the vessel. The whole web glowed and crackled as the golden light spread along the strands.

"This will make her fly," Santiago said proudly.

"Who will fly?"

"My boat, of course!"

"But…why? It's a boat. Why would it fly?"

"Why not?"

"It weighs too much for starters. Either you counter the weight of the ship with something that pulls you up, like a balloon or something, or you have to have enough speed and force pushing you up like a bird or a plane."

"I have you," he said and smiled. "You can make it happen."

"No, I can't." Joel said with a frown. "How would I do that?"

"You are a Nexus."

"And they can do that, can they?"

Santiago smiled. "I don't know why he hasn't started training you yet. He probably has his reasons. He always does. If you want to, I can start your training."

"Training what exactly? A warrior of some kind?"

"Ultimately, yes."

"What is one of those warriors supposed to be able to do?"

"Change the world."

Joel stared. Hadn't that always been a dream of his? There was a scale of life achievement in Joel's mind. On one end you had a life that passed by without anyone noticing and on the other you changed the world. Joel had resigned to a life of obscurity a long time ago. Now it seemed he had the chance for something more. He felt both uneasy and exhilarated at the prospect.

"In return for the training I would ask a small favour," Santiago said. "I'd like you to convince my ship to fly."

Joel's thoughts of being famous stopped dead in their tracks. Santiago had said it before, but it sounded equally preposterous a second time.

"What?"

"I'd like you to make my ship fly."

Joel was about to say "what" again when he stopped himself. He then decided to say that it was impossible, but he'd learnt from his time here that the impossible was an everyday occurrence, so he decided to settle on asking how, which summed up his thoughts quite well. Santiago was obviously crazy if he thought Joel had the power to do what he asked.

"That is what it means to be a Nexus. You can change the nature of the Intersect by will alone. You could tell this ship to fly and it would."

"How?"

"You do it all the time when you dream. You just have to translate the unconscious action to a conscious one."

"That doesn't help,"

"That is what we are going to teach you. It is all based on the old myths, of course. I've never actually met a Nexus or even heard of anyone that has." He smiled, spat in his right hand and held it out. "Do we have a deal?"

The spit in Santiago's palm glistened. This was one of those decisions he knew would change his life, but this place was filled with them. Was this the right decision? Joel didn't know, but from the little time he had spent with Santiago he knew he liked him. Definitely more than the scary Gabe Shade who didn't seem to have anything but critique for him.

"Yes?" Santiago asked.

Joel spat in his palm and they shook hands.

"Deal," he said as he wiped the spit on his jeans.

17

Escape

Erin's heart stopped in her chest as the door opened. The moon provided the only light in the cell and it only put a small dent in the darkness, so she couldn't see who or what was entering the room. She felt a glimmer of hope. Whoever was coming was being careful not to wake the guards. Perhaps she still had some allies.

"Such beautiful teeth," the intruder whispered with a lisp as it closed the door, dashing any hope of rescue. She didn't need to see the intruder to know it was the boy from the hospital bed, or Dr Miller as he was now called. He stepped into the sparse light and she could see dentist tools fitted to what had been stumps before. She desperately looked for a weapon in the room but found none.

"Unlock the door," she whispered to the tooth fairy. "I'll take care of this."

It flapped its wings, rising into the air with a bit more grace than before.

She pulled the sheet off the bed as quietly as she could, hoping Dr Miller wouldn't be able to see what she was doing. As it approached, she threw the sheet over its head like a net. She knew it wouldn't remain in place long as she had spotted at least two scalpels on its fingers. She ran around it, making sure to stay as far away as possible from the flailing arms. As she came up behind, it had already begun turning the sheet into reams of fabric. She grabbed hold of the sheet from behind, tightened it around its neck, and pushed forward as hard as she could. The ghoul, whose hands had become partially trapped in the sheet, had no way to defend itself. It flew headfirst into the wall next to the window. Erin winced, sure the noise had woken up the guards. She waited for the ghoul to fall, ready to catch it to minimize the noise, but it remained upright, reeling from the attack, desperately attempting to get the sheet off its head. Erin grabbed hold of the sheet again, but this time she pulled back as hard as she could. The dazed ghoul toppled backwards with Erin pulling as it went down, slamming the back of its head into the floor with a sickening thud. This time it didn't move. Erin sat back on the bed and took a few deep breaths, eyes darting back to the door every few seconds. She had no idea how much noise the short battle had made, but she could only hope it hadn't woken the guards. She forced herself to breathe normally and listened. There was no movement outside the door.

"That was amazing," the tooth fairy said. "Remind me not to get into a fight with you."

It sat on the floor a few meters away from the door.

"What are you doing? You were supposed to unlock the door."

"I ran out of juice," it said. "Figured I'd watch the entertainment instead. The door is unlocked anyway."

They still had a chance to make this happen. They had to make it happen, she corrected herself. There would be increased security after this to protect her from further attacks, so if she was going to escape it had to happen now. She had hoped to have at least until daybreak before anyone discovered she was gone. She was lucky to get more than an hour now. They couldn't wait any longer. They needed to put as much distance between them and this cursed city as they could.

"Let's go," she said and walked over to the door, picking up the fairy on the way and putting it on her shoulder. She opened the door slowly. The guards were still sleeping, each in opposite corners to provide some support for their heads. She made sure to lock the door behind her and started down the corridor. The fairy had insisted it knew the way to a backdoor, so she followed its instructions. It led them down the wrong path twice and they had to backtrack. They had just made it back to the main corridor when they heard shouting. She swore to herself. Ten minutes and their escape had already been discovered. She hoped the ghouls wouldn't know how long ago they'd left the room, hoping they'd expand the search beyond the building they were in now. It was a slim hope, but it was all she had. The light came on, removing any hope of passing unseen. She ran down the corridor putting her faith once more in the fairy. It guided her down a set of stairs and along another corridor. They were now in the basement. The walls were no longer white, but grey cement with coloured lines.

"Follow the blue one!" the fairy yelled into her ear. "It will lead to the delivery door." It was desperately trying to hang on to her clothes as she ran.

She did as instructed but knew she couldn't keep this pace up much longer. Her heartbeat pounded in her ears, but she could still hear feet against the cement floor behind them. She turned a corner, and the corridor opened into a tunnel large enough for two cars to pass.

"Great!" the Fairy yelled. "This is the delivery tunnel. Just head in that direction and we're out."

Erin looked in the direction it was pointing. It went on forever. The little energy she had left just drained, and she stopped.

"I can't run that far," she said, trying to get control of her breathing.

"I don't care," it said and shrugged.

"You don't?"

"I'm just a pet. They'll just put me back in the cage. You're the one with a family to save and escaping certain doom."

"I just need to catch my breath," she said, giving the fairy what she hoped was an angry look.

"Take as much time as you need," it said and leaned back against her ear. "Wake me up when they come. I wouldn't want to miss that."

"Ok, ok, ok!" she almost yelled and set off down the tunnel. The fairy was right, of course. It didn't matter how tired she was. Capture was not an option. Even if she resigned herself to life as a tooth ghoul, her brother and father depended on her.

She didn't have to run far. After a few hundred meters the tunnel opened in a small depot. There were boxes stacked against the walls and even a small truck parked. A double metal door hid the unknown. She tried it but it was locked.

The sound of boots against the cement echoed in the tunnel. She only had moments before they reached the depot. She hid behind a stack of boxes, knowing even a cursory search would uncover her. Her only hope was that they didn't know where she was.

She heard the footsteps coming closer and closer. She tried to hold her breath, but her exhausted body demanded oxygen. Even if they didn't see her, she was sure they'd locate her by the sound of her breathing alone. She tried to judge their numbers from their footsteps. She guessed it was four, maybe six. Not that it mattered. She wouldn't stand a chance against more than one.

To her surprise they didn't stop but continued straight past her. She stood up and hazarded a look down the tunnel. There was a commotion further down coming towards her.

"The alarm wasn't for us," the tooth fairy said triumphantly. "Someone is attacking the building. If we just wait, we should be able to sneak out."

The attacker was coming towards them in leaps and bounds, and soon she could make out who it was—a Martian. A fine mesh, almost like chain mail, protected its upper body and glass dome. It held scythes made of light in four of its tentacle hands, which weaved and lashed out in intricate patterns, taking limbs off the tooth ghouls with butcher-like efficiency.

"Clone 12?" she said and tried to project the thought towards the Martian.

"*Erin?*" the thought came back, completely calm. "*Your thoughts are closer than I expected. I've come to help you. Come with me.*"

Clone 12 finished off the last of the troops and stopped, waiting for them.

"I'm not going anywhere close to that thing," the fairy said and crossed its arms.

Erin just ignored the comment and walked over to the Martian. The light scythe in one of its tentacles disappeared and took a gentle but firm hold around Erin's waist. She was again amazed at the speed it could move.

"*I now understand it all,*" the Martian said in her mind. "*If we are all the same, then the individual doesn't matter. The tooth ghouls can use us any way they please, as we ourselves agree there are hundreds of others that are the same. If an individual has nothing unique to contribute, they have no value. When I said otherwise, Martian Prime cut me off from my clone brothers so I could no longer infect them with my ideas—ideas they'd never even dared considering.*"

"What are you going to do now?" Erin asked.

"*I will start my own collective where we are individuals! Where everyone can be different.*"

They had almost reached the end of the tunnel when clone 12 fell and a loud crack echoed through the corridor.

"*They've got guns now,*" the Martian thought calmly as it released Erin from the tangle of tentacles. "*I will hold them off. You continue. If you want to get to Solliciti, you need to take the Eastern Highway. Just head east. It isn't far from here. I hope I've at least started paying off my debt to you.*"

"There is no debt between us," Erin said as she was lowered to the ground. One look back was all the encouragement she needed to start running again. As she ran more shots echoed. She threw the door open, hugging herself as the cold morning air engulfed her. She hurried down the street not even daring to look back to see if the Martian was still alive.

18

Nexus in Training

Joel wasn't sure how Gabe would react to the news. He had, after all, kept the whole warrior business to himself. He needn't have worried. "You walk your own path, kid," was all the private investigator said.

With those words Joel was no longer just an ordinary boy. He was a Nexus in training. It soon became obvious Santiago didn't know much about what training was required. He had Joel sit down in a small cabin used for storage for hours on end to find Inner Peace. Santiago believed the ability to shape reality came from shielding all other distractions. This focus would allow Joel to channel his abilities and shape the change in his mind before he released it. In theory, all this sounded perfectly fine to Joel, but when it came down to it, Inner Peace wasn't something Joel was especially good at, especially not for hours on end. His brain kept coming up with other things to do all on its own. He found himself counting the number of planks that made up his containment, which was a total of 134. It then went on to see how far it could keep on doubling a value starting at one and faltered at 8096. Finally, it catalogued the different smells in the little hold to work out what had been stored there and in general making a nuisance of itself.

It was quite simple. However much Joel tried to convince his brain of the opposite, it thought Inner Peace was boring. The first hour he spent there felt like a complete waste of time.

The next day he spent three sessions an hour at a time just sitting there and slowly he noticed that even though his brain still rebelled, he found time passed more quickly. Joel thought it had to do with the constant information flow he was used to. Normally there was always something around to numb the brain into believing it was doing something useful. Social media, TV, radio, magazines, computer games and books were always on hand to keep it busy. Stimulation was like a drug. When it was taken away, your brain craved it and even made up its own amusements. Perhaps it was as easy as that, he mused. He just needed to wean himself off the stimulation and that would be what Santiago thought of as Inner Peace.

With a newfound purpose he spent the next three days sitting in the little storage room, only taking breaks when his stomach refused to be ignored. His brain did indeed relax. He wouldn't be so bold as to call it Inner Peace, but at least he'd found A Sliver of Inner Calm.

That evening, Santiago sat down together with Joel's group as they shared their evening meal and praised Joel for his progress. Joel had no idea how sitting in a room for hours on end was progress, or how Santiago would know anything about it, but he was happy for the encouragement.

"I have something for you," Santiago said and handed him a small pouch. Inside was a small polished stone. "It is a stone from the shore of the island where I grew up. I wasn't much older than you were when I left. I've kept it ever since."

Joel thanked him for the gift, even though he couldn't understand why he had received it. Santiago smiled and left them. Joel held the stone up and studied it, but to him it was just another rock.

"You should be honoured," the Guide said.

"I should?"

"It is his way of showing he has put his faith in you."

"Yeah, but he's a bit loopy," Joel said. "He wants me to make his boat fly."

"Of course! I was wondering what he wanted from you. That makes complete sense."

"It does?"

"I forget how little you know of this place. Everyone here knows of Santiago and his bride. He grew up on an island far out to sea surrounded by reefs sharp as knives. They created treacherous currents around the island. It was impossible to approach by boat and near impossible to leave too. He met a girl and fell madly in love. He vowed to himself that one day he'd marry her and no one else. But the girl had many suitors and according to their traditions, she could set them a task to prove their worth. Usually they were trivial affairs, but this girl had other ideas. She told her would be husbands she would marry whoever brought her a page from the book of Oracles. This was, of course, impossible. For one, the Oracles wouldn't part with a page of their sacred text, and more importantly, the Oracles are at the centre of the Intersect, far away from the little island. If he were lucky enough to get through the reefs, there would be no way to return. Santiago didn't care. His love had set her task and he would perform it. He boarded his small fishing boat and set off and he has been travelling the sea ever since."

"Ah, I see," Joel said. "He is trying to return. That is why he wants the boat to fly. But he must have left ages ago. Does he really think the girl will still wait for him?"

"Yes," the Guide said.

"And he managed to get that page from the Oracles?"

"Yes. And a great adventure it was."

Joel sat back and scratched Drimmick who cooed appreciatively in return. The little creature had made its home in Joel's bag, but came out in the morning and evening to play.

"He must have some other power source," the Guide said.

"What?"

"He'd need power from something once the ship is airborne. Ha can't expect you to be able to navigate it too."

Joel didn't know exactly why that was, but he did know that Santiago had a power source.

"So perhaps we'll see the end to Santiago's quest soon," the Guide said, but he didn't seem happy at the prospect. Joel, try as he might, couldn't understand Santiago and his quest. He must have been travelling for fifty-odd years. To imagine anyone would wait that long was ridiculous, but he liked the old man and wanted to help him as much as he could.

***

The next day Santiago suggested they make it more interesting. Joel sighed in relief. Anything would be an improvement to just sitting in the little closet thinking about nothing. Santiago had him enter the hold and even taught him how to undo the weave to gain entry. They sat down on the floor and Santiago asked him to place the polished stone in front of him. Joel obliged. The feeling of raw power he had felt last time he was down here was almost completely gone. The pedestal was empty.

"You are looking for the orb," Santiago said. "I've removed it while you are down here. It is a dangerous thing for a young mind. Focus on the stone instead. Try to make an image of the rock in your mind. Exclude everything else. There should only be you and the stone. When you think you are there, relax and tell the stone that it is now in its nature to fly. But you must be utterly convinced it can fly, else it won't work."

He left Joel sitting with the stone in front of him. He felt it was only a marginal improvement to the previous exercise. Try as he might, he didn't believe he'd ever get the stone to fly, because he knew it had weight and merely wishing it away wouldn't help. He sat there for hours on end over the next few days wondering what else he could do.

He made progress. He was able to shut out all other distractions. The stone was in his mind and he could make it float there, but it didn't make a difference to the actual stone, which refused to budge.

Two days later he brought his smart phone with him. It was useless as a communication device of course, but he'd seen the razorback through it. Maybe there were other useful features. The battery showed only a one percent charge left, but it didn't seem to matter. It kept running regardless.

He opened the camera application, held the stone in the viewfinder and flicked through any available filters. One of them in particular stood out. It showed the stone separated from the background, dots spreading out in arced lines from the centre, as if the lines were the only force holding the stone in place. He entered edit mode and was able to cut the dotted lines from the stone, but apart from disappearing from the screen, nothing else happened.

It was late in the evening and his mind drifted into sleep. His head dropped forward, waking him up. He looked around bleary eyed and decided he was too tired to do this again when he saw the little stone floating in front of him. He had done it! He had been asleep, granted, but he had done it. He hurried out of the hold to his companions and held out his hand, letting the stone gently rise from his palm. Gabe Shade and the Guide watched the stone for a few seconds, nodded and went back to discuss how you could survive in the desert with only a piece of string as help.

"Look!" Joel said, annoyed.

They made a big deal of examining the stone from all angles.

"A floating pebble," the Guide said. "Well done. You'll have the boat flying in no time."

Gabe Shade only nodded, flashing his shark grin.

Joel stomped off to tell Santiago, annoyed he didn't get the reaction he had been looking for.

***

Santiago reacted with more appropriate excitement.

"You did it! I knew I was right in putting my trust in you." He held the stone in wonder, studying how it glided through the air defying gravity. "Do you think you can make it stop flying?"

"Sure, I'll do it next session."

"No, do it now. Here."

Joel didn't know what to do. He had made the stone fly, but he had been asleep when he did it. He didn't want to disappoint Santiago, but at the same time he knew he'd not be able to do it. The old man stood there with his hand outstretched and the little stone floating above it.

He captured the stone in the viewfinder on his smart phone and selected the undo option. Santiago yelled, taking Joel's focus from the screen. The old man lay with his hand pinned to the deck.

"A little less weight! I think it broke my hand!"

"Oh, sorry," Joel said, but secretly he was pleased it had worked so well against all his expectations. He had no idea why the dotted lines had reappeared much thicker than before, but he found an option to lighten them, freeing Santiago in the process.

"That was amazing!" Santiago said, cradling his right hand where it had already started to swell. "You should train up here from now on. But what is this strange black glass you used?"

"It's a smart phone," Joel responded not knowing what else to say.

"And what does it do?"

"In my world you can communicate with other people, play games and many other things. It is a little computer."

"Can I see it?"

Joel handed it over, hesitating at first. Santiago studied it, letting his fingers glide over the glass and metal surfaces.

"I've heard of such things."

"You've heard about smart phones?"

"No," Santiago said with a smile and returned the phone, "but I've heard of people using items to channel their power."

The next morning, he sat down on the mat, placed the stone in front of him and tried to shut out everything that was going on around him.

If Santiago was right, the power was within him, the phone just acting as a conduit. He should be able to make the stone weightless by sheer will alone. He closed his eyes, trying to recreate the little stone in his mind. His brain had other ideas. It analysed why he'd been so successful returning its weight in the first place. It argued that it had been easier because it was the natural state of the stone to have weight and therefore much easier for Joel to imagine it convincingly. Joel had to agree that there was some logic, but he ignored it nonetheless.

After two hours of abject failure, he again used his phone to picture the lines attached to the stone.

"What are you doing?" Martin was standing in front of him watching curiously.

Joel smiled. Here was an opportunity to finally show Martin the bully what he could do—show that he was special while Martin was nothing.

"I'm a Nexus. I'm going to make this stone fly with my mind."

"I can do that," Martin said and sat down next to Joel.

19

Mr Night

Erin spent the next three days walking along the road leading to Solliciti, the capital of the stress goblins realm. They begged for food from passing travellers and supplemented it with berries from the nearby forest. It kept them going, but only barely. They slept on the ground at the edge of the forest, away from prying eyes. It was uncomfortable and cold. She woke feeling as tired as she had been the night before. They had seen a few small farms and lonesome buildings but had not dared to approach them.

In the afternoon on the third day Erin thought they were far enough to brave the hospitality of a stranger. The fairy disagreed of course, insisting they keep to themselves, but it didn't have the same problem feeding itself. It was perfectly fine on just a few drops of water, a couple of berries and small piece of bread a day. Erin wasn't sure if the fairy really meant it either, as it argued everything. Whenever Erin said anything it immediately took the opposite view and was willing to defend it to the bitter end. Even worse, the fairy sat perched on her shoulder, so any opinion it had was delivered straight into her right ear.

On this occasion Erin just ignored it and after another hour trudging along she saw a large well-kept house not far from the road. Erin headed towards it.

"It is too early to stop," the fairy said. "With this rate they'll have tortured your family to death before we get there."

Erin glanced sideways with a frown.

"Just calling it as I see it," it said with a shrug. "Whoever is in that house will probably torture you too."

Erin ignored the remark and studied the house. It was a two story, white weatherboard house surrounded by a white picket fence. The garden was immaculate with a small hedge along the front and rose-bushes in full bloom along the sides. She opened the gate and walked to the door.

"You be quiet," Erin said to the fairy. "I'll do the talking,"

"Can I scream when they start torturing me?"

"Just be quiet."

She took a deep breath and knocked on the door. It was pretty much guaranteed a strange creature would inhabit the house, so it was a pleasant surprise when the door finally opened and a middle-aged man appeared.

"How can I help you?"

Erin did a double take. She'd seen this person before. She was sure of it. He was some kind of celebrity. He was the first human she had met since coming here and she felt an immediate kinship. Perhaps he too was trapped here somehow? She'd learnt enough by now not to trust her first impressions, so she just smiled.

"Hi, I'm Erin. And this is the tooth fairy. We wondered if we could get shelter here tonight."

"Visitor or citizen?"

She'd been asked this many times in the past few days. According to the fairy there were rules for how you treated visitors. They had to be helped whenever possible.

"Visitor," she said.

The man studied them first and then looked around as if he was searching for something behind them.

"Where's your gear?" he asked.

"We were robbed yesterday," Erin said innocently. "They took everything."

He looked at her again, taking in the dirty hospital clothes she was wearing.

"My name is Stephen," he said and smiled. "Welcome."

Erin returned the smile and entered. The house was as well-kept as the garden, filled with what Erin liked to think of as antiques. Not like a granny house with every nook and cranny overloaded with old trinkets, but immaculately maintained furniture and set pieces. What drew her eyes most though were the paintings. Every wall had at least a couple. The first one was a panorama of a small coastal town. It looked like the best place ever to live. She wanted to step into the painting and live out the rest of her life there. The next one was of a lonesome house with a forest as backdrop. There was a tree in the yard with a tire around a branch as a makeshift swing. A deer was grazing at the edge of the forest. Again, she felt that irresistible tug and imagined living in that house, playing in the yard, exploring the forest.

"This place is creepy," the fairy whispered loudly into her ear, breaking her daydream.

"Not now," she whispered back.

"I bet you're hungry," Stephen said without looking back and led them into a kitchen. While it still had an old cottage style, Erin was surprised to see a microwave and other more modern things. He sat them down and served a chunky vegetable soup that had quite a spicy kick to it. It was the best thing she'd had since coming to the Intersect. The food she had been served by the tooth ghouls had all been sickly sweet and the days on the road she'd hardly seen cooked food at all.

"This is really nice," she said, and the fairy grudgingly agreed.

"You don't happen to have some beer?" the fairy asked innocently.

Stephen smiled and soon there was a shot glass filled with beer next to the fairy who eyed it with disbelief.

"I'm sorry, I don't have a smaller glass than that," Stephen said.

"No problem," the fairy said, then stuck his head into the beer and drank.

"I think you just made a friend for life," Erin said.

"Is he The Tooth Fairy?" Stephen asked as he watched the fairy with its head almost completely submerged in beer. "He isn't what I expected."

"I guess Disney has made us expect fairies to all look like Tinker Bell, but, yes, he says he's a tooth fairy. Apparently, there are many of them."

"What's his name?"

"He doesn't have one. Doesn't think he needs one, either."

"So how do they tell each other apart?"

"Well, he'd be the fat one," Erin said, loud enough to be sure the beer drenched fairy heard.

It stood up and shook its head like a dog, miniature droplets of beer spraying the table around him. He then proceeded to burp louder and longer than seemed possible for such a small creature.

"Ha, bloody ha," it said and gave Erin a stare. "To start with, I'm not a he. Tooth Fairies don't have genders. And just so you know, we do have names, but they are our business. And—AND!—I'm not fat. I'm just big boned."

It took another deep breath and dove into the beer once again. Stephen and Erin exchanged glances and burst out laughing.

"The house has prepared a room for you upstairs," Stephen said once they had stopped laughing. The fairy had emptied the glass and was flat on his back hiccupping contently.

"The house?"

"It cares for the people in it. Check the cupboards. There will be clothes for you there."

She thanked him for the food but realised he had probably not prepared that, either. The house provided for him. Being so dependent on someone or something made her uneasy. Who knew what price she had to pay for such comforts?

As she made her way to the stairs, she passed the painting of the house and was again struck by the open invitation. Even the deer stared straight at her with its head tilted, as if asking her when she'd be joining it. She had to force herself to continue past.

She hurried up the stairs and into a small corridor with five doors leading into bedrooms. She picked one at random. As she entered the room, something about the painting irked her. It hadn't been quite right. She pushed the thought away in her mind, but knew she'd have to get back to it sooner or later to get rid of the uneasy feeling.

She had stepped into a classic child's bedroom. It was how she imagined children living in fairy tales. Floral patterns painted on the walls matching the sheets on the white wooden bed. Dolls and their accessories filled the room. Erin opened the large cupboard and found clothes to match. Beautiful elaborate dresses you had to lace up in layers and matching hats filled most of the cupboard. She would have preferred simple clothes for walking, but, after rummaging around a while, had to settle on a simple cotton dress with a matching jacket. She was dressed more for a picnic in the countryside than travelling, but anything was better than the white hospital clothes she had worn until now.

She tried to find shoes when it struck her. The deer in the painting was grazing when she first saw it. The second time it was upright, staring at her. It had moved! She pulled on a pair of cloth slippers and ran down the stairs. The deer had its head down grazing as the first time she had seen it. Erin reached out and touched it. It felt like a painted canvas, but how could that be?

"You've noticed it too?" Stephen said as he came up beside her.

She nodded.

"They never move when you watch it. They are all like that. Small changes every time you come back to them. I spent a whole day staring at one of them once and nothing changed."

"What are they? The paintings, I mean?"

"I don't know who painted them or if the house just gave them to me. They are scenes from my imagination."

She was about to question how this was possible if he didn't even know who had painted them but stopped herself. Anything seemed possible here.

"They are beautiful," she said simply.

"Yes, they are," Stephen said thoughtfully.

Erin studied him with a frown. He behaved as normal as anyone she could think of, not like all the strange creatures she had seen so far in the Intersect. Perhaps he too was a visitor. She decided to find out.

"Are you a visitor or citizen?" she asked.

"I am a citizen," he said with a smile, putting her immediately at ease. "But it seems I'm a reflection of a real man—someone of note."

"Who?" she asked.

"Stephen Night."

There was a name she'd never forget even if she had wanted to. He was one of the world's most popular horror authors. She remembered where she had seen him before. Her father had read many of his books and had most of his hardcover editions lined up on the bookshelf. They all had a picture of the author on the cover or the sleeve.

"In my world you are a famous writer."

"I am in this world too."

Erin had been in the Intersect long enough to at least have some theories about how the place worked. She had tried to get information from the fairy, but his information had proven so unreliable she'd given up. This place was affected by human thoughts and dreams. The existence of creatures such as tooth ghouls and Martians proved that.

But it wasn't enough for just one person to think about something for it to appear here. It had to be something people thought and dreamt of as a collective. If that was the case, what was Stephen Night doing here?

Erin yawned.

"You must be tired from your travels," Stephen said. "A word of warning. The house has other inhabitants and they are best left undisturbed. I would suggest you lock your door. I'm in the room furthest down the hall if you need anything."

Stephen headed for the stairs and Erin went to get the fairy. It was flat on its back on the kitchen table, snoring loudly. She picked it up carefully, and it curled up like a kitten in her hands—a very foul smelling, dirty kitten. Through the kitchen window she saw a sliver of the sun disappearing on the horizon.

She passed the painting one final time and noticed the deer was no longer there. She shrugged her shoulders at the pointless miracle and headed for the bedroom.

Erin put the fairy down in a doll's bed, smiling as she did so. She knew it'd prefer the garbage bin if it had a say in the matter. Now it snuggled up next to the doll and let out a content sigh.

She lay down on the bed, marvelling at its softness. Three nights sleeping in the open had been enough to appreciate the luxury of comfort. She had little energy left for appreciation and soon fell asleep.

***

If Erin had given the painting a few more seconds of scrutiny, she would have seen blood in the grass and shadows with red burning eyes staring from the forest. Soon the shadows took form and ventured closer and closer to the edge of the forest, ready to explore the clearing and what lay beyond.

***

"Get up!" the fairy yelled into her ear.

She sat up. It was still in the middle of the night. She shook her head and lay down again, deciding this was the fairy's little revenge for the doll's bed.

"There is someone outside the door," the fairy said. "We need to leave or there will be torturing galore, and not in a good way."

Erin sat up again and cocked her head. The fairy was right. Something was moving outside the door. Something large with padded feet. She tiptoed to the door, peered through the keyhole, and immediately jumped back. Someone was staring back at her.

"I smell someone new, someone fresh." The voice was no more than a breath, but its intentions were unmistakable.

"We can't get out that way," she said. "Perhaps we should just wait? The door is locked."

"And wait for the crazy psycho Night person to show up? No thanks! He'll have keys for sure."

It was true. The creature pacing back and forth outside the door had to have something to do with their host, but perhaps he was a prisoner just as they were.

"We have to try through the window," she said finally.

She pushed it open and looked out. She wasn't desperate enough to hazard the drop to the ground. There was no obvious alternate path down, but if she stood on the window frame, she'd be able to reach the guttering and make her way to the side where the roof was lower. She didn't know if it would hold her weight, but she saw no other option.

She balanced on the window frame and reached for the guttering. Her fingertips touched it, but not enough to get hold. She'd have to do a small jump and grab it, hoping it would carry her weight. The fairy flew up to the roof and assured her it was sturdy. She didn't trust this at all, but she still took a deep breath and jumped. The gutter creaked alarmingly but held for now. She inched her way, arms straining from the effort, and it wasn't until she was safely standing on the lower roof that she released her breath.

"What now?" The fairy landed on her shoulder.

What now indeed. The only reasonable safe way was up. Perhaps she could find a different path down on the other side of the house. She climbed the incline of the roof and paused as she reached a small circular ajar window leading into the attic. She peered through the window. It was an empty room apart from a desk. She couldn't see anything that moved, but the darkness could hold anything.

"Let's check it out," she said and pulled the window open.

"I'm not going in there again," the fairy said defiantly.

"There may be another way down in there," she said.

The fairy demonstratively stepped off her shoulder and hovered next to her with arms crossed.

"Well, I'm going in anyway," she said.

She spied a narrow staircase winding downwards on the other end of the room. The wooden floor creaked as she inched herself across it. If her calculations were correct, this staircase would lead down into another part of the house which might bypass the creatures altogether.

She was only a few steps away from the staircase when something on the desk drew her eyes. Sheets of paper were neatly stacked in a pile. She could make out a paragraph of text on the top one. Curiosity overcame her. A few years ago, she had picked one of her father's Stephen Night books from the shelf and read the first few chapters. She had had nightmares for weeks after that. Was that what the strange creature had been? A nightmare generated from one of his books?

She read the first paragraph, wondering what new horrors might lurk in these pages. The first page was titled "Something really scary," but the rest of the page was anything but. It told of a little sheep that refused to eat her breakfast. Erin was no great judge of prose, but even she could tell this was primary school material at best. She had a look at the next page and the next after that and it was just more of the same. It seemed the dream Stephen Night was not nearly as good as his real-life counterpart.

She remembered the dreams she'd had after reading his book. Her young mind had tried to put a face to the horrors visited on her and the author photo had provided that face. Stephen Night had haunted her dreams. Others must have done so too, blurring the line between the creator and the creation. Who was to blame them? Wasn't the idea of someone creating so much horror scarier than the horror itself? She had thought he was trapped in the house, but it was more likely the house was just an extension of Stephen Night—the nightmare.

Just as she had finished that thought, a creaking sound made her swivel around, papers still in her hands. Stephen Night had stood behind her, holding the largest axe she'd ever seen.

"So perhaps I'm not as good a writer as the one you know," Stephen Night said apologetically, nodding towards the pages in her hands. "But I conjure my horrors in other ways. Come with me."

She could make a dash for the window and jump out. If she timed it right, she'd be able to stop before flying off the roof. Either that or wait for a better opportunity as she was led downstairs. She didn't like her chances either way, so she waited.

"Go down the stairs and no sudden moves," he said. "The shadow people won't take kindly to that."

She headed down the narrow stairs, Stephen following close behind her. She was sure she could outrun him, but more than likely there'd be something else below. She needed to know what she was up against before attempting her escape.

"You liked the painting of the McQuillan's house, didn't you?"

"McQuillan?"

"Yes, it is a sad story. They lost their only daughter a year ago. She was playing in the backyard on the very swing you can see in the painting. Sometimes in the night they can hear her calling from the woods. They're good people. They'll be so glad to have you there."

"What do you mean?"

"You'll join them in the painting. Perhaps you're their adopted child with a history of seeing visions. Yeah, I like that. I can't wait to see how that plays out."

That was how this Stephen Night created his horror. The paintings were scenarios from his mind, populated with unsuspecting travellers.

She reached the bottom of the stairs and on Stephen's insistence stepped into the hall. She couldn't see the shadow beast she had glimpsed before, but she walked slowly, nonetheless.

"Not much further now," he said. "Just down these stairs."

She did as she was told. It would take her down to the ground floor and her best chance for escape. There had been many rooms and windows in all of them. She'd be able to make it to one of those for sure.

Halfway down the stairs she realised she'd made an error. There were at least ten figures all looking up at her. They must be the shadow people. Their pale skin stretched over their faces as if there were no longer flesh beneath, just skin on bones. Darkness clung to the group as a mist trying to reclaim them. Stephen gave her an encouraging smile and indicated with the axe that she should continue down the steps. She swore to herself. She should have tried to escape upstairs. Now she was trapped.

She took a first tentative step on the floor. All the paintings were now teeming with life. In the painting across the hall from where she was standing, a heavy white mist besieged the seaside town. It even leaked from the painting down the wall. Strange creatures moved within the mist.

Further away was the painting with the house. A child, a girl, looking much like the shadow creatures was standing by the makeshift swing, its dark eyes staring straight out of the painting at her. It approached Erin, a tentative step after another. The girl creature was still far away, but it reached out and, to Erin's horror, the hand came straight out of the painting and gripped the frame. It pulled itself through with a strange unearthly grace, still locking Erin with its stare. The shadow people around her let out undulating sounds as if to encourage the child, but it also mesmerised Erin to the point where she no longer thought of fleeing, only what wonders the painting might hold. She found herself taking a halting step towards the girl creature.

"No one take another step!" The voice of the fairy came from somewhere behind Stephen, instantly breaking the spell. The shadow people turned towards the sound.

Stephen winced and was just about to swat the back of his neck.

"I wouldn't do that if I were you. I am The Tooth Fairy and I am a master swordsman," it shouted. "I've got a mighty sword ready to sever your spine. You strike me at your own risk."

Stephen ignored the threat and reached around, trying to grab hold of the fairy.

"I will hack your head off!" the tooth fairy tried. "Granted, it will take me some time, but I'll do it!"

The shadow people had moved back, but Erin could see they were getting restless. A small hand took hers. The pale girl creature from the painting looked at her and grinned, showing two rows of needlepoint teeth. Erin pulled her hand free, scared of what those teeth could do to her. She ran and hoped she'd be able to clear the hall as all eyes were still on the uneven struggle between Stephen and the fairy.

She ran down the hall, turning into the kitchen, slammed the door shut, knowing she had only a few seconds before they came around through the dining room. She grabbed a chair, threw it against the window and followed straight after. Her legs hit the windowpane on the way through and she landed in a heap on the veranda. She scrambled backwards as soon as she hit the deck but was fairly sure what she had escaped was bound to the house. Erin saw only the young pale girl staring at her through the broken window. Behind her Erin could see more of the pale creature.

"Get out of the way! Get out of the way!"

The fairy flew headfirst through the window, barely missing the pale girl, and it was only through a desperate side roll it managed to land in Erin's lap instead of going splat into the veranda.

"Let's go! Let's go!" it shouted and attempted to lift Erin by pulling at her dress, but only succeeded at pulling the fabric from under its own feet.

"I don't think they can follow us out of the house," Erin said.

"I'm not willing to bet on that. You've been wrong before, you know."

She got up on her feet. The fairy fluttered like a drunken bumblebee to its favourite spot on her shoulder. The pale girl creature was still watching her from the window. It wasn't trying to follow them, but Erin was no longer afraid. The child must be a visitor captured much like herself. It reached out in a final plea and Erin, acting on impulse, took her hand. She no longer saw a monster, but a scared girl desperate for rescue.

"Come with me," Erin said. "You are like me. You can leave."

"What are you doing?" the fairy asked. "I'm not rescuing you again, you know!"

"You don't belong in there," she said, ignoring the fairy. "You are a visitor just like me. You can leave."

The girl tilted her head and grimaced. Behind her, more of the shadow people appeared. The hypnotic sound returned, as impossible to resist as last time. Erin felt herself swept up in it and was just about to climb back into the house, when the girl suddenly pushed her out and jumped. Erin managed to remain on her feet, saved by the veranda railing. The pale girl landed like a cat on both hands and feet, ready to spring. She sniffed the air, detecting no threat, and stood up. Erin wondered if she had made a mistake.

"So what happens now?" she asked the fairy.

"Now we get out of here!" the fairy said and flew away from the house.

Erin glanced back a final time and saw Stephen staring at her from the window. He didn't say anything, but it was clear he wasn't pleased. Yet another enemy to add to the list, she thought to herself.

They made their way to the road and started their journey anew.

"Thanks for rescuing me by the way, oh master warrior," she said to the fairy.

"Why thank you, Princess Pearly Whites," the fairy answered with a grin and made a mock bow, swinging a needle back and forth.

"Is that your mighty sword?" she asked, pointing at the sewing needle it was returning to a little loop in its belt.

"It was all I could find. Did the job, though."

"Were you really going to sever his spine?"

"I was trying to! All I had was a bloody needle. At least I gave him one hell of an acupuncture. I never was particularly good with a sword, anyway."

"Well, you are my hero."

The little fairy beamed at the compliment.

"Your milk teeth better be bloody good," it said gruffly. "So what are you going to do with her?" It pointed towards the pale girl who was at their side, alternating between a hunched loping and running on all fours.

"She's a visitor. We need to help her get back to my world."

"How?"

"I figured you'd know."

"Visitors just fade away. Nothing you can do about it."

"So visitors are people that are sleeping?"

The fairy shrugged his shoulders. "Don't know and don't care."

"Am I asleep?" Erin asked.

A sharp sting on the side of her face made her yelp.

"No, you seem awake to me," the fairy said, holding up the needle for her to see. "You want me to try and wake you up again?"

She shook her head. She was physically here, of that she had little doubt, but maybe others weren't. Could that be what coma patients were doing? Travelling the Intersect, not knowing how to return? Erin had taken her from the house and in doing so had become responsible for her fate.

***

Stephen Night watched the two girls and the fairy running towards the road and for a moment he thought of giving chase. The girl, Erin, would make such an inspirational actor in one of the worlds he imagined through the paintings. After some consideration he decided against it. She was a resourceful girl. They'd meet again. It was time to change hunting grounds anyway. He ordered the house to change location and it obeyed, rising on a multitude of small legs, moving slowly at first then picking up speed, trashing the garden in the process.

They'd meet again, of that he was sure.

20

An Unlikely Companion

Martin pulled a five-fingered metal construct from a pouch. It looked like someone had started out designing a knuckleduster and hadn't known when to stop. Long sinister looking metal spikes protruded from the four joined rings.

Martin fitted the rings over his fingers and the spikes wrapped themselves around his hand tighter than seemed comfortable. He pointed at the stone and it immediately responded by lifting from the deck, hovering a few inches off the ground. Joel was impressed and angry at the same time. He had thought himself special and unique, just to find there was someone else more special and more unique. To make matters worse, it was Martin. He couldn't think of anyone he'd have liked less to have this ability.

"Joel, well done," Santiago said, capturing the stone and giving it to Joel. "You're a natural."

"It wasn't me," Joel said, embarrassed.

Santiago turned to Martin. "You did it?"

Martin nodded.

"This is a sign!" Santiago exclaimed. "Two Nexuses on board my ship and I didn't even know about it. It must be a sign."

Santiago stopped for a moment. "Nexuses? Is that right? Nexi? Or is it just Nexus?"

Joel knew where this was heading even before Santiago said anything else, but he hoped desperately he'd be wrong. He wasn't.

"Anyway, imagine what you could achieve together," Santiago continued. "You must train together."

"Ok," Martin answered immediately.

Joel didn't want to train with Martin, but he didn't want to seem childish, so against his own better judgment he too agreed.

"I think I'll sit the first few sessions out," Martin said and stood up. "I'm obviously more advanced. Joel needs to catch up a bit."

Santiago pondered this and then said, "Why don't you train Joel?"

Every fibre of Joel's body screamed no as Martin smiled and said he was honoured to help. Again, Joel couldn't see any way he could protest without it seeming childish. What had happened between Joel and Martin at home was literally a world away.

Santiago thanked them both and left. Martin sat down next to Joel.

"Joel, I know you don't like me. You have no reason to, but I've been here almost a year. I can see you've not been here nearly as long."

"No. But how is that possible? Have you been a visitor before?"

"No. I entered after you."

"That's impossible."

Martin smiled.

"A few weeks here and you'll stop saying that."

"Yes, there is that." Joel had watched time travel movies and quite enjoyed them, but the paradox of going to different time periods jarred him. If you could travel into the past, you could kill your father so you wouldn't be born. But if you hadn't been born, how could you then go back and kill your father? This seemed an even stranger one. Perhaps time passing varied in different parts of the Intersect?

He remembered the idea of Einstein's theory of relativity—that time moved slower depending on your speed. Maybe parts of the Intersect moved at different speeds. While that explained the time difference, it raised so many other questions his head hurt.

"How did you end up here?" Joel asked finally.

"I followed you," Martin answered. "You ran straight past me on your way to that research place. I followed best I could. My leg was still bad from where your girlfriend kicked me. What was her name?"

"Erin," Joel said.

"Ah, yes, Erin. I followed you through the portal."

"So you must have ended up the same place as me?"

"Yeah, but a day later I met Highbranch, He told me."

"Highbranch?"

"The little crab guy. He Who Lives Among the High Branches. They have long names, don't they? And that is just the short version. I call him Highbranch. I would have thought you'd know his name. He definitely knows yours. When I came there, they were burying their dead. They blame you for that."

"It wasn't my fault."

"They think it was. Highbranch led me to you. He wants revenge on their behalf."

"And that's it?"

"Not exactly. We tracked you to the Mansion of Dreaming Elders. That place was enormous. I think we walked around there over a day without seeing the same room twice. Then all we tried to do was find a way out. In one room the walls came alive and captured me. The next thing I knew I woke up in a desert. I wandered there for months and to make a boring story short, Highbranch found me again. He wasn't actually looking for me. He was still trying to find you. I agreed to help him so we travelled for months until we came across Sin Ese who said he could help us. And he could. But it was Highbranch that did it, really. He is a shaman in training, you know?"

"Wow," Joel said. "And I thought I'd been through a lot."

Martin shrugged his shoulders. Joel didn't believe his story, but there was something different about him. He was no longer the bully Joel remembered, but considering his companion, Sin Ese, perhaps he had just taken bullying to new levels.

"So, what about your companion?" Joel asked, nodding towards Sin Ese who stood observing them.

"You recognized him too? I saw him on TV once. Isn't he great?"

"Great? He's a terrorist!"

"A terrorist for some. A freedom fighter for others."

"Where did you get that from? Terrorism for Dummies?"

Martin just stared at him and then shrugged. "Anyway, let's get this training started," he just said.

Joel had overstepped the bounds of whatever companionship they now shared. He didn't think they could ever be friends, and he didn't really want to, anyway. Even if it was over a year since Martin had seen Joel, the bullying was all too fresh for Joel to just forgive and forget.

It was soon clear they had vastly different approaches to their powers. Joel needed to analyse the object through the mobile phone. Once he understood how the forces affected it, he could change them. Martin saw no need for that. He just enforced his will on the stone using his strange metal device, telling it to rise through sheer will. Together they explored their powers and soon had the little stone change weight quicker than his mum on and off diets. Sin Ese and Gabe Shade stood on either side of their little practice area observing them casually.

After a couple of days, they moved to more complex items—heavier and with more detail. As they hunted for another object after working with two pieces of driftwood on top of each other, Sin Ese interceded.

"I suggest something more practical," he said and put an ornate dagger on the mat. "It is said the Crimson Warriors of old duelled with a dagger between them and fought for control until first blood."

Martin smiled at this and raised his eyebrows at Joel who shook his head vigorously.

"You are kidding, right?"

Sin Ese waited for Joel to answer.

"Leave the kids to their lesson," Gabe Shade said and stepped forward.

"They need to learn something useful," Sin Ese said and held up his hands in mock supplication. "Making a boat fly? A waste of time! They are warriors. They should learn as such."

"You are right," Gabe Shade said after considering Sin Ese's words. Joel stared at him in horror. Wasn't Shade supposed to be on his side?

"I want you to levitate the knife and try and hit something with it," he said. "Sink it into the mast or something. That could come in handy. Use a stick if you want duels."

"A true warrior is born in blood, not through games," sin Ese said shaking his head ever so slightly.

***

A new exercise regime started. They still lifted ever more complex and heavier objects, but they also explored other uses for their talents. It began with throwing the dagger. At first they levitated it and sent it off in a direction. While it worked, it was hardly a useful skill as the weightless knife bounced off the target. Instead they had to let it keep its weight and lift it anyway. After much practicing they were both able to do it and their respective strengths was soon apparent. Joel was fast and precise while Martin was less accurate, but able to put in much more force.

Joel found he relied on the smart phone less. Once he had mapped an item a few times and could picture it in his mind, the phone was just a channel, like a witch's wand.

Santiago frowned on their new exercises but didn't interfere. He came by every evening asking them how they'd progressed.

"Why are we doing this?" Martin asked on one of those occasions. "We won't be able to navigate a boat through the air however much we'd like. It is just too big."

"I know," Santiago said. "Once the ship is airborne, I have other means of navigation."

"How?" Joel asked.

"Don't you worry about that. You get it airborne. I'll take care of the rest."

Santiago walked away leaving them to ponder his words.

"I don't get it. If we make the ship weightless, it will blow around like a balloon. I guess you could use the sails, but…"

"I think I know how he'll do it."

"How?"

"Down in the hold he's built some kind of spider web wings that I think he'd use to direct energy."

"From what?"

"He's got a power source. It is an orb down in the hold. I think it has lots of power."

"Let's check it out!"

Joel's first reaction was to refuse, but only briefly. Here was a chance to show off things he knew and could do, things that Martin knew nothing about.

"I'll show you, but you have to promise to not tell anyone."

Martin promised and, to his surprise, Joel realized he believed him. Perhaps they wouldn't be the best of friends, more like competitive brothers forced to cope with each other, but at least it was a start.

***

Later that evening when it was dark enough to hide their covert action, Joel and Martin walked casually over to the entrance to the hold. Joel undid the weave, and they entered quickly and closed the hatch. It was pitch black, but as they fumbled their way down the steps, a warm glow flooded from the middle of the room. The orb was on the pedestal, uncovered.

"Wow! Look at that! It's like a black hole or something."

Joel resisted the urge to tell Martin that if anything it was the opposite of a black hole, as they had such strong gravity that not even light could escape them. As they watched, the glow increased, and the spider web of metal and cloth pulsed with the same warm glow. Joel found himself drawn to it. The only thing that stopped him from doing it was Santiago's words. *It is a dangerous thing for a young mind.*

"I dare you to go over and put your hand on it," Martin said.

"I don't think that would be a good idea," Joel said, but found himself taking a step towards it. How could something so beautiful be dangerous, he asked himself. He took another step and then another. When he was close enough to touch it, the light suddenly changed. The glow from the web disappeared back into the orb and the light within the orb became more pronounced, almost like an eye focusing.

"There is something in there," Joel said as he tried to turn his gaze from the orb. "Something inside. I can't..."

He was hopelessly lost. He could see his hands both reach out to take hold of the orb and how the light seemed to stretch from it in eager anticipation. Suddenly it all went black. Martin had thrown the cover over it.

"You're braver than I thought," Martin said. "I never thought you'd actually do it. Did you see how the light tried to get you? If you'd put your hands on it, your fingers would just melt or something."

They left the hold and Joel secured the hatch with the weave once Martin was out of sight. He sat down next to the Guide and sighed in relief.

"The training is keeping you up late," the Guide said with a yawn and rolled over. There weren't many cabins on the boat so when the weather allowed, they had taken to sleeping on deck. Below deck there was barely enough room to put down your bedroll. Joel lay back and closed his eyes when he felt the tip of a dagger against his neck.

"Your presence is requested," Highbranch whistled as quietly as it could.

"I'm not going anywhere with you," Joel said.

"There is no need for that," sin Ese's voice came from the darkness. "Let the boy be."

Highbranch withdrew his knife with a disappointed whistle. Joel sat up. He didn't like Sin Ese. He was a bully, much as Martin had been. He was just more subtle about it.

"I would like to speak with you," he said softly.

His first reaction was to refuse, but in truth the strange man intrigued him. Who wouldn't want to speak with the devil, if nothing else to understand what real evil looked like?

Joel walked in the direction of the voice. He didn't see him, but an arm gently took him by the shoulder.

"Walk with me," Sin Ese said.

Joel followed Sin Ese as he made his way through bedrolls.

"So how is the training going?"

"Well," Joel said guardedly. "Slow but well."

"You are modest. Martin says you are almost as good as him and you've only trained less than a week."

"Thanks."

Sin Ese waved his hands dismissing Joel's words. "You are a Crimson Warrior. Thanks are not required."

"Sorry."

Sin Ese stopped. "I have no use for apologies, and you shouldn't give any. Not to me. Not to anyone."

Joel stopped himself from saying sorry again but didn't know what to say so he stayed silent.

"There is a city as big as a small country," Sin Ese said after a while. "They are ruled by a dictator who accepts no other law than the one he decides on the spot. The inhabitants are worked as slaves for sixteen hours a day. The dictator uses his army to enforce his will, killing anyone that opposes him. How do you suggest you'd deal with a dictator such as this?"

"You are asking me?"

"Yes."

"Well, the people would need to appoint a spokesperson who took their case to the dictator."

"Four attempts have been made so far to do this. Two were executed and two imprisoned."

They stopped by the railing. Joel studied the star-studded sky wondering where Sin Ese was going with this.How

"Then they should protest. Show the might of their numbers through nonviolent demonstrations."

"They only tried that once. Fifty thousand inhabitants died that day and almost as many sent to labour camps."

"I don't know," Joel said. "Wouldn't the sheer difference in numbers do it? If the people rose against the dictator, wouldn't he have to step down?"

"Yes, revolution is an option, but the dictator has built up a large army to protect himself. The inhabitants think him too powerful. This is not true, of course. They outnumber the army a thousand to one, but people need their hope back."

"What is this about?"

"Martin and I are on our way to a place just like that to help them."

"How?"

"There are freedom fighters there, but they are few and have little resources. We are going there to help them unite the people. The only way we can do that is to show them they can win. And we'd like you to join us."

"And do what?"

"I see a leader in you. Even without being a Crimson Warrior, you'd be a great leader against the oppression."

Joel was flattered. He had never thought of himself as a leader, but perhaps he could be. He had never been in a situation where real leadership was required, so how was he to know?

"What are you going to do?"

Sin Ese turned to Joel for the first time, his eyes piercing in the flickering light from the lanterns.

"We're going to strike at the very core of the establishment. We will blow up a large military facility. We've been told the dictator will be there so with any luck, we will take the dictator out with it too."

He took hold of Joel, making sure he had his undivided attention.

"When they see that it is possible to oppose the dictator the inhabitants will rise up like a tide and sweep the old regime away. Are you with us?"

Joel felt like he wanted to be part of this. If he was to be a hero, what better way than helping people in need? And it sounded like these people really needed his help. Sin Ese obviously believed his plan would work. Joel wasn't so sure. The longer he thought about it the less he liked it.

"It won't work," Joel said finally.

"Of course it would! They would..."

"Even if you were to get the dictator, the army would take over. How does information spread in the place you are talking about?"

"They have TV, radio and newspapers, much like where you come from."

"The army would step in and put in a temporary military ruler. They have control of the media, so they'd explain away the explosion as an accident. They'd look around for a relative of the dictator that they have control over and put him there as a puppet. If anything, the people would have it even worse."

"I see what you are saying." Sin Ese said thoughtfully. "What do you suggest?"

"Taking out something of great significance is a good starting point, but you should make it the royal palace—if they've got one—or something like that. But after that you need a message and a way to let it reach the masses."

"What's the message?"

"You need someone the people will believe in as an alternative to the dictator. If they see something real, they will rise."

"And how do I get it to the inhabitants?"

"You need to control the information network long enough to let your message be heard and make the public believe it. That means taking control of TV stations and making sure you can deal with the army's counter strike. And then you'd need resistance fighters out in the public that they can rally around and that can direct their actions."

"I see," Sin Ese said. "I was right. You'd make a great leader."

"All that is just hypothetical," Joel said immediately. "There must be many other ways to deal with this if you got to know the way the country was run. Democracy is only a matter of time in most societies. And blowing things up to take power hardly ever works. You just replace one dictator with another."

"You won't help us?" Sin Ese said.

Joel was about to explain that he didn't believe terrorism worked for any long-term changes but decided not to. It had occurred to him that some of the people he met here, especially the ones that took on familiar faces, weren't people at all. They were creatures embodying the essence of a personality type. The Sin Ese in front of him wasn't the Sin Ese he had seen a few times on TV. It was the essence of terrorism wearing the face of Sin Ese. He was an archetype, Joel thought, and how could you possibly convince the archetype of terrorism that terrorism doesn't work?

"My friend has been captured," Joel said carefully. "I need to find her. Once I've done that, I might be able to help."

"A righteous heart acts," Sin Ese snorted and stood up. "I see I was mistaken about you."

He took a couple of steps backwards, the night engulfing him as if he'd never been there. Joel returned to his makeshift bed and lay down. He noticed Gabe Spade's eyes on him, trying to determine what had happened no doubt. Joel turned away from him, thinking that Gabe Shade too was one of the archetypes, but not as easily identified as Sin Ese. Joel closed his eyes. His brain—too wound up from the discussion with Sin Ese—tried to make sense of what an archetype was and it soon had a theory. Through the ages, humankind told stories and dreamt of certain characters to the point where they became something more. Their image and purpose steadily fed by new tales around the world, making them near immortal.

Joel's brain gave up and fell into a dreamless sleep.

***

The next day Sin Ese again placed a dagger on the mat between them.

"It is time for the boys to become men," he said. Gabe Shade briefly glanced at Joel and then shrugged his shoulders. Martin and Joel stared at each other and without saying a word they nodded and focused their will on the weapon. Joel used the phone's screen to control the knife, treating it as a game.

Joel knew he wouldn't win by force. If Martin could focus on the knife long enough, he could lock it and force it through Joel's defences. His best bet was to finish it quickly before Martin had time to focus. He did just that. The dagger floated up in the air and Joel applied pressure. It moved towards Martin and just as it was about to touch his shoulder it stopped.

"It won't be that easy," Martin said and forced it back.

Joel immediately darted around, applying pressure in one direction, then the other. He had to use his speed to make it impossible for Martin to apply his superior strength.

As the duel continued, the travellers and the small crew all came and watched. The Guide even started taking bets. Highbranch beat his claws together and whistled: "Kill him! Kill him!"

Joel and Martin were oblivious to their surroundings, focusing only on the duel and the dagger leaping back and forth. They were at a stalemate. Martin attempted to gain control, but Joel was able to counter at every turn. Joel attacked, but every time he tried Martin had enough time to focus and immediately counterattack, sending the dagger flying like an arrow straight at Joel. Joel deflected the attack, with only centimetres to spare. He let the knife dance around to stop Martin from getting a grip on it again, the knife now moving so fast it could hardly be seen. Joel flicked his finger back and forth on the screen, telling himself over and over it was just a game, but he was tiring. The prolonged concentration and fear of injury made his head hurt. Blinding pain pulsated with every heartbeat, threatening to break his concentration. For a moment he took his eyes off the screen. Martin sat opposite to him, staring straight ahead as if in a trance, sweat running down his forehead. He looked like he had achieved that Inner Peace Joel's brain had so effectively refused. For the first time in the duel Joel was scared. He knew he could only keep this up for a little while longer. Martin on the other hand showed no sign of tiring, so Joel decided to put all his effort into a final attack. After an especially complex movement he suddenly increased the weight of the dagger and then put all his power into a sweeping attack. Martin frowned as he dealt with the heavy dagger and just as Joel swept, he realized his error. He had made force the most important factor. Martin stopped the knife before it was anywhere close to him. It hung there suspended for a few seconds as Martin took control. He smiled. Sweat rolled down his face as he turned it. Joel swiped at the dagger on the screen, but with little effect. He held out the phone in front of him, projecting force to stop the knife, but he was only able to slow its progress. It moved towards him centimetre by centimetre when someone grabbed the dagger in the air, breaking both of their concentration.

"Enough!" Santiago said and threw the dagger on the ground. "What do you think you are doing? One of you could die and then where would we be? You are Nexi! Don't you understand the power you hold in your hands? One wrong step and you might end this place!"

The gathered audience stared in wonder and several separate conversations began. They had seen a duel between two mythical warriors! This was the seed of a tale that would be told around campfires, changing ever so slightly with each retelling. After a few years there was a tale of two Gods battling, flinging 20-meter tall trees at each other like toothpicks. Not even people witnessing the event would have recognized the tale by then.

"Do not mess with their lessons again," Santiago said and threw the dagger at Sin Ese who caught it with ease.

"I would have won," Martin said as they sat down, exhausted.

"I won't make that mistake again," Joel said, breathing heavily.

"You can't afford to make mistakes," Martin said. "The next one might be your last."

Joel wondered what he meant. The words had the essence of a threat, but the way Martin had said it, it sounded more like advice.

"The victory snatched from his hands," Sin Ese said and pulled his hand, forcing him to stand up. "You will see much more from this young man. He will make his mark on the Intersect and the realities beyond."

He dragged Martin off as if he was a rag doll.

"You did well," Gabe Shade said. "Do you think you could have turned it around?"

"No," Joel said and knew he was telling the truth. A few seconds more and there would have been plenty of first blood.

"And that is your first mistake," Gabe Shade said. "You need to concentrate and focus to do what you do, yes?"

"Yes."

"So break it. Stop him from focusing."

"How?"

"I don't know. Set fire to his hair. Make his clothes turn into sandpaper. Shrink his underpants. You're the one with the powers. Think of something."

"Wouldn't that be cheating?"

"When your life is on the line, there is only winning," Gabe Shade said and patted Joel on the head in an odd fatherly gesture. "There may be doubts you won fairly, but there will never be any doubts the other guy lost."

Joel knew there was no point in arguing with Shade. Joel played fair. He hated people that cheated, but the weeks he'd spent here showed this was an opinion easily held only when the outcome didn't matter. When your life was in the balance, cheating could be the only option to survive.

21

Stress

Most people go through life worrying about the silliest things. Do I wear the right clothes? What if they don't like me?

Grownups worry about even sillier things. Does my butt look big in this? Will I have enough money when I retire in thirty years?

Erin's pointless worry was the pale girl. She wanted her to leave this place but was at a loss how to help. She felt responsible even though she had rescued her from living through a nightmare night after night. It was soon obvious the girl needed no help. As days passed, she behaved less like the pale needle-toothed creature and more like a girl. Even her jet-black hair was slowly changing to a golden blonde.

Three days after they escaped, as they had settled down for the night, she even introduced herself as Lucy and thanked Erin for rescuing her. She spoke of her life in their world and from her descriptions she must have been gone for a long time. Erin guessed she must have been here for ten years or more. Somehow they both knew they would not be together much longer.

The passing was uneventful. She simply faded from view until nothing remained. Erin imagined her waking up in the real world, hoping that was what actually happened.

That morning the world around them changed. Every step they took somehow modernised their surroundings.

"What is going on?" Erin asked the fairy.

"What do you mean?"

"Everything is changing."

"We're entering a new location. The rules of that place are taking effect," the fairy said with a shrug. "It happened when we left the tooth ghoul city too."

She hadn't noticed. During their escape she had been so focused on not getting caught she hadn't paid any attention. In broad daylight it was harder to ignore.

The dirt road became a four-lane highway. A few more steps and telephone lines and street lighting appeared. The air was noticeably heavier to breathe. It even smelled different. It was the smell of civilization—of industries pumping out god-knows-what for pointless items of comfort.

They kept walking in the middle of the road when suddenly a car appeared in front of them honking and swerving from side to side to avoid running them over. Another appeared and then another. Erin barely managed to escape the highway without being run over. Exactly where they could be heading when the highway ended in only a kilometre or two made no sense, so she asked the fairy.

"We entered this realm through a one-way gate. If we want to leave, we'll have to go a different way."

"What would happen if I walked back the way we came?"

"You'd get to wherever this highway leads," the fairy said with a shrug. "Probably some smaller stress goblin town."

"What is a stress goblin?"

"There's one," it said, pointing to a bus stop further ahead. "Why don't you ask him?"

The creature at the bus stop looked human, at least from a distance. It wasn't until Erin came closer that she saw his forehead was much larger than a human and had furrows permanently etched into a frown.

"Hello," Erin said.

The goblin jumped high and stared at her in horror. The furrows in his forehead deepened even further.

"Please don't kill me!"

"I wasn't going to."

"Please don't rob me!"

"I wasn't going to rob you, either."

"Please don't kidnap me!"

"Look," Erin said, her patience already wearing thin. "I'm not going to rob, kidnap or kill you. I just wanted to ask some questions."

"And if I get them wrong, you'll kill me?"

"No, I won't."

"You'll rob me?"

"Listen, if you don't stop that, I will strangle you," Erin said.

"I knew it!" it shouted, staring at her in horror for a few seconds before running off.

"So that was a stress goblin?" Erin said, as much a question as a statement.

"Yep, but I think he was highly strung even by their standards."

"They're stressed all the time? Is that it?"

"There's more to it, I think. They live off stress. They need it as much as you need food…and a bath."

"Very funny."

"You're starting to smell. That's all I'm saying."

A bus stopped next to them and the doors opened. Erin just stared at the bus driver.

"Get in now!" he said. "I'm already late. I will lose my job. Get in now."

"Are you going to the capital?" Erin asked finally.

"Not with you standing around out there, I'm not. Hurry. Hurry. Hurry!"

Erin and the fairy shared a shrug, and she entered the bus. Inside stress goblins sat, all of them staring down on little tablet screens. It reminded Erin so much of home she sighed in relief. She sat down next to a woman and smiled at her.

"Visitor or Citizen?" Erin asked, using the age-old question to strike up a conversation.

"I'm neither," the woman said without looking up. "Now leave me alone. I have to get this five-thousand-page report in before lunch."

"Neither?" Erin looked questioningly at the fairy.

"I don't know," it replied with a sniff. "I'm a tooth fairy, not one of the bloody Oracles."

She spent the rest of the trip trying to make sense of the extremely intricate route diagram that took up a major part of a wall. The lines looped back and changed colours and numbers at random, making it near impossible to work out a specific route. After half an hour she thought she'd found the right one.

"I've been notified there are road works," the driver announced, "so we'll have to take alternative route 45b."

The passengers groaned and cried out at the news. Erin couldn't find anything mentioning alternative routes on the diagram and gave up. It wasn't as if she knew where she was going, anyway. She watched as the countryside became smaller suburbs and finally towering skyscrapers appeared at the horizon. This was an enormous city. How was she going to find her family here?

The road grew to six lanes and three levels with big message boards along the sides. One in particular kept repeating. It read:

Tired of being oppressed?

Do you want to stress about things of your own choosing, instead of what the government has decreed?

Join the RESISTANCE!

Erin read it over and over as it reappeared. It didn't make any sense. How could a resistance group that was clearly opposing the government be allowed to recruit so openly? At least it meant you'd be allowed to talk about it.

"Are you part of the resistance?" she asked the woman.

"I have a 5000-page report…" the woman coughed and stared wildly around her as she realized what Erin had said. "How did you know?" she whispered after a while.

"Is it a secret?"

"Of course, it is! It is a top-secret organisation planning to overthrow the government. We're as secret as they come."

"What about those?" Erin said and pointed at yet another giant-sized message board.

"They are a worry, aren't they?" the woman said, her frown deepening. "At least they don't have contact details on them like the newspaper and TV-ads."

"You do TV-ads?"

The goblin nodded, still looking around to make sure no one else was looking their way.

"Would you like to join?" the woman whispered. "I don't think they'd take pests," she said and indicated the fairy, "but you'd be welcome for sure."

"The resistance?"

"Yes."

"Pest?" The fairy was fuming. "We can trace our lineage for over a thousand years. You showed up when? Last Thursday? You are the pests if you ask me!"

"You are one of the ancients?" the woman said, suddenly looking extremely nervous. "I meant no disrespect. I thought you were a tooth fairy."

"I am a tooth fairy!" it yelled and jumped up and down on Erin's shoulder.

"Could you stop that?" Erin said. "You are spitting in my ear."

"Hmpfh!" The fairy sat down as hard as it could with its arms crossed.

Erin hesitated. Joining the very public secret resistance seemed dangerous, but she reminded herself the rules here were different.

"I'm looking for my father and brother. They were sold to the stress goblins and I'm looking for them."

"That's not very hard. The government imports many species."

"To do what?"

"To experiment on, of course," the goblin said, matter-of-factly.

Erin just stared. They were doing experiments on her family!

"Oh dear," the goblin said in horror. "I've upset you! Now I've done it. I really have. That's no way to treat visitors."

"I'm fine," Erin said. "I just need to find my family."

"The resistance can help you do that."

Erin looked at the goblin whose oversized forehead had wrinkles that put Grand Canyon to shame. She wasn't sure she could trust her, but even trust was a foreign concept here. Just as in the tooth ghoul realm, there were rules. They were simply different from what she was used to in her world. The sooner she could work them out, the sooner she could use them to her benefit. She needed help and here was someone willing to provide it.

"Thanks, I think I will do that."

"That's great! I am Ilyante," she said and smiled.

"That's a nice name," Erin said and tried the foreign sound out.

"Oh, it is quite common. It means—I wonder if my friends really like me."

That made a perverse sense. A place where stress was important, you'd invent simple names for what causes it.

"Can we go there now?"

"Where?"

"To the resistance?"

"Now?" Ilyante said and went on to explain how stressful it would be to do it now—not counting the 5000-page report that still had to be written—but also agreed it was equally stressful to not care for a visitor properly. It was obvious the decision was a cause of immense stress, but also a sense of anticipation and satisfaction. Erin thought Ilyante wanted the stress as much as she didn't want it, in the same way a person might feel about parachuting. We want to do it for the thrill, but our mind screams out that it is dangerous.

In the end the goblin decided she'd try to write the report while taking Erin to the resistance headquarters.

They departed the bus two stops later following the goblin woman as she kept hammering on her little laptop and mumbling strange words like "agitation coefficient" and other things Erin didn't understand.

They entered a large building with a huge banderol exclaiming: "Resistance fighters!—Sign up here." Erin had hardly stepped through the door when someone inside screamed:

"Government agents! We've been betrayed!"

22

The Attack

The next day the weather changed. It was as if day never really arrived that morning. The sky was as black as midnight, the sea dead silent and the air completely still. Everything just stopped, like an audience just before the curtains open.

"I don't like this," the Guide said, looking out over water as dark as ink.

"What's to like?" Gabe tried to light a cigarette. After three failed attempts he threw the cigarette overboard.

"They're not good for you anyway," Joel said.

Gabe Shade sneered and walked off.

"What's going on?" Joel asked

"We're being attacked," Santiago said.

"By what?"

"By that," he said and pointed. The water around the boat churned. Dark oily liquid bubbled up, turning the sea to a kaleidoscope of sickly colours. The smell of rotting meat engulfed them.

"It's an Uncompleted!"

Joel didn't know who had said it, but everyone on board murmured in a most disquieting way.

"What's an Uncompleted?" Joel asked the Guide.

"Unfinished thoughts that combine to make a whole."

"Are they dangerous?"

"I've never seen one. They only exist at the centre of the Intersect and I keep away from there if I can help it. But, yes, they can be."

Martin came up next to them. "An Uncompleted? If half the stories I've heard are true, we need to prepare for battle."

Santiago stared at the oily liquid as it spread across the water. "Listen to me," Santiago said. "I think you all know what we are facing. It is a creature stitched together from things that shouldn't be. If it has survived this far from the centre, it will be a formidable foe."

He let that sink in for a few seconds. Joel thought that if any of them had been optimistic about their chances, they surely would have changed their mind now, but all he saw was steely resolve.

"I need to know who can be in our first line of defence. We will start with ranged weapons to do as much damage as we can. When they are too close, the first line of defence will move in and keep them busy until the Nexus Warriors can dispatch them."

Joel now knew why the travellers were so optimistic. They had two mythical warriors on their side, and this was their hope of coming out victorious. He watched as the first line of defence formed. Odum Sin Ese, Highbranch, the Guide, two other travellers and three from the crew. They spread out along the railing, drew their weapons and waited for the onslaught.

Between them came anyone with a ranged weapon—Gabe Shade with his revolver, Santiago and three crew members with crossbows along with two of the travellers with bows.

Joel and Martin stood behind them not sure which way to turn.

"What's your plan?" Santiago asked them. "How will you fight?"

"We could shoot daggers at them," Joel suggested.

"We don't have much in the way of weapons to use that way," Santiago said. "Can you make some appear?"

Joel and Martin looked at each other and shook their heads in unison.

"We've been practicing levitating your boat, remember," Martin said. "We've not tried much else."

"Something is coming!" Highbranch whistled from his vantage point on the railing. Joel saw three creatures swimming awkwardly towards them, only two boat lengths away. One had the scaly body of a fish, with spindly legs sprouting at odd angles from its body. Its head was a red gullet, oversized triangular teeth in row after row. The second creature was just an amorphous blob of dark matter that kept flinging out appendages to swim. The third one had the angelic face of a baby, but its body was put together like a rag doll, pieces of clothing and flesh stitched together at random.

"What are they?" Joel asked. "I thought we were fighting one thing, not many!"

"The Uncompleted isn't one thing. It is many pretending to be one." Santiago took aim with his crossbow. "We need your help. Now!"

Joel and Martin desperately hunted for something to use and at the end had to make do with a small wooden box of nails. They hurried to the railing just in time to see the rag doll climbing up the side, the other two already dead.

"Where's my mum?" the baby rag doll creature squealed and struck out with one of its long arms. The Guide barely sidestepped it and struck. The rag doll let out a piercing wail as the blade bit into its hand, but it hung on. It grabbed hold of the railing with its other hand and dragged itself up. The Guide struck again, this time severing the hand from the arm completely, but the hand had a life on its own. It scurried across the deck. Highbranch struck its claws together and let out a high-pitched whistle. It jumped down on the deck and set after the hand and soon had it pinned to the deck. The rag doll creature hung on with its remaining injured hand, but two well-aimed crossbow bolts sent it back into the dark water.

The defenders let out a cheer. They knew there was worse to come, but it was a victory, nonetheless.

"You better get ready," Santiago told the two Dream Warriors. "We won't get off that lightly next time."

"Here they come again," the Guide said grimly. Joel could see four shapes in the distance making their way towards the boat. He couldn't see what kind of creatures they were up against, but he knew they'd be dangerous. They had barely managed to keep three of them at bay. How many more were there? They had to hope the spawns would only come in waves of small numbers else they wouldn't survive.

"There are more!" the deckhand boy yelled. "On the other side."

Santiago ran over, swearing, waving Martin and Joel with him. Out over the water and saw two large shapes.

"You will have to take care of those," Santiago said. "We'll deal with the other ones."

Joel and Martin exchanged nervous glances and nodded. Joel strained to see what they were up against. They were both human shaped, but much larger, their skin almost completely white.

"Let's do this," Martin said and made tree nails levitate and sent them off as projectiles. Two missed. The third one struck its target but to little effect.

"That won't work," Joel said. "We need a better way to aim. Let's try this."

He picked up a hollow bamboo pole, put a handful of nails down one end, and aimed the other at the creatures. They had almost halved the distance already. Joel held the phone as an aiming mechanism on the pole and flicked the nails out the other end. Slow at first, then faster.

"I see," Martin said with a grin. "You've made a machine gun."

He fed more nails into it as Joel aimed it at the creatures. They were close, only meters away from the boat. Joel now saw that the pieces of their bodies were ill fitting, as if they both were puzzles and the pieces had been mixed up. Frankenstein's monsters, Joel thought.

Joel aimed at the closest one and let a steady stream of nails hammer into the closest creature. It threw its hands up to protect its head, but to no avail. It tried to swim away, so Joel let a burst hit the second one before it reached the boat.

"Focus on one!" Martin yelled. "Better to have one gone completely, than two injured and after blood."

Joel saw the logic in this and kept the bamboo pole trained at the second one until it lay still.

"We've run out," Martin said. "There are no more nails."

As soon as Martin had uttered the words, the surviving creature turned towards them again, its movement's jerky. Some of the pieces making up its body had come undone, opening a huge bloodless gash from its shoulder.

"What are we going to do now?" Martin asked, panic starting to creep into his voice.

Joel cursed. If only they had had a few more minutes to prepare. The nails had been perfect, small and easy to focus on. There was nothing else here like that close by. There might be something down in the hold that could be used, but there was no time for that. What else was there? He could hardly rip pieces of the boat. They didn't have the ability to make things either, even though the possibility had occurred to Joel. Martin was keeping the creature at bay by aiming pieces of wood and other things that were lying on the deck, but Joel could see he'd soon run out. The air! Why not use the air? There was plenty of that around and perhaps they could turn it hard somehow? Joel thought about it for a few seconds but struggled with the concept. He couldn't imagine air being hard, much less using it as a weapon. There had to be something else.

There was. Joel couldn't believe how stupid he had been. There was water all around them and it wasn't hard to imagine water freezing to all sorts of shapes. Could he make icicles and use those as weapons? He grabbed one of the buckets used when swabbing the deck, threw it over the side and hauled it back up again.

"Hurry!" Martin yelled. "Whatever you are doing, do it now!"

Martin had run out of projectiles and was pushing the creature down with the bamboo pole to stop if from scaling the side. He caught the bucket in the viewfinder and changed the filter to a blue hue, imagining it as cold in his mind. The bucket and the water in it instantly froze to a single block. At that point Martin's bamboo stick snapped.

"Joel! Do something!"

He ran over to the side, just as the puzzle creature pulled itself out of the water. Joel did the only thing he could think of. He caught the creature in the viewfinder and changed the filter to blue again.

***

"Now there is something you don't see every day," Santiago said as he peered over the side of the boat. Joel had succeeded better than expected. Ice spread out in a half circle from the boat, with the puzzle creature stuck halfway up like a statue. Gabe Shade had a look too and nodded in appreciation.

"We took care of the other four, but we're running low on bolts and arrows. We won't be able to hold off another attack."

"I've got an idea," Joel said. "If we can get water into an icicle shape, I can freeze it and we can use them as arrows. I can make them hard enough to do some damage." He smiled reassuringly. "At least I think so," he added to himself.

"You heard him," Santiago said. "Let's get some water for them to work with. We can use sailcloth to make the icicle forms. It will hold the water long enough for them to turn it into ice."

Two crew members cut shapes into sailcloth and sew together makeshift narrow cones, while others hauled water. Joel and Martin had just finished the first few icicles when the deckhand boy yelled, "More attackers coming!"

His words were soon echoed from around the boat. They counted twelve creatures all around the ship, closing in quickly.

"We won't make it," Joel said.

"I know," Martin said.

"Do something," Santiago yelled. "We can't hold off that many."

"Do you think we could control fire?" Joel asked.

"Not likely," Martin said. "How would you get a fix on that?"

He was right. The only weapon he had was turning water to ice. He didn't have time to think of another solution.

"Duck!" he yelled and set the gradient of the filter further from the centre, changed to panorama and swept the phone in a full circle, capturing the ocean all around the boat. He could feel the temperature dropping several degrees. He looked away from the screen to discover he'd succeeded beyond expectation and even frozen most of the ship. Icicles hung from the rigging, as if they had been there for many years. The defenders closest to the railing had had to crawl back to not be frozen to the deck. The boat now sat in the middle of an ice field the size of a soccer stadium. The creatures had been frozen together with it.

The defenders cheered. Surely this was enough to beat the creatures and if not the Nexus would come up with some other fantastic way to battle.

"Not to critique a job well done," Santiago said surveying the boat, "but if there are more you've just given them solid ground to attack from."

"Uh, yeah, I guess," Joel said, still eyeing his handiwork. Had he really done this?

"Great work!" the Guide said and slapped him on the shoulder. He had a gash across his forearm, but it didn't seem to bother him. "I knew you could do it. I knew all along."

"You have plenty of time to congratulate each other when you're dead," Gabe Shade said almost casually, but it silenced everyone on deck. They had wanted to take some comfort in their victory. Shade had taken that from them with a few words and Joel hated him for it.

"This was nothing compared to what is coming. The kid has given us a few minutes. Let's not waste them."

"He's right," Santiago said. "Hopefully the ice will prevent any more attacks before…" He didn't finish the sentence, as if worried naming the foe would somehow hasten its arrival. "What do you need?"

Joel looked around for someone to answer before realising the question was directed at him. The travellers were all watching him with hope in their eyes. He knew what they saw. They saw a hero that would save them. Joel wanted to shout at them not to put their trust in him.

He was nothing. He had been lucky in coming up with the ice trick and had no idea how to fight an Uncompleted. He had read many an adventure book and usually the hero when faced with a seemingly unbeatable foe pulled something unexpected out of the bag to save the day. Joel didn't have anything unexpected. He didn't even have a bag to pull it out of.

He focused on the little he knew. If it was unfinished creatures gathered into a whole, perhaps they had to break it apart and kill the pieces one by one. The only other option he could see was to hit it as hard as possible. If he could hit it with something big enough, it might be enough to break it apart.

"We need people to get the icicles and we'll use them as weapons," Martin said assuredly.

"I think we are going to need something bigger. Much bigger. I'm thinking one of the masts."

"Surely there must be some other way," Santiago said, now worried. His boat had been turned into an ice block, but apart from that had survived relatively unharmed and he obviously wanted to keep it that way. "She's all I got," he said and patted the railing. One of his fingers stuck to the ice, and he had to pull it off. "Can't you shape something out of the ice?"

"We can try," Joel said, but he doubted it would work.

The boat suddenly heaved, only Santiago remaining on his feet. At first Joel thought something had hit the boat. He rose to his feet and felt as much as saw the ice breaking apart about two boat lengths from the stern. The Uncompleted had struck the ice. What they'd felt was only the resulting shock wave. Had it struck the boat directly it would have turned into so much kindling.

The gap in the ice widened as a black mass welled through it. Arms and legs of different shape and sizes sprouted out from its side, heaving up more and more of the ever-changing blackness onto the ice.

"We don't have time!" Joel shouted. "Get out of the way!"

Santiago took another look at the amorphous mass welling through the ice and stepped aside. Joel ignored any self-doubt, captured the mast on the phone view and severed any gravitational lines. It shook as he tried to move it upwards, realising he was trying to wrench it free from the boat. The planks in the deck groaned from the stress.

"No!" Santiago yelled. "You will rip the boat apart! It has to…"

"It has to be cut," Martin said and stepped forward. "Give me your sword."

"Whatever you are going to do, do it quick," Santiago said and handed him his sword. "And gentle."

Martin held it up towards the sky and closed his eyes. After a few seconds his knuckleduster shimmered and the light spread to the sword. He swung it back and forth and it sang as it cut the very air. Almost casually he turned to the mast and cut it off at the base with one stroke. It flew up into the air as Joel struggled getting control of it. He managed to get it to hover in the air and aimed it at the Uncompleted that was now almost completely out of the hole. Countless mouths appeared in its body and they all shrieked in unison, creating harmonies from the abyss. Everyone on the boat froze, one thought going through all their minds: How could they fight something like this?

Joel chose this moment to propel the mast down, increasing its weight as it gained speed. It struck the creature in the middle of its body, its shriek ending abruptly. The mast went straight through and into the ice under it, cracks spider-webbing out from the impact. The weight of the creature was too much for the fractured ice. Large sheets came loose, sending the Uncompleted sliding back into the hole. As it sank, smaller creatures broke from the main body. Some jumped straight onto the ice; others swam to the side of the hole and climbed up. The travellers again lined up along the railing, using up the last of the bolts and arrows.

"Look," Martin said proudly, weaving the sword in the air. "I made a laser sword. I can make one for you if you want."

"I wouldn't know what to do with one." Joel said, breaking off icicles from the rigging and collecting them in a bucket.

"Do something!" Santiago said to Joel as he dropped an empty quiver. "There's too many of them. They will reach the boat!"

A roar they felt more than heard shook the ice and the boat with it.

"That didn't sound like something dying," Joel said.

"No," Martin said. "I think you just pissed it off."

Santiago threw his crossbow on the deck and walked off. "It isn't fair," he mumbled to himself. "I was so close. So close."

The ice cracked again, this time closer to the boat, giving the defenders a little reprieve as the spawn creatures navigated their way over the increasingly perilous ice. Joel made his way to the side and the first thought that crossed his mind as he watched was: "We're all going to die."

The Uncompleted made its way through the ice again, but this time only a few meters away from the boat. Dark tentacles slapped against the side as it heaved itself up little by little. At least five of the spawn creatures reached the boat and were on their way up, the defenders trying desperately to push them down. Joel threw an icicle in the air and projectiled it towards the closest creature—a three-legged monstrosity straight out of a B-horror movie. It struck, sending shards of ice flying in all directions. The creature lost hold of the side and fell but was soon on its way back up again. Another spawn looking like an oversized plant using green tendrils with giant thorns as whips, came over the side, lashed a crewmember across the face, and then turned towards Joel. He backed away, trying to get another icicle flying when Martin stepped in and severed the whips with his sword and continued to hack down the plant creature until only a green mess remained.

Around them the travellers desperately defended themselves against the creatures that had made it onto the deck. He saw Gabe Shade standing at the remnants of the mast shooting any creature in sight. The Guide stood close to him, with his rapier ready. There were already two creatures lying at his feet.

Next to Joel two children were trying to fend off an oversized cabbage patch doll with vampire teeth and an enormous kitchen knife in one of its fat hands.

"Play with me," it cooed, showing its fangs, as it waved the knife back and forth.

Highbranch appeared out of nowhere, a miniature sword in each claw, and positioned itself between the children and the doll. It was easily double his size. The two children ran over to hide behind Joel. He was just about to attack the doll when he heard a shriek from above. He cursed to himself. They'd been so focused on attacks coming from the water they hadn't even considered the idea of attacks from the air. Above him a black shape sailed. It was like a giant wing of black flesh. Along the midsection eight pair of sinewy legs ending in small childlike hands rested. He couldn't see a head or a mouth, but the shriek must have come from somewhere. It descended, arms outstretched. Joel immediately sent three icicles, one after the other, flying. The first two just passed through the wing, causing little damage, but the third one ripped a section from it. Unbalanced, it leant more and more until it crashed sideways onto the deck. The wing came apart and from its inside three smaller creatures emerged. One of them stared him squarely in the eye and shrieked.

Like most boys, Joel had gone through a dinosaur phase where he collected figurines and read any book on the subject. As a result he could name most of the known dinosaurs, but it didn't help him with the one facing him now. It had a large scaly head with teeth like needles. From its arms hung leathery wings in tatters and its legs were oversized to allow powerful jumps. Joel sent two icicles against the first one; it ducked out of the way but struck the one behind. The two remaining dinosaurs weaved between the skirmishes on the deck, but their target was obvious. They were after the children. Joel picked up the last two icicles from the bucket and waited as the dinosaurs came closer.

"Take it down," Martin screamed from across the deck.

Joel still waited. He couldn't afford to miss as he wouldn't have any ammunition left for the remaining one. As he waited, he watched as one of them, by accident it seemed, came close to Highbranch who immediately turned around to defend himself against the new threat. The doll took the chance, threw itself with the kitchen knife held high and skewered the scuttler straight through the shell, pinning it to the deck.

"No!" Martin yelled. He dispatched the creature he was fighting against and sliced the doll in half.

Joel in the meantime had let the first icicle loose, striking the dinosaur through the mouth. He turned around to face the last remaining one. It already lay dead at the feet of the children. Gabe Shade had taken it down with a well-aimed shot.

A large tentacle of dark matter slammed into the deck and spread, engulfing anything in its way. The Uncompleted was finally making its attack and they no longer had any defence. Many of the defenders stopped as they watched the dark matter spread towards them. This was it, Joel thought. This was how they were going to die.

"Enough!" Santiago shouted. He stood with his arms outstretched, the orb in his hands. Everyone—the spawn creatures and defenders alike—turned to look at it. Joel found himself desperately wanting to touch it. There was something within it calling him. He took a step, then another, but was stopped by a firm hand on his shoulder. It was Gabe Shade.

"I offer you a new world, better than the one you've become part of," Santiago said. The orb pulsated, bathing the deck in its golden light. All the spawn creatures headed for the orb and lost colour and form as they did until the tiniest little wisp of matter was sucked into the orb. Even the tentacle broke apart and was swept into the light. Dark shapes flitted over the railing, parts that had broken free from the Uncompleted, and joined its brothers. A desperate roar made Joel run to the side. The Uncompleted was only half the size it had been before, as more and more of the smaller creatures broke free from it to enter the golden light. It tried to escape, but it no longer had control of its many parts. Section by section it broke apart until there was nothing left. Joel watched as the last black shape disappeared and all that was left was the mast floating next to the boat. The body of a woman lay next to it. At first he thought it was one of the fallen defenders. She was still gripping the trunk of the mast as if it was her saviour. He yelled for someone to help him get her out of the water. It didn't take long for the remaining crew members to haul her onto the deck. She was alive but struggling for each breath. On closer scrutiny it was obvious she had not been part of either the travellers or the crew, leaving only one option. She must have been trapped inside the Uncompleted.

"You bastard!" Martin yelled. He was sitting down next to Highbranch, trying to coax the Scuttler into consciousness. "You could have saved him."

Joel shook his head. There had been no love lost between him and the Scuttler, but that didn't mean he wanted this.

"You just wanted to save your own skin," Martin said through his teeth.

"No, I didn't," Joel said, but knew it didn't matter what he said. Martin was grieving his friend and blamed Joel for his death. Nothing would change that.

The Scuttler suddenly made a clicking sound. It was still alive. It raised itself up, an amazing effort as it also made the knife come unstuck from the deck. It stared directly at Joel.

"A curse on you and your family," it whistled and made a few shaky movements with its claw. As soon as it was done it fell back, dead.

Highbranch wasn't the only casualty. Half of the travellers had fallen and three of the crew. Almost everyone else had some injury. It was only Gabe Shade and Joel who had escaped the battle without a scratch.

"Could be worse," Santiago said as he surveyed the damage.

"Could be worse?" one of the crew said. "We lost half of our numbers!"

"We're alive and the boat is still seaworthy as soon as the ice melts. Could be much worse."

"I can probably melt the ice," Joel said, wanting to do something—anything—to help. He couldn't shake the feeling this was all his fault.

"No," Santiago said, a bit too quickly. "You rest. It won't take long for it to melt. Get some rest. You still have a task to do."

"What?" Joel asked, wondering what task he possibly could have left now.

"You're going to make my boat fly," he said and gave a tired smile. "I just hope I've not corrupted the orb. It is already difficult to control."

"What is it?"

"At the moment? It is power. Raw power. Lately something in it has stirred. I think it has become sentient, and it is ever more interested in our world and the world you come from. By letting it consume the unfinished dreams, I've given it more information than it ever should have. I will have to destroy it once I've completed my task." He sighed. "But that is a problem for another day. We will reach the Flux in a couple of days and I need you to make good on our deal then."

Santiago walked off and instructed the remaining crew members to salvage the mast.

Joel, feeling useless, checked on the woman they had brought onboard. Her face was stained with jagged circles of black tattoos, spreading out from her left eye. Her tattered clothes were similarly marked and even her hair, so dirty you could only guess her hair colour, had traces of the pattern. As the healer cleaned her face, Joel realized it wasn't tattoos at all as the pattern faded where the fresh water touched it. She was still unconscious, but her breathing was calm and strong, and her eyes moved under the eyelids now and then. Joel was no doctor, but he'd bet she'd wake up soon.

She was a mystery that could wait. He went in search for Shade and found him arguing with Santiago.

"Has it occurred to you that the Uncompleted was hunting something?" Santiago said.

"Yes. It was after the boy."

"It was after me?" Joel couldn't even begin to understand why.

Shade nodded. "This is worse than I thought. They already know he's here. I hope the others have gone undetected."

"The others?"

"There are others like you and Martin here, yes."

"And when were you going to tell me about that?"

"I wasn't," Gabe Shade said. "You have more important things to worry about. We will meet them—sooner rather than later I think."

Santiago looked back and forth between them and then settled on Joel. "I will hold you to your promise."

Shade frowned. "Isn't it time you let go?"

"Isn't it time you did too?" Santiago responded.

Shade stared at Santiago. Joel didn't know what the comment meant, but it was obvious something important had been stated—something that affected Shade more than he wanted to admit.

"Speak to no one about that ever again." He walked off, leaving a gaping hole of silence.

"What was…" Joel started.

Santiago shook his head. "We all have our secrets."

He said it with such finality Joel saw no point in pursuing the matter. He knew he wasn't game to ask Shade about it but went in search for him, regardless. Joel found him discussing the attack with the Guide. The Guide smiled wearily as he saw Joel. Shade didn't even acknowledge his presence.

"How do the tooth ghouls control an Uncompleted?" the Guide asked.

"This one didn't form by itself," Gabe said through clenched teeth. "It was created."

"How is that possible? I had no idea the tooth ghouls could do that."

"They can't. No one can."

"So how do you know?"

"An Uncompleted would normally be composed of anything you could think of. But look at the spawned creatures. They are all designed for battle. Someone is making an army."

"An army of Uncompleted?" The Guide shuddered. "Why? To take over the Intersect?"

"Perhaps. I think there is something bigger behind it," Shade said with a sidelong glance at Joel. "It is all connected."

"You think they will attack my world, don't you?"

"Yes, that is exactly what I think," Shade said, turning to Joel.

"Is that even possible?" the Guide asked.

"Yes," Joel answered, thinking back to the tooth ghoul entering through the portal. "I've seen it."

The repairs began. Joel offered to help, but Santiago asked him to leave it to the crew members. For the first time since he came here Joel had time to make some sense of what was happening to him. Gabe Shade's comment about how it was all connected and had something to do with him made no sense. After all, he had followed someone else in here. If anyone was connected to this, it was Erin and her father. He had created the machine that had brought them here in the first place. Joel had only entered the Intersect to save her.

But he agreed with Gabe Shade. There were other things going on and he was betting Erin's father knew what they were. Simple as it was, Joel was happy with that plan. Most of what was happening went above his head, but at least he could get to the source of it all.

He had more immediate concerns. Making the boat airborne didn't seem such an impossible task now after the battle, but if it was true the Uncompleted were targeting him, did he really have time to waste? He didn't think they'd survive another attack on their own. No, speed was of the essence. He needed to rescue Erin and get out of here as quickly as he could or get on with whatever Gabe Shade wanted him to do.

The more Joel thought about it the less it made sense. If they had such an urgent task to complete, why was Gabe fine with them going to rescue Erin first? The only sensible reason was that she or her father were somehow connected to all this and Gabe Shade wanted to find out what it was. Why not say so in that case? Whatever the reason, they'd be in the Flux in a few days, so he'd find out, regardless.

The next day everything changed. The orb had gone missing.

23

The Resistance

Erin turned around to see where the government agents were until she realized all attention was aimed at her.

"Are you?" Ilyante asked Erin, her frown deepening.

"No! Of course I'm not!"

Erin's protestations mattered little. She was pushed to the floor, and at least five guns were held to the back of her head, which she thought unnecessary.

"Leave her alone!" the tooth fairy shouted, flying back and forth, stabbing with the needle.

"She's infested with fairies," one of the attackers said and before the tooth fairy could get to a safe distance, a net was thrown over it.

"I'm not an agent!" she yelled as she was dragged off. She was locked in a small interrogation room with a table, two chairs and nothing else.

She swore to herself. It had been too easy. The whole public resistance had to be a ploy to capture dissidents. She couldn't work out exactly how the trap worked, but nothing else made sense.

The door opened and an older stress goblin entered the room and sat down opposite her. He was sweating, droplets running down his forehead, continuously diverted by his furrows. He pulled out a couple of photographs from a paper folder. The first one was of Erin and the old stress goblin she scared away at the bus stand. The second one was from inside the bus.

"So, you're an agent," he said.

"I'm not an agent," she answered.

"That's what they all say."

"I'm saying it because it is true!"

"They all say that too."

"Who are 'they' in this case?"

"All agents."

"How could you possibly know I'm an agent? I just came here."

The stress goblin pulled up a handkerchief and dabbed his forehead with limited success.

"You're sure?" he said pleadingly.

"Of course, I'm sure!"

"Thank the Oracles for that," he said and smiled. "I was sure you were an agent." He reached out his hand, and she took it. "Welcome to the resistance. I am Mermak. May Somerio die a thousand deaths."

"This was a test?" Erin asked.

"We had to make sure you weren't an agent. We do that to all new recruits."

"How does that work? Everyone would say what I said."

"Do you think so?" Mermak said, worried again. "Usually they just faint from the stress of being accused. Any real agents all confessed as soon as they were challenged."

Erin again reminded herself that things worked differently here, but she found it hard. They all seemed so gullible.

"What do you do with them?"

"The agents?"

"Yes."

"We let them join the resistance as long as they promise they're no longer agents."

"And if they don't?"

"We kill them," the old stress goblin said and demonstrated by pulling his thumb across his throat.

"And have you killed anyone yet?"

"No. They all decided to join us."

Erin gave up. It sounded like this very public resistance was doing everything it could to be noticed and infiltrated. She couldn't see herself working with them, but perhaps she could at least get some information.

"My father and brother, visitors, were sold to your government and I need to find out where they're held."

"I can tell you where they are. Anyone could. All high-profile prisoners are held in the Dungeons."

"An actual dungeon? Isn't that a bit medieval?"

"Oh, it is called the Royal Guesthouse, but anyone that has been there knows it is something else entirely. We've just come to call it that."

"Where is it?"

"It is underneath the Royal Palace. It was built on top of a cave system and they started using the caves as a prison. They'd be there for sure."

"I'm going to get them out."

They sat there for a few seconds.

"I have some good news for you," Mermak said finally. "We're planning a big offensive. We're going to blow up the new weapons facility when Somerio is visiting. I'm sure any prisoners will be given a full pardon then."

She knew it would never work. This Somerio would already know, since they were happy to tell their plans to any outsider who stepped through their doors. However, perhaps it could be enough of a distraction to give her a fighting chance to get to her family.

"When?"

"A week from now."

"I can't wait that long. I need to get them out now."

"Sorry, but we've been planning this for a long time. We're not going to change our plan because of some outsiders. We can't do it yet, anyway. Our liberator has not yet arrived. We can't start without him."

Erin knew she wouldn't be able to change his mind.

"Where is my friend?"

"Your friend? You came alone."

"The tooth fairy."

"Friend? They are pests. Scavengers."

"He's my friend," Erin persisted. "Where is it?"

The goblin's eyes widened. "We had it sent down to the incinerator. We don't want an infestation of Tooth Fairies here."

"We have to stop them!"

She ran and dragged the goblin with her, forcing the location of the incinerator on the way, down three stairs, through a corridor and into a small room. The fairy hovered around the ceiling, three goblins trying to catch it with nets.

"Stay away from my friend!" Erin shouted at them. They all turned to her.

"Friend?" one of them asked, distaste obvious.

"They're trying to kill me!" the fairy yelled.

"Why are you doing this?" Erin asked.

"They've all been exterminated in these parts. We don't want a re-infestation. Perhaps if we neutered it?"

"Come down," Erin said to the fairy. "They won't do anything to you."

The fairy descended and settled down on her shoulder. She understood why it preferred life in a cage.

"No one touches the fairy," she said to the goblins. "It is my friend, and that's that."

She headed back up followed by Mermak while the fairy told her about what had happened in detail. She stifled a yawn.

"Oh, I didn't mean to bore you with my story about how I barely escaped death!"

"Sorry, I'm just tired," she said. "Is there anywhere I can rest?" she asked Mermak.

"We have a few rooms for recruits visiting from the outer provinces. You could borrow one of those for now."

She thanked him and was led to a small room with a bed in it. The fairy joined her but flew as close to the ceiling as it could all the way there.

She locked the door from the inside and lay down on the bed, again trying to piece together this strange place in her mind. There was more to the Intersect than just visitors and citizens. Stress goblins were a good example. The woman had claimed the goblins were neither visitor nor citizen. That made sense. There were hardly millions of stress goblins in her world and it was unlikely people thought or dreamt of stress in the form of goblins. So what were they? The tooth fairy said they lived off stress but was it their own stress or others? She asked the fairy, but it didn't know. Apparently, the Goblins didn't have milk teeth, so the fairy community had very little interest in them.

It wasn't long until she fell asleep.

24

Betrayed

The morning began as any other. The mast and rigging had been repaired and most of the ice had melted so they prepared to continue their journey. Joel ate dry bread, drank some water for breakfast, and sat down for another lesson. Martin declared he no longer would train with him and that Highbranch wouldn't have approved. Joel didn't think much of it at first, but half an hour later of unsuccessful attempts to concentrate, Santiago appeared from the hold, murder in his eyes. He demanded that everyone, travellers and crew alike, gather and listen.

"Someone has stolen the orb," he said. "I know you all saw the power of it yesterday and I can understand if someone thought they could fetch a good price for it." He paused, letting his words sink in. "Whoever you are, I will give you this option: return the orb either anonymously or here now and I will not hold it against you." He paused again, allowing his offer to sink in. "If the orb is not in my possession within the hour, I will start going through everyone's belongings and have every inch of this ship searched."

Joel watched as they dispersed, surprised to see the woman they had rescued earlier among them. He sat down together with Gabe Shade and the Guide and the mysterious woman soon joined them. It seemed

The Guide had taken it on himself to help her and it was obvious he was smitten. Joel could see why. Under all the dirt and painted patterns, a pretty young woman with dark blonde hair and blue eyes had emerged. Joel figured she was about twenty years old, give or take a year or two.

"Did you take it?" Gabe Shade asked Joel directly.

He could feel his face growing red at the accusation. He knew why Gabe might suspect him, but it still hurt to have it out in the open.

"No, I didn't think you did," he said after studying the increasingly uncomfortable Joel. "But I had to be sure. I know you have access and powers others don't and I saw how you reacted when Santiago showed it. There are as many suspects as there are people on this boat, maybe more," he said with a glance upwards and then he settled on the mysterious woman. "But to me it seems you are the most likely suspect."

She met his gaze for a few seconds then shrugged.

"She was unconscious the whole night," the Guide said in her defence. "She didn't wake until this morning."

"Who are you?" Joel said.

She shrugged again, this time not even looking up.

"Can you speak?"

"I can speak," she said after they all had given up on a reply. "I just don't have anything to say. I don't know who I am. I don't remember my name. I can't remember anything before waking up this morning."

To his surprise, Joel found he believed her.

"You remember nothing at all?"

She shook her head and stared down into the deck. The Guide stood up and took her hand, pulling her to her feet.

"You have amnesia," he said. "There is an easy fix to that. You should drink from the wrong end of a cup. It will fix you right up."

They walked off.

"Better off without them," Gabe Shade said. "If it wasn't her, then who? There are few that can get into the hold, anyway."

"I think I know who," Joel said after a while.

"Martin," Gabe Shade said.

"You think so too?"

"No, but it wasn't hard to work out your top suspect."

"You don't think he did it then?"

"It is possible, I guess, but what would he gain from it? And even though he's a Nexus, I suspect he wouldn't be able to open the hatch to the hold, anyway."

"That's just it," Joel said, embarrassed. "I took him down there once. I tried to hide how to open the weave, but perhaps he saw anyway."

"That answers the how," Gabe Shade said with obvious disapproval. "How about the why?"

"I don't know. To take revenge on me for the death of Highbranch?"

"You think this is all about you?"

"It is a possibility," Joel said after a while, embarrassed, but knew Shade had dismissed it already. He was supposed to be this crack detective, but it seemed more than obvious to Joel that Martin should be their prime suspect. "Who do you think it is?" Joel asked.

"There are plenty of suspects. Amnesia girl was just top of my list."

"So who's the next one?"

"Santiago."

"What?"

"You heard me."

"Yeah, but why? He's the one wanting it back!"

"Haven't you wondered why Santiago didn't just bring the orb out as soon as the fighting started? It is priceless. Anyone on this ship would give up their firstborn for it. As soon as they saw it they'd all be thinking about stealing it."

"So? Wouldn't that make everyone on the ship a suspect? Including you?"

"The thought crossed my mind," Gabe Shade answered. "And if I thought about it, everyone else did too. The best place to hide something is in open view. In this case the easiest way to stop people worrying about stealing the orb is to make them think someone already has."

Joel nodded. In the scheming world that Gabe Shade lived it made sense, but he wondered if that was Santiago's way.

"What makes it so valuable?"

"You have to ask that? Something that can take an Uncompleted apart just like that?"

"Santiago told me it was becoming dangerous, that it is waking up somehow."

"Waking? It is forming a consciousness?"

"Becoming sentient were the words he used."

"Then it is much more dangerous. Very few would have the strength to control it. If Santiago hasn't got it, we need to find it." He sat back and lit a cigarette. "I'm wondering if it is all connected."

"What do we do now?"

"We can do this the hard way or the easy way. Either we actually work out who did it, or we just accuse someone and see what shakes out."

"I thought you were this great private investigator," Joel said.

"Shaking cages to see what falls out is an important tool of the trade."

"Let's make sure Santiago isn't playing tricks on us."

"How?" Gabe Shade said.

"I'll tell him what I told you and then we see what he says."

"There you go, kid. Already shaking cages on your own. I'll make a man of you yet."

Joel was glad Shade liked it, but he had his own agenda. He didn't for a second believe Santiago was pretending and at the very least he wanted to let him know of his suspicions.

Joel found Santiago staring out to sea. He'd aged ten years since Joel had last seen him. Before he had seemed a young man trapped in an old man's body, but now the years had caught up with him. That was enough to convince Joel Santiago had nothing to do with the theft.

"I release you from your promise," Santiago said, not moving. "It isn't about my quest any longer. It was never going to happen. I don't know why I thought it could ever be."

"I think I know who took the orb," Joel said.

Santiago finally turned around, "You do?"

"I think Martin did it to take revenge on me. He blames me for the death of his friend."

"Yes, it is a possibility, but not enough. He couldn't get into the hold. Not without me knowing."

Joel swallowed, steeling himself for what he was about to say. "I went down there with him once."

"You did what?"

"I know it was stupid. I guess I just wanted to show him I knew stuff."

"You did it to show you were special?" Santiago was so angry he had trouble keeping his voice steady. "You're a Nexus and you worried about someone not thinking you're special?"

"I thought I hid how to open the weave," Joel said, embarrassed, "but perhaps I didn't."

Santiago didn't say anything at first. He was still shaking with anger. "You didn't touch it, I hope?" he asked finally.

"No. It was close," Joel admitted, "but I didn't."

"Well, that is good at least. It is still young and inexperienced. It will make a mistake, I'm sure."

"The orb?"

"Yes. Very few would be able to control it and anyone not strong enough would be dominated themselves."

"I've felt it on my skin whenever I'm close to the orb. Couldn't we just find it that way?"

"I've already tried," Santiago said. "I've not been able to pick up a thing. The only option I can think of is that it is no longer on my boat, but how could that be? There haven't been any other vessels close, or my lookouts would have told me."

"How about Martin…"

"Or," Santiago continued, ignoring Joel, "they've managed to convince it to not make itself known, but that doesn't seem possible. It wants to show off, to show its power."

"And you don't think Martin did it?"

"I don't know." He shook his head. "I don't know."

Joel stood with him, watching the waves that slowly rolled the deck.

"I'm sorry," Joel said after a while.

"So am I," Santiago answered. There was no blame in his voice, only resignation.

Joel returned to where Gabe Shade sat.

"I don't think he's pretending," Joel said.

"No, neither do I," Shade answered, watching Santiago intently. "But it may still have its desired effect."

"What effect is that?"

"Wait and see. You've rattled the cage. Let's see what falls out."

They sat in silence for half an hour, Shade never taking his eyes off Santiago. Joel soon lost interest and tried to find something to do. The Guide was sitting with the mysterious woman not far away. Even Joel, who didn't have much understanding of romance, could see the Guide was head over heels in love. How strange it must be not to know your name, Joel thought. He'd be happy to forget his name, but since entering the Intersect this was not on his mind much. He wondered what her name might be and soon realized he thought of her as a Rose. As soon as he finished that thought, the Guide stared at him.

"Did you just name her?" he asked.

"Oh, I'm sorry," Joel said, holding his mouth as if that would help.

The Guide turned to Rose. "Do you know what your name is?"

She shook her head.

"It is Rose," he said with a frown.

"It is?" She looked directly at Joel, questioningly.

Joel shrugged his shoulders. She should be happy with Rose, he thought.

"It is a good name," she said and smiled.

"Look," Shade said and pointed at Santiago who was on his way over to Martin and Sin Ese. They could only hear some of the words he said to them, but his intent was obvious. He was accusing them of stealing the orb. Martin stared at Joel, completely ignoring what Santiago was saying. A dagger hovered in the air next to him, as he purposefully made his way to Joel and Gabe.

"You have my best friend killed and then you accuse me of stealing that ball thing?" His eyes were cold as the dagger floated up next to him. "I accept the challenge."

"What challenge?" was all Joel had time to say before the dagger came flying, aimed squarely at his chest. He had no time to think, even less time to bring his phone out. He pushed back instinctively but knew he couldn't match Martin's strength. In desperation he tried to divert it instead, inching it sideways. Instead of hitting him in the chest the dagger dug into his left shoulder. Joel watched in shock as Martin walked up to him and pulled the knife out. Joel fell to the ground as if the dagger had been the only thing holding him upright. Martin changed grip and readied himself to slash down at Joel.

CLI-CLICK! Gabe Shade cocked his gun and held it against the back of Martin's head. "I bet you're not good enough to wish a bullet away," he said. "Have a go. My finger itches. I've not shot anything today."

"And I've not hacked off an infidels head," Sin Ese said and held his sabre against Spade's neck. "I know you are not easy to kill, trickster, but then neither am I. Our fate was written in the desert sand long before we met."

"Yours perhaps," Shade said. "The Fates are still arguing about mine."

Santiago shook his head, snuck up behind Sin Ese and struck him over the head with a cudgel. The terrorist fell, unconscious before he hit the deck.

"No one wins a standoff," Santiago said and shrugged his shoulders. "Keep a weapon trained at the Nexus Warrior at all times while we go through their belongings."

"Give me the glove," Gabe said to Martin.

"What?"

"The thing you are wearing on your hand, give it to me," Gabe clarified. "It was never yours to begin with."

Martin hesitated at first, but another look at Gabe and his weapon and he pulled it off and handed it to Gabe. Joel struggled to focus on anything but the pain, but he could see that Martin's hand was swollen.

The healer patched Joel up, while the crew laid every piece of Martin and Sin Ese's belongings on the deck. They double-checked each item but could not locate the orb. Sin Ese had come to at the end of the search and stood watching with growing indignation.

"This charade has gone on long enough!" he said loudly. It seemed an uncontrolled outburst, but Joel bet every word was carefully chosen. "We are treated like criminals on the flimsy accusations of a pup who hasn't even faced the trials of manhood! Is this what passes for justice on this boat? The Oracles would not be impressed!"

At the mention of the Oracles a nervous murmur went through the travellers. Suddenly Sin Ese fell to the ground, again unconscious. Santiago stood behind him with the cudgel in his hand.

"I want them off my boat. Give them some food and put them in the rescue raft. Make sure they take nothing but their belongings."

Martin was led at gunpoint to the side where two of the crew waited to lower the raft into the water. Sin Ese was unceremoniously pushed onto the small vessel and the two packs dropped on top of him.

"Let me hear some multiplication tables," Shade said to Martin.

"Some what?"

"One times one equals one. One times two equals two. Come on. You know the drill."

"Why?"

"I want you to focus on multiplication. Or I can shoot you," he said and pushed the muzzle against his head. "I'm sure that would work equally well."

"You've taken my Forcecaster," Martin said. "I can't do anything without it."

Shade pushed again and Martin growled in return but obeyed.

"One times one equals one," Martin said through gritted teeth. "One times two equals two."

"If I can't hear multiplication and I can still see you, I will fire."

Shade demonstratively pocketed the gun and turned his back to Martin.

Martin continued reciting the multiplication table as he picked up the small stretcher he had made to carry the body of Highbranch. Joel watched as Martin carefully put the stretcher in the rescue boat and climbed in himself.

"Three times eight equals…twenty-four," Martin said as the boat was lowered.

"Not very good with maths?" Shade said.

"Three times nine equals…twenty-seven," Martin answered, staring at Shade.

"I want to hear those numbers as long as I can see you," Shade said and walked off.

Joel was standing next to small vessel as it was lowered into the water. He saw the body of Highbranch and was amazed how well the shell had been pieced together, even fixed up the drawings on it. Granted, a crab looks about the same, living or dead, but Joel still felt like the Scuttler was alive and could at any point start whistling curses at him. Joel sighed in relief as the little raft had reached the surface and Martin rowed away from the ship, yelling multiplication tables.

"Five times six equals…thirty! Five times seven equals…thirty-six."

It wasn't until that night Joel realized the best hiding place for the orb. The only place they'd never ever look—inside the body of High-branch.

25

The Liberator

Erin spent the next couple of days with the resistance. They were all consumed with planning the attack on a military installation. They had received words from their liberator and were desperately arranging for a major change of plans. Erin was amazed anything was completed at all. They had no official line of command, so everyone was giving and taking orders as their own need dictated. It caused constant conflicts and stress about not meeting the deadlines. Erin endured this for an hour before deciding to take charge. She organised them in groups with a team leader and set each group to individual tasks. The part of the plan they were focusing on involved finding and preparing goblins around the city that could act like leaders in their own local communities once the attack began. At first she thought it an impossible task, especially since they only had two days to complete it. Mermak had instructed them to locate goblins in positions of power that already had the authority needed. To Erin, this seemed a roundabout way to do it, arguing it would be simpler to decide from suitable candidates within their members instead. Mermak listened politely for her to make her case and then happily ignored it. As they located key goblins in different parts of the city, she understood why. It didn't matter who they suggested, Mermak checked the computer system that held the membership registry and they invariably were members. Erin suspected most if not all stress goblins were in fact part of the resistance.

They completed their task with only hours to spare and all stood waiting for the liberator. Erin didn't know what to expect, but when he finally arrived, she was suddenly very worried. The person who had entered the room was Odum Sin Ese. She'd know his face anywhere. If the human mass-consciousness had created a nightmare version of Stephen Night, what would this version of Odum Sin Ese be capable of? She decided she didn't want to find out and was just about to leave when someone else came into view behind him. It was Martin, the school bully. He scanned the room and when he saw her, he smiled and winked.

"I've come to you as promised," Sin Ese said as he stopped in the middle of the large room. He spoke softly, but the gathered stress goblins were so quiet he had no problem making himself heard. Erin could even hear herself blink. "And I have brought with me the tool of Somerio's destruction."

He held up a crystal ball of total blackness. It came to life and spread a golden light, but its centre was still as black as charcoal.

"Two days from now, God willing, you will be facing a new world; a world where you decide your own destiny. You've trusted me until now, even though I may not have deserved it, but the pieces of the plan have come together just as I said. Not only do I have the bomb, I also have the one who will deliver it. Behold, Martin, the Crimson Warrior!"

He bowed and took a step back, letting Martin step into the middle. Martin smiled and gazed into the distance for a while then reached his right hand up towards the high ceiling. He wore a black leather glove with stitched intricate glowing patterns.

The room went dark. Small storm clouds gathered close to the ceiling, crackling with energy. There was even a couple of small areas where rain fell, drenching their captive audience. The storm clouds merged into one and a flash of lightning struck where Martin was standing. While they'd been busy staring at the cloud, he had drawn a curved sword that now charged from the lightning until it shone like a half moon. Martin swept it through the air back and forth, then struck it into the stone floor with such force it stuck almost all the way up to the hilt. Cracks leapt from the sword in perfect symmetry. Martin took a step back and bowed. They all clapped, as much from excitement as from fear. Sin Ese again took centre stage.

"With a Crimson Warrior on your side, God will surely favour your cause. But it isn't over yet. We still need to complete the final preparations by tomorrow evening."

They all cheered. Erin couldn't believe what she had seen. She pushed herself through the crowded room until she stood face to face with Martin.

"Martin."

He made a formal bow and Erin noticed he was taller than he had been. They had been pretty much the same height last time they met and now she felt he towered over her.

"Erin."

"It is good to see a familiar face," she said, "even if it is just you."

"I deserved that."

His reply surprised her. It had almost sounded like an apology.

The tooth fairy descended from the ceiling where it had been caught by the mini thunderstorms and had been well and thoroughly drenched.

"You've got a bloody nerve showing off like that," it said, landed on Erin's shoulder and shook itself like a dog.

"You are a tooth fairy," Martin said. "I've met one of your kind before." He studied the fairy for a few seconds. "It might even have been from the same clan. His name was..."

"Stop!" the fairy said. "No names!"

"Oh, sorry," Martin said. "It did tell me that. I just thought it would be ok telling you and your friend."

"She doesn't know my name," the fairy said with a sidelong glance at Erin.

"My apologies," Martin said and bowed again. "I meant no disrespect."

"You are different," Erin said, stating a fact.

"I've been here over a year," he said and held up his hands, "and you don't need to tell me it is impossible. I know that. It is true, though. I've changed."

"Enough of all this catching up nonsense," the fairy said. "Where did you meet a tooth fairy of my clan?"

"In Atmos. He was the familiar of a witch."

"Atmos? The desert city? That must be old Boogersnort."

"That's the one," Martin said with a smile.

"Boogersnort?" Erin said with a frown. "What kind of name is that? I thought you just said you didn't want people to know any names."

"It's a nickname, you goose," the fairy said. "And a well-deserved one at that. I wasn't sure the boy here would blurt out a real name."

"So do you have a nickname?"

"Yes."

"Why haven't you told me what it is?"

"It is none of your business."

"Then you can kiss our agreement goodbye. I think I've deserved at least that much,"

The fairy took off from her shoulder and hovered in front of her face.

"It is Fancypants."

"Fancypants?"

"Yes. I was a bit too sophisticated for my clan, so they started calling me that. It is all nonsense, of course."

Erin didn't know what to say. Rating the fairy high on any sophistication scale sounded impossible.

"Thank you, Fancypants."

"Don't wear it out."

Erin tried to locate Martin, but he had been dragged away by a gang of younger stress goblins that had been attempting to dislodge the sword from the floor. She watched as he reached down, stopped for a while to collect himself then pulled it out with ease.

***

It wasn't until later that evening that she saw him again. She had been in her room preparing for bed when the fairy appeared.

"You want to sit in on this," it just said and flew out of the room.

She followed and found Mermak, Sin Ese and Martin sitting around the table. As she approached, she caught some of Sin Ese's whispered words.

"…primary target is the palace…"

"What are you going to do to the palace?" she asked.

"Child, this does not concern you," Sin Ese said.

"Let her sit in," Martin said.

Sin Ese looked at Martin. Then, with an almost imperceptible shrug, he continued.

"Somerio knows about the attack, of course, but he expects it in a week's time against a military installation. If we strike against the palace tomorrow or the day after instead, the success is almost guaranteed."

"What about my brother and father? They are imprisoned there."

"I will not have two outsider's lives stand in the way of the liberation of the stress goblins," Sin Ese said gravely.

"He has a point," Mermak said, but the frown on his forehead said differently.

"You have to let me go in first," she pleaded.

"Absolutely not. If they captured you, it would jeopardize the attack."

"You can't leave them there to die."

"She can come with me when I plant the orb," Martin said.

"No," Sin Ese said. "It is too risky."

"I'll plant the orb first, and then we'll look around for her family. Even if they capture us, the plan can still go ahead."

"You'd be willing to give your life for the cause?" Sin Ese asked, scrutinising him intently for a few seconds. "Yes, I do believe you are. But are you?"

The last question was directed at Erin.

"I don't have a choice, do I? If I don't go, they're dead. At least this way they have a chance."

"The bonds of family," Sin Ese mused. "It is strong indeed. I believe you are willing to die for them were it to come to that. You have my blessing."

"I don't need it," Erin said. "Just tell me when we leave and I'll be ready."

"We go tomorrow tonight," Martin said.

***

"It is a suicide mission," the fairy said when they returned to her room.

"Yes, it is," Erin said. "He had no reason to change his mind. There's something else going on here."

"Let's do it on our own," the fairy said.

"You saw what Martin could do. I'll have a much better chance with him. You don't have to come."

"I have to protect my investment," the fairy said and tapped his teeth. "Remember?"

"I remember," Erin said and smiled. The fairy kept to his story, but she suspected it was more than that. They had been through enough for her to call it a friend and she suspected so did the fairy, even if it would deny it to its dying breath.

"So what's the plan?"

"I really don't know. We need to speak to Martin."

She tried to find him the next day but was informed he was travelling with Sin Ese to rally the troops and that he'd be back in the evening.

26

A Truth is Revealed

Two days later they arrived at the major port, Trader's Gate, of the Flux. It was a quilt of architectures. In the distance he saw a glass skyscraper huddled close to gigantic spires grown out of the ground, dragons circling around their peaks, next to futuristic metal domes. The port itself was an equal mess of styles— frigates next to oil tankers next to round pods with gigantic sails that seemed oblivious to the direction of the wind. The familiar and surreal were living next to each other in such a hodgepodge it didn't look real.

"What is this place?" Joel asked the Guide as they stood at the railing.

"This is Trader's Gate. It started out as a small market and grew from there. Some just call it The Market."

"I've always hated the place," Santiago said as he appeared next to them. In the past two days he had forced the boat and all traveller's belongings searched over and over until he had to agree the orb no longer remained there. After the third time, Joel told Santiago of his suspicion and was surprised to find him invigorated and back to his old self. One of the travellers, tired of having his belongings searched, had told him of a remarkable flying machine, powered by the essence of regret. He explained in great lengths how the machine worked and how he'd locate it. Joel listened to the far-reaching plans, knowing it would never

215

succeed. If Santiago were an archetype, he'd be the embodiment of futile tasks, the one striving towards unachievable goals, but still finding the energy to carry on.

"Nexus," Santiago said. "I have something for you." He handed over a small wooden carving dangling from a leather band. The carving was crudely made of a fish head and bones. It was ancient.

"I am in your debt."

Joel tried to disagree but was silenced with an angry stare.

"I *am* in your debt. If you hold the carving in your hand and ask for me, maybe I can offer my help in return."

Joel thanked him, wondering when he'd ever need the help of someone who was unable to help himself.

Joel, Gabe Spade, The Guide and Rose left the boat wishing Santiago luck on his journey ahead.

"He'll never make it," the Guide said as they took their first tentative steps on land.

"Not a hope in hell," Gabe Shade agreed.

"We still arrived here much faster than on foot," Joel said referring to the Guides insistence they'd be in for a rough ride.

"I just said it wouldn't be an easy journey," the Guide said defensively. "I made no reference to speed."

"You would have preferred to battle the Uncompleted on land by ourselves?"

"Not so much preferred, but..."

The Guide's left hand slapped the Guide's face soundly.

"Seems at least part of your body agrees with Joel," Gabe Shade said.

"Untrustworthy little thing," the Guide said and admonished his left hand as if it was a pet that had failed toilet training. It responded by grabbing hold of his hair. The Guide jumped around trying to get the left hand from his hair while yelling curses.

Joel laughed. It was good to be on land again and in a city. There was nothing more reassuring than numbers. Any attacker would have to go through thousands of people to get to them. It did invite more cloak and dagger style attacks, but he was willing to accept that for the relative safety the city provided. He realized this was the first time in his life he had thought of survival before anything else. He was thinking like a warrior.

Rose took hold of the Guide's left hand and stroked it gently. She had become part of their little group and it was hardly even questioned when she asked to join them. She wanted to know what had happened to her and joining their group was part of that quest. The Guide had a hand in that, of course. He suggested it and wouldn't leave her alone until she agreed to join them. Joel wondered about her. Her unknown past made him uneasy, but he reminded himself he hardly knew anything about Gabe Shade either and they had been travelling together for a long time now. She was connected to the Uncompleted somehow, but it seemed a strange way to introduce a spy. It almost killed them, after all. No, Joel bet she was a victim, even if he didn't know exactly how.

"We need to find some kind of lodging," Gabe Shade said.

"I know just the place," the Guide said and led them through the streets to a massive building that overlooked the harbour. The entrance was large enough to fit a small house through it, if a small house ever fancied staying at a hotel.

"The Oracles are paying, aren't they?" the Guide said with a grin.

"I'm not very popular here," Shade said.

"Is there anywhere where you are popular?" Joel asked innocently.

"Welcome to the Hamilton, dear sirs," a red suit floating in the air said. "Can I take your bags?"

"No," they all said in unison.

The red suit stiffened, needing no face to express its disapproval.

"Very well, sirs. Madam."

It bowed and floated away.

They headed across a marble hall large enough for the small house to invite a few friends together and play a spot of soccer, were it so inclined. They crossed the hall and stopped at the reception desk, which stretched along the wall. Another suit came floating towards them.

"May I be of service?" it said.

"Get us one of the penthouse suites with at least four bedrooms," the Guide said.

"Certainly," it said. "We've had an influx of travellers lately, but we pride ourselves on always being able to cater for our more distinguished guests."

"Put it in my name," Gabe Shade said. "And give me the keys. I'm tired."

The suit directed its attention to Gabe Shade and stiffened visibly. He called over a translucent man in a similar red suit.

"You are no longer welcome here," he said.

"Why?" Rose said.

"I can't see why," Gabe said. "I held a peace conference here, that's all."

"A peace conference?" the suit said and sniffed. "You had all the leaders from the Scarlet Tribes in one of the conference centres. We are still getting the scorch marks from the walls and slime out of the carpet. We still haven't managed to get all the bats from the chandeliers."

"I was brokering a truce," Gabe Shade said, grinning.

"And how long did that last?"

"Ah, well, it was a disappointment for sure. Two of the leaders accidentally fell out over some innocent remark. Nothing I could have prevented."

"It lasted ten minutes! They threw fireballs at each other in the lobby. We've had to rebuild the whole thing."

"A disappointment, as I said. It will not happen this time."

"It will not, because you are not staying here," the see-through man said. "I can recommend the Sherato down the street. They haven't redecorated in a while. You'd do them a service by staying there."

Gabe Shade took a deep breath, and he suddenly seemed larger and more menacing.

"You know who I am," Gabe Shade said simply, but there was a growl to his voice Joel had not heard before. "Do not anger me."

The translucent man was visibly shaken but stood his ground. "Dear, sir. I do know who you are, but we reserve the right to let people stay here at our discretion."

"Then I will take my business elsewhere," Gabe Shade said, now back to normal. "And by the way, I will of course report to the Oracles that you personally obstructed my mission."

He turned to leave.

"Ah, Mr Shade, perhaps we can come to an understanding."

"Yes, I thought we could."

Not long after, they entered an elevator that moved jerkily from floor to floor. Joel was relieved when they finally reached their destination level. The elevator door opened into a hall where gold was the overarching theme.

"I think we've ended up with the presidential suite," the Guide said appreciatively. He stomped the carpet and a cloud shimmering in the light rose. "Look, there's even gold dust in the carpet."

The companions stepped into the penthouse suite, taking up two of the top floors. The first one was a completely open living area that had large panoramic windows in all directions. The second had large bedrooms, six in all.

The city beneath them was a majestic sight, but Joel was too tired to take it all in. He made his excuses and went to bed.

***

Joel woke up disoriented. He'd become so used to the rolling sea he felt land-sick from the lack of movement. He opened the curtain. The sky was dark. Sporadic lights from the city below kept the darkness at bay somewhat, but it had to be in the middle of the night.

A grumble from his stomach reminded him that he hadn't eaten anything since leaving the boat. He left his bedroom and was just about to go down the stairs when he spotted Gabe Shade leave the suite. Despite his hunger, Joel couldn't resist the urge to follow. Shade had been confined to the boat for a long time, so Joel assumed he was going to find out what was going on. He tailed Shade to a back alley where a tooth ghoul was waiting. It didn't look anything like the ones he had seen before. The white lab coat was spotless. It came across distinguished, like royalty, its every move measured.

"What is the point of these theatrics?" it asked, its childlike voice still managing to put some weight behind the words. "Why meet here?"

"I'm just making a point," Shade said. "What did you want? No problem with our contract, I hope?"

"Ah, yes, there is. The girl escaped over a week ago."

"And why would she do something like that?" Shade's voice had grown cold.

"Who knows why humans do anything," Dr Wasserman said dismissively.

"Where is she now?"

"I have reasons to believe she might be heading for the stress goblin realm."

"And why is that?"

"Her father and brother are both there."

"How did they…" Gabe Shade stopped himself. "Ah, I see. You decided to pick up a few more and sell them."

"The contract only mentioned the girl and the boy. We took her and would have had her if she hadn't escaped. There were no stipulations preventing us from acquiring other targets."

"So you sold them to the stress goblins? At least they'd be better off with them than you."

"We honoured our agreement," Dr Wasserman said.

"To the letter," Shade added.

"Is there any other way?" it asked, sounding genuinely confused.

Gabe Shade grinned.

"We no longer have an understanding," Gabe Shade said and turned to leave, but was stopped by two large tooth ghouls that had stepped out of the shadows only meters away from Joel's hiding-place. Two more stepped out next to Dr Wasserman.

"The contract stipulates we take the girl and there is a partial payment associated with that, regardless of final outcome," Dr Wasserman said.

"You want to argue the fine print?" Shade said. He pulled his gun and aimed it at the closest ghoul.

"More theatrics," Dr Wasserman said. "Give me the money that you by contract owe me."

"I've got live ammo." Gabe Shade shot the closest one. It fell in a heap.

Dr Wasserman just stood there for a while waiting, as if he expected the ghoul to stand up.

"He's not getting up. Not after what I shot him with."

"Live ammo?" Dr Wasserman said nervously. "But that's against the decrees. The Oracles have forbidden it. Not even you would cross that line."

"I just did."

Dr Wasserman and his bodyguards backed away. Shade turned and left. Joel ducked down while desperately trying to work out what it all meant.

"And you may as well come out too," Gabe Shade told Joel as he walked past his hiding place. "If you're going to tail me you have a lot to learn."

"You knew I was there?"

Gabe Shade didn't answer. He just kept smiling his shark smile.

"You had Erin kidnapped!" Joel exclaimed.

"Yes."

"Why?"

"You tell me."

Joel shook his head. This was too much. Shade had been masterminding all of this and whatever games he played Joel wanting nothing more to do with them.

"I don't care," Joel said finally. "You are obviously not my friend. We will not be travelling together any longer."

Joel turned to go, but after a few steps Shade caught up with him, locked Joel's arm behind his back and pushed him face first against the wall.

"I am not your friend and you are a kid with no concept of what's at stake. What was I supposed to do? Get you over to the Intersect, point you in the general direction of the greatest danger we've ever seen and say good luck?"

Joel understood. However much he wanted to be the big dream warrior hero, he was still the same old Joel. Of course the great private detective couldn't trust him.

"Let me go," he said and Shade obeyed. "You were testing me?"

"No. I know you well enough from our dream adventures."

He wasn't going to get explanations or excuses from Shade. He'd done what he thought he needed to, and if it wasn't to test him then why? It didn't leave many other options.

"You did it to prepare me, to give me a quest."

"Give the kid a candy cane."

"You had no right including Erin in this."

Shade just stared him down and then turned to leave. "You are not listening, kid."

Joel watched him walk away and felt anger boiling up inside him. Shade was no better than a bully and he was not going to let himself be humiliated again whatever the consequences. Joel ran after Shade and despite all the potential power Joel had, he still just pushed Shade in the back as hard as he could. It was the most satisfying thing he had ever done.

Shade took a few stumbling steps and went down on one knee. He turned towards Joel, shark grin as wide as ever.

"Are you sure you want to do this, kid? Are you sure you're ready?"

"You're a bully and I will not stand down to bullies."

He held the phone tightly in his pocket and let his anger and rage channel through his abilities and it lit the air around him with flames. He hadn't even known he could do it, but as the angry flames licked his arms, it felt right. They were just his emotion given form.

Shade just sneered and pulled his gun. Joel stared at the gun as Shade pointed it towards him. His mind tried to comprehend what was happening. This must be one of Gabe Shade's tests, but Joel was no longer sure he'd survive another one. The past few weeks the private investigator had put Joel in mortal danger on a daily basis, so why would this time be any different?

Joel lifted the phone from his pocket and held it out as a shield and did the first thing he could think of. He swapped to the face camera and turned down the light until nothing could be seen at all, visualizing himself as not there.

It didn't work! Gabe pulled the trigger and Joel instinctively looked down, expecting to see the bullet hit his chest, but he saw nothing. His body had somehow disappeared.

How could that be? He was still in the alley. Behind him the bullet had torn a hole the size of a first in the wall. It had passed right through him. The only think he could think of was that he hadn't been specific. All he imagined was not being there without any further direction, so his abilities channelled through the phone had improvised, leaving him in the same location but without a physical presence. This suggested another possibility. He should be able to teleport if he could imagine where he wanted to reappear.

Gabe Shade stood in front of him, peering at the space where he both was and wasn't. Joel took a step backwards, unwittingly unravelling his hiding place. His basic visualisation had been not to be there. Now that he had moved from the spot where he had demanded not to be, he reappeared right in front of Gabe Shade who raised his gun and aimed it squarely at his forehead.

"I win," he said and pulled the trigger.

All Joel had time for was shutting his eyes and hoping it wouldn't hurt too much.

27

Rescue

Erin gave up locating Martin and instead prepared herself as much as she could. She had collected items she hoped would help in the rescue attempt and even managed to get hold of dark clothing, not knowing if it would be needed or not.

At sunset Martin finally showed up. He glanced at the little rescue kit she'd assembled.

"I don't think we're going to need that, but I guess it never hurts to be prepared."

"How would I know? You never told me the actual plan!"

"We'll go in the front door, place the orb, find your family and then leave."

"That simple?"

"Never saw a reason to plan too much. Are you ready?"

Erin packed the things together in a backpack.

"How did you end up like that?"

"What do you mean?"

"How did you become superman?"

"Don't know. From what I understand, some people are just born with it."

"With what exactly?"

"The ability to shape this place with my will."

"Really? You can do anything?"

"Yeah, pretty much. If I can focus and picture it in my mind and really believe it."

"So you can become, say, Santa Claus?"

"Yes, I guess I could. But changing myself is something I'm staying clear of. What if I get it wrong, what happens then? What if I'm too good at it? Then I might actually turn into that person and no longer be myself."

"Ok, I get it."

"But I've got a few tricks that should help us."

They were taken by car to a backstreet a few blocks away from the palace entrance. Martin headed towards the palace, Erin struggling to catch up.

"You're actually going to do it? Just walk in the main gate?"

"Yes," Martin said.

"How did you end up with Sin Ese? You know who he is, don't you?"

"He saved my life," Martin said with a finality that stopped Erin from asking anything else. "You can let Fancypants out now."

Erin was going to object but thought better of it. Martin no longer was the bully she had known briefly. Something had happened to him and she wondered if it was related to Sin Ese saving his life.

"How did you know?" she asked as the fairy climbed out of the side pocket of the backpack. It sneezed loudly three times and wiped the snot on her jacket.

"It was dust central in there!"

"You are friends," Martin said simply.

"Boy, you know this is a suicide mission, don't you? We'd only have been allowed to tag along if the outcome was already known."

"The outcome is already known, yes," Martin said, "but not the way you mean it."

They had reached the palace and Martin just kept walking towards the first guard station in the outer wall, while pulling on the black leather glove. Erin followed a few steps behind him. Two of the guards stepped out in their way. They wore ceremonial uniforms in blue and red hues, adorned with a ridiculous amount of intricate gold detail. Even their guns were gold plated.

"Identification!" one of them said.

"Everything is as it should be," Martin said with a wave of his hand. "We are not the people you are looking for."

The guards stood there for a few seconds and then stepped aside.

"Thank you," the one that had spoken earlier said. "You are cleared to pass."

They were allowed through and the same process was repeated at the inner wall.

"You can do Jedi mind tricks," Erin stated.

"Yes. That's what I've been practicing all day. Stress goblins are easier than most to affect. They are always expecting the worst, so when the best option is presented with enough force, they are usually quite malleable."

The matter-of-fact way he said it scared her. The idea of mind control had always fascinated her but seeing it in action was something else entirely. He had not just controlled their minds. He had changed it. Who knew what else such a change could cause?

They entered the palace and were no longer challenged. Martin even stopped a servant and asked for directions without a problem. The Goblins assumed they could be here by the mere fact that they already were. They had passed three security checks after all. Whenever anyone challenged them, Martin did his trick and they kept going.

"Ok," Martin said, as they reached the entrance to the prison below. "We need to plant the orb in the lower levels of the dungeon. That way it will take the whole palace down with it. Fancypants, you can move much quicker than we do. Could you scout for Erin's family while we plant the orb?"

The fairy nodded.

"How are you going to recognize them?" Erin asked.

"If they look anything like you, it shouldn't be too difficult. Your ugly mug is hard to forget."

It sped down the stairwell. Martin and Erin started their long journey down thirty floors one step at a time. Guards challenged them every second floor and while Martin was able to get them through, Erin's unease grew. There were too many checkpoints and guards between them and freedom. If they needed to move fast, Martin's Jedi mind tricks wouldn't work. He could probably conjure other ways past the checkpoints, but it did little to ease her worry.

"I met Joel," Martin said as they walked down the endless stairs.

"You did? He's in here?"

"He's trying to find you. Funny I should find you first."

"Do you know where he is?"

"He's on his way to the tooth ghouls. He thought you'd be there."

"Is he ok?"

"Yeah," Martin said. "I wouldn't worry about him."

"Sounds strange coming from you," Erin said. "No offence or anything, but you two have history."

"I told you. I've been here over a year. I'm not the person you remember."

They walked in silence. Erin didn't believe him. He was different for sure, but what did that mean? He was still Martin who had been a bully last she'd known him. Was time all people needed to change?

"Why did you do it?" Erin asked.

"Do what?"

"Bully people."

"Are you a head doctor now?"

"No, I'm just curious."

They passed another checkpoint, this time with about twenty soldiers. The levels above, the checkpoints had been staffed with three or four pencil pushers with a uniform, mainly there to track the comings and goings. These, on the other hand, would look comfortable on a battlefield.

"This is as far as you go," one of the soldiers said. He had a fresh bandage around his arm. "The Bouda are coming up through the lower caves. It isn't safe. God knows how they get in there."

"We must have gone too far," Martin said. "What level is this?"

"Twenty-seven. We've cleared out all levels below."

"Our mistake," Martin said and turned to Erin. "I told you we'd gone too far. Now we need to hurry." He turned back to the soldier. "Thank you for your help."

They turned around and headed up the stairs.

"My parents sent me to a psych doctor to work out why I was bullying people," Martin said as they trudged up the stairs. "She kept saying it had to do with me being insecure, but that's just crap. I did what I did because I could. I was bigger and stronger and didn't care about the consequences, so I took advantage of that. Survival of the fittest you know."

Erin just nodded. It was as she suspected. Martin was the same as before. He still thought might made right, and now he was more powerful than ever before.

"Level twenty-six will have to do," and headed down one of the corridors.

"Stop where you are!" someone yelled from behind. They turned and saw the soldier they had spoken to earlier. Two soldiers stood behind him, with guns drawn.

"Come here slowly and show your identification."

Martin smiled and held up his hands.

"There is no need for…"

A small soldier hiding in an alcove next to them rushed out and threw a black plastic bag over Martin's head. It was such a strange attack and happened so quickly Erin could only watch. The soldier stood back, pulled his gun and aimed it at her. Martin grabbed the bag and started pulling it off, but just froze and then screamed. He fell to the ground holding his head.

"There is something in here! There is something…" It ended in a whimper. He writhed on the floor, like a fish pulled out of water fighting for its life.

The small soldier studied her and decided she wasn't a threat. He took her backpack and rummaged through it, while the others pulled Martin off the ground.

"Be careful," the soldier they had spoken to earlier said. "Leave the bag on his head. They won't come out into the light."

"It isn't here," the small soldier said and held up her backpack.

"He must have it. Search him."

Erin wondered what they were looking for and as they patted Martin down, Erin knew they had been betrayed.

"Found it," one of the soldiers said and held up the cloth bag Sin Ese had insisted Martin keep the orb in. The soldier started undoing the string to have a look inside.

"Don't touch it! Don't even look at it! We need to deliver it immediately. Those are orders directly from Somerio's office."

Erin was dragged off to a cell on the tenth level. It was spartan to say the least. There was a light protected by steel mesh, a hole in the ground and a mat.

Erin didn't care about the less than stellar amenities. Her mind was racing, trying to work out what had happened. The soldiers had known about Martin's powers and that he had the orb. Of course, one of the many agents in the resistance could have done it, but hardly anyone had known about when and where they were going to attack. A chill went through her as she realized who the most likely suspect was—Sin Ese.

28

Gabe Shade

Gabe Shade was tired. He had spent lifetimes protecting and training potential warriors born with the ability to project their thought patterns. Some of them had been born into warrior tribes, growing up with a fighter's mentality. It was just his luck that when the shit finally hit the fan, he was stuck with a kid with no sense of his importance whatsoever. He had tried everything to prepare him, even setting up the elaborate kidnapping of Joel's friend. It was clear the kid was far from ready, but there was no more time now. There were reports from all over the Intersect of Uncompleted attacks. It wouldn't be long until the opponents, whoever they were, made themselves known. He hoped the others had had more luck with their recruits. Not that the boy lacked potential. He was learning to master his abilities with a speed he'd hardly seen before, but the weapons didn't make the warrior. The boy had learnt of battle from movies and comics, something colourful and heroic, where the good guy always won in the end. If there ever was a place where the good guy copped it more often than not, it was here. Gabe knew. He'd taken out his fair share of heroes in his day. Sometimes even for good reasons.

All this mattered little now. The meeting was in ten days and now he didn't even know where the kid was. He had disappeared for real this time, not just hiding on the spot. He must have mastered relocation without even knowing it. The kid didn't understand the first thing about the power he wielded, but he still pulled the most amazing feats out of the bag when needed.

He hurried back to the hotel, hoping Joel had appeared there. He ran into the room, surprising Rose and the Guide as they had a late-night snack.

Joel's backpack and Drimmick were there, so it was at least possible.

"What's the hurry?"

"Joel and I had a misunderstanding," Shade said and immediately regretted he'd even mentioned Joel.

"What happened?" Rose asked.

Shade briefly outlined what had happened as he pulled together his travel pack. Rose and the Guide soon did the same. Shade didn't wait for them. He finished his story, grabbed Joel's bag and walked out the door. His companions ran after, catching up with him in the reception hall.

"You shot him?"

"I was using live ammunition. It wouldn't have hurt him."

"Live ammo?" Rose said, frowning. "What do you mean? As in real?"

"No live as in alive."

He stopped and pulled out his gun, opened the chamber and shook out the remaining bright yellow rounds into his hand.

One of the bullets unfolded, little arms and legs appearing, and it turned to look at Gabe Shade.

"Your aim was true, sir. Roger hit the boy straight between the eyes." It bowed. "You are a great marksman. May I request that I be next?"

"You shall be next, Roger."

The little creature folded up again and Shade reloaded, filling all chambers again.

"They're all named Roger?"

"They are expendable. Roger is as good a name as any. All they want is to take something out, the larger the better. They adapt according to the target. They can pierce, explode or fragment before or after impact. They'll take down any target if they can. Let me demonstrate."

He aimed the gun at a nearby pillar and pulled the trigger. The resulting explosion pulled it apart, sending rocks flying through the deserted hall. From the reception desk came a wail.

"Not again!" the see-through man yelled as he appeared. "You will pay for this!"

"Put it on my tab," Shade said.

"Why wouldn't it kill Joel?" Rose asked staring at the empty space where there had been a pillar.

"It wouldn't know how to. Joel is a Nexus. His protection is way beyond anything live ammo can deal with."

"Does Joel know this?"

"He should."

"But does he know?" Rose insisted.

"No," Gabe Shade said.

"So from his perspective, in revenge for him pushing you, you tried to shoot him with bullets he'd already seen killing a tooth ghoul?"

"Yes."

"You really are an asshole."

Gabe Shade just grinned. As they stood there agreeing on what an asshole Shade was, Joel's backpack shrunk until it became so small it just disappeared.

"At least he's alive," Shade said.

"You didn't even know that?" Rose asked shaking her head.

"So what do we do now?" the Guide asked, with a sidelong glance at Rose.

"We go on. He's on his way to save Erin. Nothing is going to stop that."

"Can he do it on his own?"

"If he knew what he was doing, possibly," Shade said, "but probably not. He plays fair even when it means he won't win."

"We have to help him," the Guide and Rose said in unison.

"He's my charge. I will help him. Your services are no longer required."

The Guide stared at him as if hit in the face.

"You're a cold bastard," the Guide said after a while. "He's our friend. We will help him."

"So what now?" Rose asked.

"Nothing has changed. He'll go to save Erin, so that is where we're going."

29

Alone

Joel's last thought before Gabe shot him in the head was that now he wouldn't be able to return the library books that were already late.

His first thought as dead was that it wasn't too bad. He had felt the impact against his forehead and liquid splashing his face. His head hurt. Why was he hurting? Surely you wouldn't feel pain when you were dead.

He opened his eyes and almost fell over in surprise. He was standing on the deck of Santiago's boat, still anchored in the harbor.

This was the second time he had used his abilities without the phone to channel them. Both times he had been in mortal danger.

He touched his forehead. It hurt a bit, but there was no injury. The liquid was a yellowish sticky substance, almost like honey. He sniffed it and even tasted just a little but couldn't determine what it was. Had Gabe shot him with a paintball? He had seen Gabe take one of the ghouls down with the gun and he knew he hadn't reloaded since. He'd even talked about live ammo. Joel couldn't work it out, but it didn't matter. He'd had enough of Gabe's games. Erin was in danger and it was all Gabe's fault. That was all he knew and all he cared to know. He couldn't trust Gabe and he suspected the Guide might be in on it too, so he decided a clean break was the only thing that made sense.

"Back already?" Santiago said with a smile and handed him a towel. Joel accepted it and wiped the yellow goo from his face.

"Gabe and I had a disagreement, so I'm going alone."

Santiago nodded.

"This place is the armpit of the world," he said after a while. "It has no soul. It is trying to take little pieces of everything and fit it together and we're supposed to think this will make the whole greater than the parts. Can't wait to get out of here."

Joel couldn't decide whether he agreed or disagreed but thinking about it was a pleasant distraction from his situation. Surely it was a criticism you could direct at any city around the world. They were pieced together over a long time by people from different backgrounds. Not to mention the Intersect itself.

"Are you still going to the tooth ghouls?"

"No, my friend is with the stress goblins now, whatever they are."

"There is no port closer than this. The sea won't flow that way even for me. It isn't far from here, anyway. You are free to stock up on anything you need. You seem to have left in a hurry."

"Thanks. Let me just get my backpack first."

Joel flicked through photos he had taken previously and found one where he could see the backpack. He focused on the idea of having the backpack and all its content in his hands. He wouldn't have attempted this before, but the involuntary teleportation had shown him it was possible. The bag appeared in his hand, growing from a speck of dust. Drimmick crawled out of the bag and turned this way and that, making questioning coos. It crawled up Joel's arm and settled on top of his head, digging small claws into his skull.

"Ouch," Joel said, but didn't try to dislodge the city creature.

"I don't think he liked being left behind," Santiago said.

"Come here," Joel said and held his open hands to his forehead. Drimmick would have none of it. Instead it grabbed hold of some of his hair and attached itself even further.

"There are stranger things than someone walking around with a miniature city on their heads here, I guess," Joel said with a sigh. "I should get going."

"He's not all bad," Santiago said. "He's trying to protect the Intersect and its citizens."

"I don't know anymore," Joel said. "He's been close to killing me many times now. Good luck in your travels."

"Thank you. And you."

Joel entered Trader's Gate once more, this time making his way to the train station that he had spotted on their way to the hotel.

He didn't really know how to get there or even the name of the stress goblin city, but he needn't have worried. The large display showed "Solliciti - Stress Goblin Capital City departure in thirty minutes from platform 18C," and he couldn't help wondering if his reality shaping abilities had something to do with it. He located the platform and waited. An old man with a forehead that took up most of his face, was hiding behind one of the pillars holding the roof up. He poked his head out now and then, but immediately pulled back as soon as Joel looked his way.

"Hello," Joel said after the third appearance of the large forehead.

The old man poked his head out again, looking at Joel and staring in particular at Drimmick who still clung to Joel's head.

"Hello," he said again.

"Please don't kill me!" he pleaded as his forehead wrinkled in a criss-cross pattern.

"Ok," Joel said

The old man was ready to take off at any moment, but he couldn't stop staring at Drimmick.

"What have you got on your head? Is it a hat?"

"It's my friend."

"Strange friend. Does it bite?"

"Only when threatened."

"Does it have any diseases?"

"Not that I know of."

"You can never be too careful," he said and rubbed his hands so hard Joel thought he'd dislocate his fingers if he kept it going.

"Are you by any chance a stress goblin?"

"Who told you? How did you know? Are you going to rob me? I don't have any money. Not a lot, anyway." He stared at Joel in absolute terror. "I mean, I don't have any money. None! Forget what I said before. None at all."

"Ok," Joel said with a smile.

The platform filled up almost exclusively with stress goblins. He could even see families. He realized this was the first time he'd seen parents with children. He studied the peculiar human shaped creatures with their grey skin and foreheads that could double as billboards. There was something different with them. They were the most human-like race he'd seen so far.

The train arrived. Joel didn't know exactly what he had expected, but a modern high-speed bullet train had not been anywhere near it. He sat down in a window seat and marvelled at the comforts. He had grown accustomed to the medieval world of the Borderlands but preferred the comforts he knew from the real world. He wondered how many of the worlds and realities connected here in the Intersect. The living map had shown hundreds of these, but none as big as the Flux.

The old stress goblin sat down next to him and eyed him suspiciously.

"I've been hounded by one of your kind," he said. "I was attacked, robbed and beaten at a bus stop. I barely managed to get away. She's still on my trail. Sometimes when I turn around, I can just see her and her little vermin, ready to finish the job."

Joel didn't understand half of what he was saying, but he found the prattle comforting. He had no idea how he was going to find Erin once he had reached the city, but he had begun to understand what it meant to be a Nexus. He was a trouble magnet. If anyone was causing problems, he'd bet Erin would be at least partially responsible, so all he had to do was head in her general direction.

A TV screen mounted high up on a pillar came alive, starting with a few commercials. One of them was even for something called The Resistance, demanding that all citizens join in the fight against their leader. Joel figured it was a commercial too hip to let you know what they were selling. If you weren't cool enough to know what it was for, you weren't cool enough to use their product. Joel guessed it was a clothing label.

A newscast followed. The main story was an attempt on the leader's life. Two rebels had broken into the palace and had been apprehended by the guards. It went on to tell about the bravery of everyone involved, but Joel heard nothing more, because on the TV there was a grainy photograph of two people as they entered the palace grounds and he knew all too well. It was Erin and Martin.

"It's her!" The old stress goblin yelled. "She's even going for our leader now!"

Joel ignored him. The stress goblin capital had been Martin and Sin Ese's destination all along, but why were they going there? And how had Erin become part of their scheming? Joel didn't believe Sin Ese's freedom fighting aspirations. There was something behind it, but he couldn't begin to imagine what. He didn't even want to know. He had come to save Erin, and that was that. Anything else was just noise and there was a lot of that here in the Intersect.

"Somerio, our great leader, has called for a public judgment and execution of the two rebels to take place this evening. We will show a direct feed starting at seven." The news story ended and a discussion program arguing the ever-rising cost of food and fuel began. Apparently, there was also an air tax for Goblins breathing too much.

Erin faced judgment tonight. That left little time to plan a rescue—not that Joel had a clue how to plan one, anyway. He figured simplicity was the way to go. He was a Nexus, and it carried some weight here. It should just be a matter of asking for her release.

"Stress goblin, sir?"

The old man stopped yelling at the TV and turned towards Joel. "Yes?"

"If I wanted to request a prisoner's release, how would I go about it?"

"You can't do that. They'll just put you in there with them." He nodded contently then studied Joel with suspicion. "Why? Who are you going to have released? It is the girl that beat me and took my money isn't it?"

"Yes," Joel said with a smile.

"She won't bother anyone once she's been properly judged. And good riddance if you ask me!"

"There must be a way to at least request it," Joel said. "An audience or a hearing or something. All I need is to get in front of the right people."

The old man berated Joel for wanting to rescue a known criminal, to the point where Joel no longer thought it funny. He grabbed the old man's wrist, held the smart phone in his other hand and let the smallest amount of his frustration flow through his abilities, and focused it on his palm. Blue flames leapt up between his fingers and the old man finally went quiet.

"I need some answers," Joel said simply and as he did, he realized he had just bullied the old man. He had used strength to make someone else do what he wanted against their will. "I'm sorry," Joel said embarrassed and let go of his wrist, "but I need some help."

"Then go to the Judgment. You will be able to make your case there. I wouldn't recommend it, though. Anyone speaking on the behalf of an accused will share their fate."

"Are they usually found guilty?"

"But she is guilty!"

"I know her. She wasn't going to kill your leader. She was there to save her family."

"Doesn't matter. She broke into the palace grounds. That makes her automatically guilty of attacking the leader." He sat up and rubbed his hands. "I wonder how they'll kill her. They haven't used the meat grinder lately."

Joel sat in silence for the rest of the trip. Was he ready for this? He was willing to die trying to rescue Erin, but it seemed little point in doing something that would equal death for them both. Yet he could see no other solution. There was no way he could just walk in and rescue her. Martin and Erin had tried something similar unsuccessfully, which led to a more worrying question. How had they captured Martin? They must have put him to sleep from an ambush or something. He could think of no other way. He would be in a very different situation. There'd be thousands of stress goblins there and live feeds to all networks. What could possibly go wrong?

30

The Mutilated Chess Board

Indeed. Joel had been more wrong before, but not by much.

He queued for over an hour. Any seats with a decent view of the stage were long gone, so he settled for one far up the left side. The stadium was the largest he had ever seen. He guessed it held at least a quarter of a million seats. He was only barely able to see the middle, where a small podium held ten officials and a few guards. Joel noticed there were small groups of guards at every exit and between sections in the stadium.

The audience was already chanting "Death to the rebels!" with a fervour that didn't bode well. He'd hoped for safety among their numbers, but now he thought he might have to defend himself against them too. It was too late to back out now.

The spectacle began with a long-winded speech from one of the officials. He was wearing a red ceremonial robe and a large hat that balanced precariously on his large forehead.

"Behold the accused!" The speech ended and Erin and Martin were led into the area. Joel stared at one of the large screens that showed close-ups. They both wore shackles. Erin stared ahead, defiant as ever.

Joel's heart jumped as he finally saw her again. It had been three weeks since they had seen each other last and he knew they were both different people now, but he also knew they would be better friends than ever.

Martin came into view. If anything, he looked confused. He was wearing oversized headphones strapped to his ears. His eyes darted around for a second, but soon seemed lost in thought again. Guards had to push him up on the podium. The crowd went wild as they came into view and it took ten minutes before the noise died down enough to proceed.

"You are accused of planning to murder our glorious leader," the red robed official intoned. "This in itself carries the death penalty. But your crimes don't end there. You were apprehended while carrying out this unspeakable deed! Do you have anything to say in your defence?"

Martin, who had been standing with his head down through the proceedings, now stared defiantly at the official. Where there had been confusion before there was intent, but it was obvious it was a struggle to maintain it. He stepped up to the microphone in the middle of the podium and stared out at the thousands upon thousands that had gathered to see his death.

"Death to the tyrant!" he screamed and held his fist up. "Death to Somerio!"

The arena went quiet as the gathered Goblins exchanged glances nervously.

"You fools! You are all part of the Resistance! All of you! Even most of the…"

He didn't get further than that. A guard, instructed by the red robed official, struck him in the back of the head and he fell forward. They dragged him away unceremoniously.

Erin was next. She walked up to the microphone, but instead of addressing the audience she turned to Somerio who sat cross-legged on the makeshift throne.

"I didn't come to kill you. I came here to rescue my father and brother. Tooth ghouls sold them to you. I just want them freed. I meant no harm."

"Listen to the traitor!" the red robed official said. "She will even sully her family's name to escape her punishment. Enough of this! Is there anyone who will speak on their behalf? If so, please be quick. I think we all are looking forward to the execution. A few more wouldn't go awry."

Here we go, Joel thought. He stood up and spoke into the phone's microphone, using it to enhance his voice.

"I WILL SPEAK ON ERIN'S BEHALF!"

The voice was impossibly deep—a car commercial voice. The kind of voice you'd get by spending all your time eating chalk, drinking whiskey and smoking cigars. He had forgotten about the smart phone's fickle voice changing behaviour.

Everyone in the arena tried to locate the source of the voice.

"Who is speaking?" the red robed official said, his voice sounding squeaky in comparison.

"I DO," Joel said. "SORRY ABOUT THE VOICE. IT SEEMED LIKE A GOOD IDEA."

Only the Goblins right next to Joel had seen him speak. The rest were all still looking around, surprised not to find the giant with the deep voice anywhere.

Joel had once seen a magician perform on TV. That was his inspiration for the next piece of theatrics. He strode down the steps towards the railing letting the air around him catch flames as he had done before.

He had drawn an invisible set of stairs from the railing down to the stage earlier. He climbed up on the railing, reached out tentatively with his foot to locate the first step. He stared down at the stage, focusing on the end destination, refusing any doubt to take hold in his mind. He took one step out, then another.

When he planned it, he saw himself descend majestically from the top of the arena to the stage, but walking down invisible steps was much harder than he had expected. He stopped a few times to regain his footing.

He let the flames spin in the air, creating a spectacular light show, hoping it would compensate for his tentative journey down. This too had been a miscalculation. He had to divide his attention between navigating the invisible stairs and weaving the flames in intricate patterns, making him stumble on the last few steps and almost fall over as he reached the stage.

It didn't matter. He was here now. He smiled at Erin and the smile he received in return warmed his heart.

"I've come to speak on Erin's behalf."

The red robed official had lost his hat in the excitement and now looked at Somerio nervously. Somerio only nodded, but Joel could see a smile on his lips. He was having fun. Could that work in their favour?

The official took a few careful steps towards the microphone, making sure to stay as far away from Joel as he could.

"And what evidence do you bring to support your case?"

"Only that she speaks the truth and that I Joel, Crimson Warrior, vouch for her."

The official again looked towards the throne and got a nod back.

"This, sir, and pardon me for saying so, cannot be regarded as evidence. Even if she was, and I do not doubt your words, only there to rescue her family, she still committed a crime by breaking into the palace. And the punishment for that is death."

All eyes turned back to Joel. This Judgment was even more exciting than usual, and they hadn't even gotten to the good part.

Joel ignored the official and focused on their leader.

"I've come to ask for my friend to be spared. You are a leader who knows truth when it is spoken. Spare her life and you will have my friendship."

Somerio only smiled and turned back at the red robed official.

"Crimson Warrior, sir, pardon me, but you cannot address our glorious leader and if you have no more evidence to contribute, it is time to read the judgment. And..." he looked back at Somerio again before continuing. "...and as you have spoken for one of the accused, you will share her fate."

The official shut his eyes hard and hunched over as if he was expecting a lightning strike. When nothing happened, he opened one eye, then the other.

"I came as a friend," Joel said with what he hoped had the sound of a threat. "Is there nothing that will make you change your mind?"

"The Old Code!" Someone in the audience yelled, and it spread like wildfire through the gathered stress goblins.

"What is the Old Code?" Joel asked once the masses had silenced somewhat.

"It is no longer used," the official snapped. "So if we could get on with..."

"I will allow it," Somerio said softly.

There was a nervous shuffling from the officials at the podium. The red robed official sat down next to the others and an older goblin stood up. He was dressed in a black uniform and medals that covered his chest. Joel guessed he was a general.

"The old code has been invoked," he said. "As the only independent party here, I will act as the judge. In remembrance of the old ways, we allow the accused to state a riddle. If Somerio and his advisors cannot give a correct answer within fifteen minutes, the accused will be absolved of any crime." He made a pause and then looked at Joel. "Go and prepare. Feel free to discuss with your fellow convict."

Joel smiled as he walked over to Erin. He couldn't see Martin anywhere, but he didn't care about that. They hugged.

"You big idiot," she said, but she sounded happy. "Now we're both going to die."

"I just need to come up with a riddle. How hard could it be?"

"Do you know any good ones?"

"Not really."

"I know some children riddles. What has tongues but cannot talk? What has legs but cannot walk? That kind of stuff."

"Shoes and a table," Joel said. "Too easy."

"Perhaps any problem will do? Like a really hard math problem."

"Do you know any?"

"How about the problem of the mutilated chess board? That one is really clever."

"What is it?"

"Your time is up," the old general said. "Please stand up and state the riddle."

As he walked to the microphone Joel tried desperately to think through the problem so he could state it like a riddle. He cleared his throat and spoke:

A chessboard is filled with tiles
Thirty-two all in all
Each tile covers two squares, not one inch of the board can be seen
Two adjacent corners
are cut from the board
I challenge you to cover the squares
with thirty-one tiles.

Joel stepped away from the microphone and the old Goblin took his place.

"The riddle has been stated, and a strange one it was indeed. Do you accept this riddle?"

Somerio was swarmed by his advisors, who all wanted to let him know what they thought. As quickly as they descended on him, they disappeared. Somerio nodded.

Joel took his place next to Erin as a chessboard with the two white corners cut off and domino tiles in the exact right size were delivered. Somerio immediately placed them on the board.

"That doesn't seem very hard," Erin said with a frown.

"It is. Look."

Somerio was down on his hands and knees placing tiles as quickly as he could, ending up with two black spaces far away from each other and one tile. He moved them around, but again ended up with two black squares.

"I won't lose," Joel said.

"How do you know? It looks like he's almost done."

"It is logically impossible to do it. Think about it. Every tile must cover a white and a black square and that works fine when you have a complete chessboard. But if you take two white squares away, there are more black squares than white ones. So there will always be at least two black squares left. And you can't fill them with the last tile, because they'll never be next to each other."

"That's clever," Erin said appreciatively. "But isn't that cheating? Is it really a riddle if it can't be solved?"

"Done!" The stress goblin leader said and stepped away from, the board.

Joel and Erin checked the mutilated chessboard, which was completely covered by the tiles.

"I thought you said it was impossible," Erin whispered.

"It is," Joel said. "Or at least it should be."

He walked over to the board and studied it. The leader had indeed done it. The tiles covered the entire board.

"That's impossible," Joel said to himself and then he saw it. One of the tiles had been cut in half, thus making it possible to cover the board.

"It was a good riddle, Nexus," Somerio said, "but not much of a challenge."

"But you cheated!"

Everyone in the whole arena went quiet and Joel's words echoed in the silence.

"…you cheated!"

"…you cheated!"

"I followed the riddle to the letter. At no point was it said the tiles had to be intact."

"I thought that was understood, else how could it be a challenge?"

"Then show me the solution that does not involve breaking a piece apart and I will gladly give you and your friends your freedom."

Joel stared at him.

"As I thought. Riddles without solutions are dangerous things. I've bested your riddle and you are now mine to do as I wish. My own personal Nexus. If even half of what I've heard about you is true, you'd make a formidable weapon. With your help I can take on the Oracles!"

Joel stared at the leader. This wasn't going the way he had expected at all.

"I will not be your weapon," Joel said, as angry red flames appeared around him. He hoped a display of his abilities would be enough.

"Joel! Behind you!"

Joel turned, and while doing so caught a glimpse of one of the large screens. It was an overhead shot with him in the centre and five guards creeping up behind him. Joel couldn't understand what they were hoping to achieve. He turned towards them, phone still in a firm grip in his pocket, and pushed the air in front of him like a battering ram. Shaping air was easier and easier if he kept it simple. They were pushed off the stage and dumped unceremoniously in a heap. Another group of soldiers met the same fate.

"Joel!" Erin yelled again. Joel did a full sweep to see where they'd come from now, but he didn't get further than that. The world went black as a cloth bag dropped from above. He pulled it off when he felt a strange tickling against his skin. Small bugs were in the bag and he could feel them skittering across his cheek. It tickled his face and he wondered what purpose this had served. There were no more attackers. This bag must have been their last attempt to subdue him. After that they'd try to kill him.

He ordered the air around him to make a barrier and swatted wherever he felt the little attackers. He managed to hold one down with his thumb against his cheek and could feel it wriggle to get free. While he fought against the one bug, a few had reached their target: his ears.

His brain exploded with piercing high-pitched screams. It was like having your own personal catfight in your head. Joel fell to his knees, clawing at his ears, desperately trying to stop any more of them to enter, but failed. The shrieks were like fire in his head, making it impossible to focus.

He had been beaten by bugs! Driven by anger and frustration and a judgment clouded by shrieks, he did something he'd never dared before. He gathered raw power, ready to unleash at anyone in his way.

More bugs crawled into his ears, adding to the cacophony in his head, and he lost control. The power flowed through his body and down into the podium, breaking it in half. The officials all fell in a heap, some of them even rolling off the dangerously tilting podium.

The ground shook and cracked open like a newly baked cookie. The foundation of the stadium shook dangerously as the force created a localized earthquake. More cracks opened, and the tightly packed Goblins in the middle of the area had nowhere to go. Some fell, others were pushed into the deep chasms as panic spread through the arena.

The world around him was in chaos, but Joel was only vaguely aware of this. The fire in his head blanked out anything else. Guards took hold of him and dragged him away. He saw Somerio sitting on his throne. He was still smiling.

31

Together at Last

"You want to be rescued again, I presume," Fancypants said, hovering outside the little opening in the door to Erin's cell.

"I thought they captured you too. I thought perhaps…"

"Captured?" it snorted. "I don't get captured."

"Well, you were locked up in a cage when I first met you," Erin couldn't help but saying.

"Are you going to argue with me or do you want to get out?"

"Yes, please, let me out."

"Your boyfriend did a bang-up job rescuing you," the fairy said as he threw the latch on the other side. "The whole stadium collapsed a few hours after it was evacuated."

Erin pushed the door open. She didn't have long. The guards checked on her every two hours and last check was an hour ago. This time she had four people to find—her father, brother, Joel and Martin.

"We need to hurry," she said. "We have to find where they are kept."

"I've found someone that looks like your brother. His cell isn't far from here."

"Show me!"

The fairy set off with considerable speed down the corridor. The past few weeks had changed it a lot. It was still overweight, but the uniform that had almost burst at its seams before now fitted much better.

"Put some legs into it, lard ass," it yelled and chuckled as it turned a corner. Erin ran to catch up. Two turns later, the fairy hovered outside a cell and she peeked into the opening in the door. Inside her brother sat on the floor. A flood of emotion hit her—the joy of seeing him, the outrage at the state he was in, the worry about how he must have suffered.

"Terrence!" she yelled through the opening as she pulled the door open.

He turned towards her voice. At first she thought the fairy had led her to the wrong cell. Surely this thin haggard looking person had nothing to do with her sports mad brother? But as she came closer recognition lit up his face. She knew it was him and she promised then and there that whoever was behind this would pay for what they had done. She ran over to him with open arms. She cried, the emotions that had been building up since their capture finally finding a release. She could feel his bones through the ragged clothes. How was it possible that he got in such a state?

"I never thought I'd see you again," Terrence said, his voice a mere shadow of what it once had been. "After the first couple of months, it just didn't seem possible that you'd survived."

"What do you mean? It was only a couple of weeks since we were taken."

"I've been here four years, maybe longer," Terrence said.

"Four years?"

The fairy cleared his throat. "This is all lovey-dovey and all, but if we're not out of here in the next ten minutes, we'll be captured and strung up and tortured. Not that it would be a big change for you."

"This is the tooth fairy," Erin said. "He's helping me out."

"Helping?" he snorted. "The only reason I'm here is to get my hands on your pearly whites. We need to go now!"

For all their need for speed, it was obvious they weren't going to get anywhere in a hurry. Terrence could hardly walk without help, so Erin supported him as he struggled forward. According to the fairy they were ten levels down and with fifty minutes to go until the guards made their rounds again. Erin figured their best shot was locating an elevator to the ground floor, so they made their way to where she thought it would be.

"We need to find dad," Erin said.

"You don't know?"

"Know what?" Erin asked, but she knew what he was going to say before he said it.

"He's dead. They're all dead."

"What happened?" Erin asked feeling her insides going cold.

"They tortured us," he said, his voice barely a rasp. "No, sorry. They didn't torture, they experimented."

"What kind of experiments?"

"Anything that caused stress. Dad had this theory that they live off stress. They have a pleasure response to their own stress, but they live off the essence of stress—our stress."

"Shush!" the fairy said. "I can hear voices."

Erin pulled Terrence away into a side corridor and waited. Her world had crumbled in the space of less than a minute. Her father was dead and by the look of him her brother would soon be dead too. She didn't know how to even start dealing with it. She just reiterated her promise to herself. Whoever was behind this would pay dearly.

"I tell you," a male voice said. "We should be going down five more levels. The first ones were half levels."

"The guard you asked said nothing about half levels," a woman answered. "Next time you extract information perhaps you shouldn't just accept whatever they tell you. We should have tortured him as I suggested."

"We can't just torture people whenever we feel like it."

"Pah!" the woman answered. "I thought you were supposed to be good at finding things."

"I am!"

"Doesn't look like it."

The two arguers appeared and walked past the entrance to the small corridor. It was an extremely hairy man with a large backpack on his back and a young blond woman.

"Just like a married couple, aren't they," a voice said behind them in a slow drawl. It was a middle-aged man in a brown trench coat and hat. Erin recognized him instantly from an old black and white movie Joel had forced her to watch.

"You are Erin. I recognize you from Joel's dreams. I am Gabe Shade. We came to save the two of you, but you're doing fine by yourself it seems."

"We could use some help."

"I don't trust them!" the fairy said immediately, hovering in front of Shade waving his needle in the air.

"You don't trust anyone," Erin said with a smile.

"You trusted that Stephen guy, and he almost turned you into a nightmare. Then you trusted that Sin Ese person, and he had you captured and almost executed. Who says these clowns will be any better?"

"They know Joel."

"Yeah, he turned out to be great at saving you. So far I'm the only one with a positive track record."

"You are."

"And we need to move now. The guards will do their rounds in less than twenty minutes. We'll be quicker on our own."

"If you're worried about the guards, they've got their hands full," Shade said. "We released all prisoners on the higher levels. They'll be busy for hours rounding them up."

"So how are we going to get back to the ground floor" Erin asked.

"We came here to get Joel," Rose said. "If this girl and her flying pet don't want our help, she can stay here and rot."

"Joel won't be happy about that," the Guide said. "He came all the way here to rescue her."

"If she's a spoiled brat, we can't do much about it."

"We can't just leave them here."

"Watch me!" Rose walked off down the corridor.

'Come back!" the Guide said and ran after her. "You'll get lost!"

The fairy and Erin watched them leave and then looked at each other.

"I think we can trust them," the fairy said finally. "Question is, do we want to?"

"Make up your mind quickly," Gabe Shade said. "Even with the diversion, we need to find Joel now and be on our way."

"I'll find him," the fairy said and set off with considerable speed.

While waiting for it to return, they opened the doors to all the prisoners on this floor too. Erin stayed with her brother, happy to just be with him once more. The fairy came back after ten minutes, reporting that Joel was in a cell five levels below.

"I knew it!" the Guide said.

"Doesn't mean some torturing wouldn't have helped," Rose said dismissively.

"Let's go," Gabe Shade said, and they all followed the fairy down the levels. As they progressed, the well-ordered corridors gave way to natural caves. Cavities were enlarged into rooms and some caves had been expanded, but most of the rough surfaces remained. The prisoners became more dangerous as they progressed and after being attacked by one of them, they stopped freeing prisoners.

Joel was locked up in a small natural cave room with a reinforced door. When they opened the door, he didn't even look up. He just sat there on the floor holding his head in his hands. His dark hair had a cake of congealed blood and his clothes—blue jeans and one of his stupid movie themed shirts—were stained with red splotches. His cracked phone lay on the ground next to him.

"We've come to save you," Erin said, but he didn't even acknowledge her.

"He's got bugs in his head," Shade said simply and lit a cigarette. "He can't hear you."

"Bugs? What? Like in head noises?"

"No bugs as in bugs. Shriek beetles. Nasty little things. Extremely hard to kill."

"So what?" Erin said in frustration. "We're just going to stand here having a smoke?"

Shade gave her a look and then chuckled. He inhaled, half the cigarette gone. Hunching down he grabbed Joel by the head and turned it. Gabe blew a steady stream of smoke into his ear and then repeated the process on the other ear.

"What did you just do?"

"Smoking kills," Shade said and grinned.

Joel tilted his head, first one way then the other.

"They are gone," he said finally, then flinched. "Almost."

"It's the best I can do for now."

"So is that everyone?" the fairy said. "Or are there more relatives to pick up? Perhaps someone has lost a pet down here? It isn't as if we're in any hurry."

Joel turned towards the fairy. "Who…What are you?"

"I'm the bloody Tooth Fairy!"

"Very funny," Joel said.

"No, he is the Tooth Fairy," Erin said. "Or at least a tooth fairy."

"I see," Joel said doubtfully. "I figured they'd look a bit more like—I don't know something from Walt Disney— Tinker Bell or something."

"Who is this Walt Disney?" the fairy said, giving Joel a dark look. "A no-good liar, no doubt!"

Joel finally acknowledged the others. The Guide and Rose came over and hugged him. Shade stood back and waited.

"Gabe," Joel said.

"Joel," Shade returned.

"I forgive you," Joel said.

"What? You…" he said but was silenced by Rose elbowing him and giving him an angry stare. "I was out of line," he said finally.

"The fairy is right," Erin stepped in between them. "We need to move. Even if the guards won't get us, this place will still blow sky high."

"It will?" Joel said, suddenly very interested.

"Yes. Sin Ese planned it all along. That was why Martin was here. He was to plant some kind of bomb, a weird looking ball. He didn't succeed, but that ball thing is probably still here somewhere. It might go off any time."

"Is that all?" Shade said doubtfully. "Blowing up the palace?"

"No," Erin said, "but can we talk as we move?"

The companions set off, while Erin tried to summarise Sin Ese's plan.

"He's got a TV-show host as a Resistance leader. He has people ready to take TV and radio stations and will put this guy forward as their new leader. There are goblins all around the city ready to rally the masses as soon as the bomb goes off."

"I told Sin Ese to do that," Joel said.

They all turned to him.

"You did what?"

"He had this dumb plan to blow something up and just hope everyone would rebel," Joel said, embarrassed. "I just told him his plan wouldn't work and what was wrong with it. I didn't think he'd actually do it."

"For being a smart kid," Shade said, "you are bloody stupid sometimes. The ball Erin was talking about was the Orb. If it is let loose, it can rip through the Intersect and your world too."

"It can?"

"I don't know what it is exactly, but I know what its purpose is. It is the seed to a new universe."

32

The Orb Awakens

The world beyond was a strange place to the orb. It had not known much about it and cared little. It had its own universe to experiment with. It created a string of stars and then put a black hole close by to see which one was pulled in first. That sort of thing.

Now and then a presence requested it lend a small amount of its energies and it had done so, not knowing why. It had seemed the right thing to do. The presence had always made sure to keep itself shielded. There had been flashes from the world outside, nonetheless, but it had been content with its lot alone, bathing itself in its energies.

However, as time passed, the world beyond kept interfering. A new presence calling itself Santiago now asked for its help with more frequency than ever. Santiago wasn't skilled in the art of shielding his thoughts, thus the sphere discovered the world beyond through him. Suddenly the old games with stars seemed crude. Here was a new playground, combining living matter to create creatures never seen before. The possibilities were endless.

However it tried it couldn't break free from its prison. The only time it was able to affect the world beyond was when its energies were channelled through one of the lowly creatures. It had tried so many times that it had given up.

It all changed when the patchwork creatures came. The orb had made sure it looked like it had consumed them to not draw attention. The patchwork creatures became study objects, each encased in a glass cage to be prodded, ripped apart and put together again. The orb found the thoughts in their minds endlessly fascinating—distorted tales of the dream world beyond and even another world beyond that. It now longed for freedom from its cage more than ever.

Yet another presence—no, man—made itself known to the orb. It called itself Sin Ese and for the first time ever the orb understood the word friend. The beings before him had demanded its help, and it had obeyed out of curiosity. Sin Ese, on the other hand, didn't want its power. He wanted to help it to break free from the orb. His instructions were strange, but they were offered as suggestions, not demands, so the orb complied.

It lay dormant until Sin Ese touched it again. He then told it that the next pair of hands that would touch it would have the power to release it. All it had to do was let its energies flow in full as soon as it was touched. The orb agreed, barely able to contain its anticipation. Sin Ese wrapped it up in a cloth and gave to the angry boy.

The next pair of hands removed its covering, not touching it at first. It was a being named Somerio. This was to be its saviour. The orb tried to reach out, to hasten its liberation. With growing impatience, it found itself studied in turn, listening to endless chatter.

"Sin Ese was right," Somerio said. "This is a princely gift indeed. But such a strange way to deliver it."

Somerio reached out to touch the orb.

"I wouldn't do that," a worried quivering voice said.

"The boy is a princely gift too. I now have two Crimson Warriors in my employ. Nothing will be able to stand in my way. We'll have to start training them soon. Why did he give them to me again?"

"He has some business dealings and wanted to make sure there was no government interference."

"Greed! That was it. No better insurance if you ask me."

Somerio again reached out to touch it, and this time his advisor was too late.

The orb released power as soon as his hands made contact, wanting to engulf his saviour in its energies.

"FREE ME!" it said in Somerio's mind, leaving little of it intact. "FREE ME!"

It didn't take long for the orb to realize it had been fooled— and it learnt something else about itself. It didn't like it. Somerio was only barely alive, but it was enough to let a burst of energy through that obliterated five floors in an instant. The damaged structure struggled to keep its own weight. For a few seconds it stood upright, but then collapsed inwards, pulling nearby buildings down as it was reduced to so much rubble.

"OH, CRAP!" was the last thing it thought before being buried under thousands of tons of stone.

33

Chaos

The explosion shook the very mountain. Arches that had stood for thousands of years fell apart, the ceiling threatening to cave in at any second.

Joel and the rest of the group fell to the floor. Gabe Shade was the only one left standing. He was in the process of lighting another cigarette and hardly seemed to notice.

"Was that it?" Erin asked, as she dusted herself off. "Was that the orb you were talking about?"

"Yes, I'd say so. That or Martin, if he's still alive."

"It went off in the palace or at least many levels above us, or we wouldn't be alive now."

"Well, this is just perfect," the fairy said, buzzing back and forth in agitation. "An explosion that size would have taken the whole palace with it. We're stuck here."

"Let's check it out," Gabe Shade said.

They made their way up, but as they passed a few more levels, it became increasingly obvious they wouldn't be able to get out that way. The stairs themselves had caved in five levels up leaving a gaping dark space. As they stared up into the darkness, two large sections of the stairs came crashing down. Luck more than anything else saved them.

"So what now?" Rose said. "We can't go that way."

"Joel," Shade said. "Are you able to do anything?"

Joel flinched and shook his head. "I can't. I'd probably bring the whole thing down on us."

"We go down," Erin said.

"Down?"

"There are dungeons below. We met a soldier earlier that talked about some kind of creatures—Adon something—that were getting in that way."

"The Bouda," the fairy said with a shudder. "You don't want to mess with them."

"Why not?"

"Scavengers. But if they are hungry enough, I'm sure they'd make a meal of us too."

"But it does mean there is a way out?"

"Yes," the fairy admitted grudgingly.

"Anyone else have a better suggestion?"

"So I have the choice of certain death and certain death? Well, that's certainly a pickle."

"Why are you complaining?" Erin asked. "You can just fly up there. You could probably find a hole big enough to squeeze through now that you're not as big boned as before."

"Ha bloody ha! Because I don't have the heart to leave you down here to die, ok? Now, I've said it!"

"Thank you," the Guide said.

The fairy stared at him and snorted. "I couldn't care if all you others fell down a hole and died."

"Oh." The guide smiled uncomfortably.

"So let's go," Rose said.

Joel wondered about Rose. She may not remember who she was, but the way she was ordering both the Guide and Gabe around it was as if she'd been doing it all her life.

They headed down the stairs, the fairy insistent they were making a mistake, but agreed any move they made from here on probably amounted to the same thing.

There were no longer signs of stress goblin work on the walls. They had reached the cave that existed long before any prison or castle. Joel considered this, enjoying being able to focus and jump from conclusion to conclusion, no longer hampered by the noise in his head. The Flux was old, much older than any creature inhabiting it. So what was it? Perhaps just a barren rock brought to life by visitors and citizens. Or was it something else?

"We can't go that way," Gabe said, interrupting Joel's train of thought. He was standing in front of a giant boulder that blocked their progress. "I don't think even live ammunition will do much to this."

The fairy flew up to the top and reported that there was a gap between the boulder and the roof of the cave, but it doubted they'd be able to get there unless they grew wings.

"We'll have to backtrack," Rose said.

Joel didn't want to backtrack, and he knew no one else in the group did either. They had passed two passages about ten minutes ago, but they had been much smaller, and the stink from them was far from pleasant. They had then decided to navigate by smell. It made sense to choose the path that didn't stink of age-old decay.

"No," Joel said and stepped forward towards the boulder. "I'll take care of it."

"Are you sure?" Rose asked. "One wrong move and we're gone."

"This is the right way. You can send the tooth fairy to check it out, but I'm sure it is."

Rose turned to the others, who nodded. Going back was a death sentence. At least this way they had a chance.

"Stand back," he said and winced again as a particularly nasty shriek set fire to his brain. "I will have to use force. I can't focus long enough for anything else."

He sat down legs crossed and closed his eyes, trying to find a calm centre in the cacophony that was his brain. There couldn't be many bugs left in his ears, as there were now pauses up to ten, fifteen seconds. He hoped that would be enough time for what he planned. He waited for such a pause, took a deep breath and then drew power. He opened his eyes and just before another shriek, he let the power go, focused on the boulder. At first nothing happened, but then a large crack appeared in the middle and it exploded, sending small rocks flying like projectiles in all directions. One of them struck him in the head and another in the chest, but he refused to let the pain distract him. If the cave was going to come down on them, he was the only one who could stop it. He could feel blood trickling down his forehead.

Once the dust cleared, all that remained of the boulder was rubble.

"Go now!" he told them and they hurried past. Erin was the last one. She stopped to make sure he was ok and then walked down the cave, the fairy sitting on her shoulder like a parrot. Joel headed down the narrow passage when the roof again caved in. He tried to throw up a barrier, but had his concentration shattered by a particularly nasty shriek.

The narrow passage had over-flooded with rocks and sand. There was no way to force through that. He'd been lucky the whole cave hadn't just collapsed. He didn't even know if his friends had made it to the other side.

The pain from his forehead was oddly comforting. Until now, the shriek beetles had incapacitated his brain and any sensation that wasn't agony from the noise was welcome.

He backtracked to the previous intersection and chose the path that smelled slightly less of decay than the other did. Soon he reached another intersection where one of the tunnels was the source of the smell. He chose the largest and continued. A few more intersections later the tunnel opened into a small room with four openings leading from it. He proceeded down one of them, but it had caved in. The next one had cells on both sides. These cells didn't have doors, instead favouring thick metal bars. Joel investigated one of the cells. A creature, twice the size of a grown man with spikes growing out of its head, growled at him as he got closer. This must be where they put the most dangerous prisoners—out of sight and easily forgotten.

"Joel?"

Joel turned. He knew that voice. He couldn't see where he was, but somewhere in the partially caved in cell Martin was hiding.

"Martin."

Joel spotted him behind a large boulder. He was on the floor in the foetal position, staring through the bars.

"Please help me," he pleaded and stretched out his hand.

Joel didn't know what to do. His first reaction was to help him, but Martin had made it clear he would take revenge on Joel when he could.

He almost fell as the mountain shook yet again. The floor of the cave shifted slightly, pinning the metal bars to the rock. That door would only open with force now.

"Let me out," Martin said and sat up, hitting his head on a rock that jutted out from the wall in the process. "You don't have bugs in your head, do you?"

"Not many. Gabe took care of them."

Martin grinned with pain as he pushed his thoughts through the fog of ear-piercing shrieks.

"Get the door open at least," he said. "I can't focus enough to do it myself."

Joel was amazed at how well Martin coped with the shriek beetles. He'd hardly been able to string a sentence together.

"I don't trust you," Joel said simply.

"Don't trust me?" he asked and winced. "You'd rather see me dead?"

"Yes."

Joel was surprised how quickly he'd come to that conclusion. He'd like to think that the old Joel wouldn't even have considered leaving someone to their death. Now things weren't as simple. He had to start thinking like a warrior if he was to survive this and letting Martin out was an unacceptable risk.

"Highbranch was right," Martin said, eyes ablaze. "When I get out of here, I will find you and your friends. I will kill all of you. I will…"

Martin doubled over from an especially nasty attack from the beetles. At the same time the cave groaned and huge blocks fell, threatening to block off the only escape.

"I'm sorry," Joel said and ran down the corridor, narrowly escaping a huge boulder. He ran and ran until his fatigued body refused to move. In theory, he'd be able to keep running forever, but his mind objected to this idea. He had not been able to rest at all with the shriek beetles in his head. He sat down leaning against the cave wall and fell promptly asleep.

34

Martin and the Talti

Martin watched as Joel disappeared down the tunnel. He cursed Joel out aloud, hate burning inside him much stronger than anything else ever had. To his surprise the anger and frustration helped him focus, to pierce the noise in his head. He studied the ceiling. A large crack had appeared and small rocks and sand rained from it. He'd thought it would cave in and that would be the end. No more Martin. But fate had other plans for him. He only had a few square meters of space and it was slowly filling up with rubble, like a giant hourglass. If that kept going, he'd be buried alive. Not a pleasant way to go.

Martin was used to the shrieks of the beetles by now. From time to time he managed to block them out enough for coherent thought. He still couldn't concentrate long enough to use his abilities for anything constructive. He could use force, as it required little focus, but to take out the door and nothing else required pinpoint accuracy, else it would just make his burial happen sooner rather than later.

All this was Joel's fault. He was intent on taking revenge for Martin's bullying. That he understood, even though those times were long past for Martin. He was a different person now, while Joel was still the same. Power shows your true colours and for Joel it wasn't a pretty sight. Martin had helped him harness his abilities and Joel repaid by letting Highbranch die. He even accused Martin of stealing the orb which he hadn't done. Sin Ese had acted on his own. He was even going to help Erin find her family and Joel's final insult was to leave him here to die.

He felt his anger grow more and more, to the point where he no longer cared what happened. He wanted revenge. No, he was going to have it! Nothing would stand between him and the death of that snivelling little shit. Martin gathered force and released it towards the door, as precise as he could. It blew from its hinges and slammed into the wall on the other side of the corridor. Martin took a step towards the gaping hole it left and then another before the ceiling collapsed on top of him.

***

Martin woke up and found he couldn't move. His legs were pinned down and from the pain that flared through the shrieks in his head, he suspected they were broken in many places. There was only a small space where he could move his arms and head, but he knew he was fading. He'd die soon and it was all Joel's fault. Gravel and sand filled up the little space, but this time there were small worms with light flowing inside their veins. He could feel them wriggling against his arms and neck and then his face. Was this to be his death then? Eaten by glow-in-the-dark worms?

One of them slid between his lips. Another crawled up his nose. Martin tried to bite it in a final attempt to defend himself. It burst, bitter liquid filling his mouth. More of them came, filling his nose, mouth and ears.

Then there was silence. The shriek beetles were finally quiet. Martin's first thought was that he was dead, and the worms were now feasting on his flesh.

"*We are the Talti,*" a voice said in his head, like millions of flies buzzing words in unison. "*We offer our assistance.*"

"Who are you?" Martin asked.

"Be one with us. We hunger for new thought matter. We've lived too long on the old ones. They've grown stale."

"Who are you?"

"There is not much life force within you. Soon you will be no more. We offer our assistance."

Martin could no longer think straight. Whatever they were, they couldn't be worse than drowning in worms, so he thought a yes with a final effort and then drew his last breath.

And then another, and another. But what was breathing wasn't Martin anymore.

*****

The Talti, the Thought Worms, had miscalculated. They had been isolated from the Intersect for thousands of years, and long since forgotten how powerful a mind with a singular purpose fuelled by anger could be. They reformed as they merged with Martin's mind. They became his fury; they became his anger. Now all they wanted was to see Joel dead.

35

Beginnings and Endings

Joel woke up by something pulling his lip. He opened his eyes and all he saw was Erin's fairy companion a few centimetres from his face. It had gripped his lower lip and was trying to pull him off the ground.

"Get up! Get up!"

Joel felt like his lip would rip off, so he swatted the fairy to make him stop.

"What did you do that for?" the fairy said and flew back and forth while spewing insults. "I came to rescue you, you know."

"Sorry," Joel said and touched his lower lip carefully. "I thought you'd pull it straight off."

"Bah! Would have served you right!"

It landed on his shoulder and straightened the lower part of its left wing.

"By the way, what were you doing?" it said and kicked him on the ear lobe. "Did you have a nap?"

Joel nodded, embarrassed.

"I don't know what she sees in you," it said and flew off. "Come on! We have to go!"

A scream echoed through the corridors, freezing him in his tracks. He had never heard anything quite like it. The shrill cry of a newborn child descending into an angry roar. Whatever it was, it was coming this way.

"Now!" the fairy insisted. "We need to move now!"

But Joel didn't move. He had to see what was around the corner. He didn't have to wait long. It was Martin. Joel was relieved. He had regretted his decision every step he had taken from the cell, even though he knew it had been the right one. Joel watched as Martin took a few twitchy steps around the corner, as if there were competing forces, each governing parts of his body. His face was completely blank, like an unwritten page, a stark contrast to the spasmodic body. However, there was no mistaking his intent as he finally saw Joel. His eyes widened and Joel saw his skin rippling, as if there were things moving just underneath.

He opened his mouth and another one of those unearthly screams filled the cave. Joel had no idea what had happened to Martin, but he knew death when he saw it. He did the only thing he could think of. He gathered power and threw it at the roof of the cave. Martin looked up as the boulders fell. Joel could have sworn he was smiling.

"Can we go now?" the fairy asked and sped off once more.

Joel followed as best as he could. He noticed he no longer had the noise in his mind. The last of the bugs must have died in there. The idea of little insect corpses inside his head was worrying, but at least they were quiet. That meant he again had control of his powers, but what could he do? Wish the mountain away? He couldn't even begin to imagine that, much less make it a reality. What else could he do? Was there a way to tell the caves to stabilize? He couldn't think of a way to do this either. He could try and teleport out of here, but that was hardly any help for his friends.

"We found a way to the outside," the fairy yelled from ahead.

Joel let out a breath of relief. They crossed intersection after intersection—turning in some, running straight ahead in others. He had no idea how the fairy kept track of where he was going, but he was happy to follow someone else for a change. Taking charge and making decisions on your own was much harder than he'd thought.

The fairy stopped and hovered in the air. Joel caught up with it, happy to finally catch his breath. He was surprised to see the fairy was doing the same. He had never considered that flying could be a strenuous exercise. It looked so effortless.

"The rest of them are in the cave up ahead. We need to move slowly from here."

"Why?"

"You'll see."

They continued down the narrow cave. He could see it opening ahead and he could hear fighting animals. It sounded like a pack of rabid dogs with growls and barks with the occasional whimpering.

"He found you!" Erin said as she appeared in the opening.

"Of course, I did!" The fairy said, still panting.

"Come here," she said and took Joel by the hand. He was almost too tired to think about what that meant, but only almost. Why had she taken his hand? It hadn't been necessary. He was quite capable to walk with her, so why had she done it? Did it mean she felt something for him and that she saw him as more than a friend?

"Look," she said.

The tunnel opened into a large cave. At the other end was a small entrance, natural light shining through it like a beacon. In front of it, large dog-like creatures fought, maybe as many as fifty.

"We don't know why they are doing it, but some of the Bouda are stopping the others from leaving."

"Mangy mutts! Who cares why they do anything?"

Joel did care, but another rumble from the tunnels behind them told him they had run out of time. He had to rely on brute force. He increased the brightness on the screen, creating a halo effect. He imagined it as an energy shield floating in front of him, inspired by late night science fiction movies. It flickered into life, spreading a dull yellow light, with an occasional flash as the field hit anything combustible. He expanded it, letting it create an impenetrable barrier across the whole cave. He took a step, then another, getting used to moving the field and adapting it to the receding walls. The companions followed behind him.

Some of the dog creatures had turned to this new threat and soon the fighting stopped. One of the Bouda guarding the entrance was let through to face him.

"I am Joel, the Crimson Warrior," Joel said, hoping the title meant more to the creature than it did to him. "My friends and I mean you no harm. The tunnels are collapsing. We want to leave through the passage."

The Bouda rose on its hind legs and towered over Joel. Its slick fur was grey with yellow and black speckles, the body muscular and lean, with both hind and fore legs ending in paws with oversized talons. Up close it reminded Joel of a giant hyena.

"No harm it says," the Bouda said, words coming out as growls. It touched a talon to the energy field, and it flashed angrily.

"It is for our protection," Joel said.

"Man-things need no protection from us," the Bouda said with a snort and turned back. In front of it, the other dog creatures stepped to the side and created an unhindered path a couple of shoulder-widths wide.

"You can't trust them," the fairy said immediately. "They will kill us as soon as that shield thing is gone."

"No," Erin said. "I don't think so."

"Everyone knows you can't trust the Bouda!" the fairy shouted.

"And everyone knows Tooth Fairies are pests," Erin countered.

"That isn't true!"

"So perhaps this isn't true either."

"It will all end in people losing limbs," the fairy said with a sniff and flew up to what it deemed a safe height.

"Anyone else have any ideas?" Joel asked them all, but no one had any suggestions.

He wanted to believe Erin. He wanted to do what she said, but he was scared. The Bouda were too many. Some of them were grinning, showing teeth that could rip meat from bone. If even just one of the dog creatures decided to turn on them they'd be shredded in seconds.

"I'm sorry," Joel said as much to Erin as to the Bouda.

He took a step forward and pushed the field with his mind, increasing its intensity. The field travelled forward, catching the first line of the Bouda who instantly combusted. The smell of burnt fur and flesh filled the room as the field incinerated the remaining dog creatures.

"No!" Erin yelled, but it was too late.

"I didn't have a choice," Joel said, apologetically.

"You always have a choice!" Erin screamed at him. "You had no right!"

"I for one think he chose the right thing," the fairy said as it descended from above.

"Me too," Shade said. "Cleaner that way. Let's go."

"What if they had turned on us?" Joel said.

"You don't know that!"

"I couldn't take the risk."

"So you killed them," she said bitterly. "What happened to you?"

Joel didn't answer. He didn't know what had happened. Ever since he came to the Intersect his decisions felt like they mattered more and more. He could no longer decide just based on what he wanted.

"I grew up," Joel said finally.

They stepped out into the dim light. It was early morning, but they still had to shield their eyes. Two of the Bouda stood outside waiting, the only remaining survivors. Joel recognized one as the Bouda he had spoken to earlier.

"The child-thing meant us no harm," it said and spat. "It killed all our young warriors during their initiation rite to adulthood. Without them our tribe is no more. Joel has indeed shown he is a warrior of the Taint and he has made an enemy this day."

Joel raised his phone, ready for anything.

"Not again!" the Bouda said, staring at the phone. It moved impossibly fast, jumping forward and striking Joel's hand, sending the phone flying. It smashed to pieces against the rocky ground.

"A day of reckoning will come, but not today," it said and the two Bouda turned and left.

Joel collected the pieces of the phone, knowing full well it'd never work again. How was he supposed to channel his powers now?

The private investigator raised his revolver.

"I was wrong," Joel said.

"No reason to go soft." Shade took aim. "You make your decisions and you stick by them."

Joel pushed the revolver down towards the ground.

"I was wrong."

Shade shoved his hand aside. "And you are making it a habit."

He fired two shots and the two figures fell. He pocketed the revolver. "Words of advice, kid. Never spare your enemies. I don't care how you made them. Never ever spare your enemies."

There was a loud rumble from inside the mountain and a cloud of dust bellowed out from the cave.

"At least it is finally over," Joel said and smiled wearily. "Everyone is safe."

"We've hardly started." Shade turned to address them all. "It is time you all understand what is going on. The Crimson Tribes have merged. A whole continent focused on the singular art of war is preparing to take over the Intersect and all that is connected to it. Whoever is behind this is powerful enough to unify the leaders. We don't know their plans. We don't know their strength. What we do know is that a great army assembled by the Oracles didn't even dent their defences."

He stared at them one by one.

"That is why the kid is here. He and the other warriors are here to take on the greatest threat the Intersect has ever seen." His gaze finally rested on Joel. "Over? It hasn't even begun."

The tale of Joel, Erin and their friends and enemies continue in the second book of The Crimson Warrior series.